Elatsoe

Elatsoe

Darcie Little Badger

illustrated by Rovina Cai

LQ

LEVINE QUERIDO

Montclair | Amsterdam | New York

This is an Arthur A. Levine book

Published by Levine Querido

LQ
LEVINE QUERIDO

www.levinequerido.com • info@levinequerido.com

Levine Querido is distributed by Chronicle Books LLC

Text copyright © 2020 by Darcie Little Badger

Illustrations copyright © 2020 by Rovina Cai

All rights reserved

Library of Congress Control Number 201995698

ISBN 978-1-64614-005-3

Printed and bound in China

Published August 2020

First Printing

*This book is dedicated with the deepest love to
my grandmothers Jean and Anita "Elatsoe"; my father,
Patrick; my mother, Hermelinda; my brother, John; my
darling, T; and, last but not least, to all the dogs we've loved.*

⇝ ONE ⇜

E LLIE BOUGHT THE LIFE-SIZED plastic skull at a garage sale (the goth neighbors were moving to Salem, and they could not fit an entire Halloween warehouse into their black van). After bringing the purchase home, she dug through her box of craft supplies and glued a pair of googly eyes in its shallow eye sockets.

"I got you a new friend, Kirby!" Ellie said. "Here, boy! C'mon!" Kirby already fetched tennis balls and puppy toys. Sure, anything looked astonishing when it zipped across the room in the mouth of an invisible dog, but a floating googly skull would be extra special.

Unfortunately, the skull terrified Kirby. He wouldn't get near it, much less touch it. Maybe it was possessed by a demonic vacuum cleaner. More likely, the skull just smelled *weird*. Judging by the soy candles and incense sticks at the garage sale, the neighbors enjoyed burning fragrant stuff.

"Look, a treat!" Ellie put a cheese cube in the skull's mouth. Although ghosts didn't eat, Kirby enjoyed sniffing his old favorites: chicken kibble, peanut butter, and cheddar. He'd been her best friend for seventeen years—twelve alive and five dead—and Ellie was confident that if food couldn't persuade him to be brave, nothing would. "Yum, yum!" she said. "Smells cheesy! Skull Friend won't hurt you!"

Kirby, in a fine example of the English springer spaniel breed, hid under the bed.

"Fine," Ellie said. "We have all summer." She'd spent five dollars on a gag, a gag that would not be abandoned after just one wasted cheese cube.

Kirby had progressed a lot since his death. Ellie still wasn't allowed to bring him on school property, but since the sixth-grade howl incident, Kirby hadn't caused any trouble, and his cache of tricks had doubled. There were the mundane ones: sit, stay, heel, play dead (literally! wink, wink!), and track scents. Moreover, the door had been opened to a bunch of marvelous supernatural powers. He just had to learn them without causing too much incidental chaos.

Ellie ate the cheese and chucked a squeaky yellow bear plush across the room. It stopped mid-arc, suspended two feet above the gray carpet. The air around Bear Buddy shimmered, and its head squished twice: *squeak, squeak!*

"Good boy," Ellie said. Maybe, for Kirby's peace of mind, the skull should make a funny sound. A rattle? A wee scream?

Bear Buddy flopped out of Kirby's mouth and landed on the hardwood floor with a pathetic half-squeak. Strange. Usually, he returned the toys to Ellie. Kirby wasn't the kind of dog who treated fetch like a game of keep-away.

"Bring Mr. Bear Buddy!" Ellie said. "Bring it."

In response, Kirby turned fully visible, as if somebody had flipped a switch from "shimmery transparent" to "opaque."

"You okay?" Ellie asked. It took effort for the dead to be seen. He rarely became visible without her clear command to appear. "What is it? Are you still scared? Does this help?" She covered the skull with an old sweater. Instead of relaxing, Kirby tucked his tail and darted from the bedroom.

"Hey!" Ellie ran into the hall, but he wasn't there. "Kirby!" she called. "Here, boy!" He popped through the stucco wall, whining. Paranormal vibrations hummed through her bones. She felt like a tuning fork, one resonating with worry.

He was anxious. *Terribly* anxious. Why? The skull? No, he couldn't see that ridiculous thing anymore.

When Ellie's grandfather had a heart attack, Kirby threw a fit, as if he could sense Grandpa's pain. Maybe, to ghost dogs, emotions resembled radio signals, and the signals were strong when they belonged to a loved one.

Could somebody be in pain? Somebody Kirby knew?

Ellie's parents were at the movies with their phones turned off. Sitting in that dark theater. Enjoying a rare but treasured date night. Would it also be their last?

No. *No.*

Maybe?

She tried calling them both. No answer.

They were probably fine. That said, every time Ellie left the house, the oven was *probably* turned off, but she still double-checked its knobs.

Ellie had to know, with absolute certainty, that her parents were safe.

The six-screen theater was five miles away from home. Three miles if she cut across the river using the old railroad bridge. It had been closed to traffic for years; Ellie couldn't remember the last time a train crossed the Herotonic River on its rusty tracks.

Sometimes, as Ellie walked home from school, she noticed people on the abandoned bridge. It drew even greater crowds at night. Darkness protected graffiti artists. They climbed forty, fifty, sixty feet above the river to paint the highest trusses. She wondered if the risk was worth the payoff. From the deck, a plummet into the Herotonic River might be survivable (if the artist could swim and the river was calm). Much higher? Perhaps not.

It was possible—likely, even—that those who climbed bridges at night were more resilient than mere humans. If so, Ellie didn't want to meet them. She could handle mundane dangers, like violent men with guns or knives, but every tunnel, bridge, and abandoned building in the city was allegedly home to monsters. She'd heard whispers about clans of teenage-bodied vampires, carnivorous mothmen, immortal serial killers, devil cults, cannibal families, and slenderpeople.

Even if most of the urban legends were fictitious, Ellie had a ghost dog companion. When it came to strange stuff, she could not be too open-minded.

At the front door, Ellie slipped into tennis shoes and a reflective athletic jacket. Her bike had red lights on its handlebars and seat. They might alert drivers to her presence, but she needed something stronger to illuminate her path across the bridge. After a moment of frantic searching that left half of the kitchen cabinets yawning open, she grabbed a battery-powered flashlight from the clutter drawer.

"Heel, Kirby!" she said, and they stepped outside together.

Ellie lived near the top of a small mountain. The ride downhill would be quick, if not safe. She fastened her helmet and pedaled her bike to the crack-latticed cement street. From a hundred-year-old oak tree that dominated her modest lawn, a barn owl hooted twice. When Ellie pinned it with her flashlight beam, the bird lighted from its branch and silently flew away. "Damn it," Ellie said.

Many owls—*most* owls—were just ordinary birds with a greater reputation for wisdom than they deserved. Ellie regularly volunteered at a raptor rehabilitation center. There, a great horned owl named Rosie fought everything that moved, including the bald eagle in a neighboring cage, veterinarians, handlers, rustling leaves, and its own shadow. Ellie's grandmother often said, "A wise woman knows how to pick her battles." Ellie would add that an unwise bird nearly dies by attacking its reflection.

The second kind of owl, though, Owl-with-a-capital-*O*,

was a bad omen *times ten*. Owl will wait until your life skirts the precipice of tragedy and shove you straight into the abyss.

As Ellie sped downhill, her wheels *click-click-click*ing double-time, the neighborhood was all cricket chirps and empty streets. People started work early in her blue-collar town. They might not be sleeping at 9:00 P.M., but they were settling down. Television screens projected talk shows and sitcoms through uncovered windows.

Near the base of the mountain, the buildings she passed abruptly changed from private homes to businesses. Ellie's brakes hissed against butyl rubber as she took a sharp turn onto Main Street. To the right, three men smoked pungent cigars outside a tavern called Roxxie's; she parted their sour-smelling mist. "Hey, slow down!" one guy hollered, and she could not decide whether he sounded angry or amused.

Brick factory buildings flanked the river, their facades crumbling, their windows dark and occasionally cracked. They used to manufacture plastics in town, and the chemical footprint persisted. White signs warned would-be fishermen: WARNING! CATCH AND RELEASE ONLY! HERO-TONIC FISH AND WILDLIFE CONTAMINATED WITH PCBs! Near the bridge, somebody had vandalized a CATCH AND RELEASE ONLY sign with a skull-and-crossbones.

Ellie walked her bike across a rocky strip of weeds between the street and bridge. Long grasses brushed her cotton pants, every tickle unnerving. She imagined disease-filled ticks scampering up her legs. Their bites would stitch a quilt of welts and ring-shaped rashes across her flesh. Her father counted every tick he extracted from dogs and cats at the public shelter. Every year, the number rose. They were either more abundant or more efficient hunters. Ellie had not decided which was worse. Before her, steel trusses jutted from the wide bridge deck and cut the sky into diamonds. At sunset, the slices of empty space resembled jewels on a giant's necklace.

A metal walkway ran along one side of the bridge. The smooth, narrow surface was easier to bike across than gritty cement. Ellie jumped on her bike, then shifted to a higher gear and accelerated. Her legs burned from her calves to thighs; although she biked often, she also biked slowly, always mindful of her surroundings. But it was nighttime. Darkness obscured the view, and there were no pedestrians to avoid.

Or so she thought. Halfway across the bridge, part of a low diagonal beam shifted. Somebody was trying to climb the great structure.

Key word? *Trying.* As Ellie approached, the person slipped a couple inches and dropped something. The object, which was suspiciously shaped like a spray-paint can, fell into the river. "Just passing through!" Ellie shouted. She mentally reached for Kirby. He was at her side within seconds, an invisible comfort. Dead or alive, dogs could skip from deep-nap-unconscious to awake-and-ready-for-anything almost instantaneously. She envied their skill.

The person flattened against the wide beam the same way squirrels put their bellies to the ground and froze when they were trying to escape notice. Ellie stopped, balancing on her bike wheels and one steadying foot, ready to ride at a moment's notice. Kirby was wagging his tail, acting like he knew the wannabe Spider-Man. Did he? Was this why Kirby had been so upset earlier?

"You okay?" Ellie asked. She shone her flashlight on the climber. It illuminated his backside, an awkward angle. The butt did look familiar.

"Stand back!" he called. "I'm gonna hop down." Okay, his voice sounded really familiar, too, but she *must* be mistaken.

"Jay?" Ellie asked. "You cannot be . . . Hey, careful! Don't fall in the water!"

In an attempt to dismount from the beam, the climber swiveled around, chest against the metal, his feet dangling several feet above the deck. Then, he dropped onto the walkway with a graceful *thunk* and roll. Yep. Ellie had seen that somersault before. It *was* him: Jay Ross. She and Jay met when their mothers attended the same Lamaze program. They weren't next-door neighbors, but they lived on the same block. Went to the same school. Celebrated their birthdays together. Point was: Ellie knew Jay, and he'd never done graffiti more permanent than chalk on the sidewalk.

Second point: Kirby also knew Jay well. Maybe Ellie didn't have to worry about her parents after all.

Ellie propped up her bike on its wobbly kickstand. "What are you doing?" she asked.

"Ellie?" Jay lifted one hand, his index finger extended, and poked her in the middle of the forehead. "It is you!" He laughed and ducked his head, embarrassed. "Sorry. Just had to know that you were solid. This bridge is supposed to be haunted."

"It is," she said. "My dog's here. Are you okay?"

"Kirby? Heeeey boy! Are you taking a walk?" Jay leaned over and wiggled his fingers, enticing the dog closer. Always excited to greet an old friend, Kirby ran up to him. Jay petted the shimmer-over-hot-asphalt mirage that signaled an invisible ghost, mindful not to put his hand through Kirby's body. "Ellie, did you catch my paint?" he asked.

"The river caught it."

He lightly smacked his own forehead. "Always bring a backup. Of course I'd mess this up."

"And what is 'this,' exactly? Should I be worried?"

"I just . . . It's personal. Don't worry. I can't continue without paint, anyway."

"Right. Are you walking home? Want to borrow my jacket, so cars can avoid you?" For probably the first time ever, Jay wore black from chin to toe. His tennis shoes, sweats, and turtleneck were ripped from a catalog of cartoon burglar apparel. In fact, at certain angles, he resembled a floating head. A head with short blond curls and wide-set hazel eyes. He and Ellie looked pretty different, which used to annoy her. As children, they'd pretend to be twins, but strangers didn't believe that a white Celtic-and-Nordic-American boy and a brown Apache girl came from the same family.

"Thanks," he said, "but it's fine. I'm wearing a yellow tank under this. Look." He whipped off the turtleneck so quickly that its fabric fluffed his hair with static electricity.

"That wouldn't do you any favors if you fell into the water," she said. "Climbing human pyramids doesn't qualify you for this."

"Oh, no, I don't climb. I'm the base during stunts," Jay said, as if her misunderstanding of cheerleading procedures was the real issue.

"You should find a safer spot to vandalize. Or not vandalize at all. How about that?"

"Ellie, I'm not here to paint," he said. "It's *Brittany*." He slumped on the tracks with his knees tucked against his chest. Jay looked sad. Puppy-in-the-rain sad. As much as Ellie loathed romantic relationship talk—she'd never been on a date, didn't plan to go on a date, and didn't know how to counsel or console friends about the whole "dating" thing—she couldn't leave a puppy in the rain.

"Brittany?" she asked. "Your girlfriend Brittany, or the Brittany in chess club who hates you?"

"Girlfriend," he said. "*Ex*-girlfriend. I guess both Brittanies hate me now."

"Sorry. I didn't know."

"It just happened yesterday night." He rapped a metal bar behind him. "The last time we came here, she drew a heart on the bridge. It has our names in it. Jay plus Brit. I just want to draw a zigzag crack down the middle, like it's broken."

"Uh-huh." Ellie paused, thoughtful. "So. Twenty minutes ago, did you feel a strong emotion? Fear, maybe?"

"Not really," he said.

"Damn. We can brainstorm a safer graffiti plan tomorrow, okay?" she said. "Gotta go."

He stepped back, nodding. "What's the rush, Ellie? Do you want company?"

"Ah, no thanks." She threw one leg over her bike and balanced on her tiptoes. "I'm worried about my parents because . . . well, it's probably nothing. Doesn't matter."

"You have my number," he said. "Need anything, give me a call."

"Same here." She reached out to ruffle his hair, and Jay tucked his chin to help a five-foot-nothing buddy out. His scalp shocked her.

"That's supposed to be lucky," Jay said, smoothing down his hair.

It occurred to her that luck could be bad.

Mounting dread chased Ellie across the bridge, down a web of streets, and through the cinema parking lot. She spotted the Bride family car, a battered-looking minivan, near the entrance. Her parents were the kind of people who enjoyed Monday night movies because the low traffic freed superior parking spots and theater seats. Flushed from the two-wheel exercise, Ellie leaned against the ticket booth and asked, "When does the movie *The Lonesome* let out?"

"Fifteen minutes," the employee said. His red vest, an usher uniform, was a couple sizes too loose. It made him seem too young for the night shift.

"Can I wait in the lobby?" she asked.

"That's fine. Just stay behind the velvet rope."

He seemed ambivalent to her bicycle, so Ellie wheeled it inside to prevent theft. Her mountain bike had new high-performance tires. Although their performance rating was based on grip, maneuverability, and durability, Ellie figured that they also performed well at attracting thieves. Plus, her bike was neon green, not the most subtle color.

Inside the lobby, several Formica-topped tables were clustered beside the concession stand. Popcorn kernels crunched under Ellie's tennis shoes and became lodged in their squiggly treads. She sat and basked in butter-smelling air, comforted by the relative calm. Her parents had made it to the movie theater in one piece; they weren't trapped in a burning wreck along the highway. If her mother or father had experienced an in-movie health crisis, one painful enough to trouble Kirby, there'd be EMTs outside and several missed calls on her phone.

Still, Kirby didn't tuck his invisible tail and run through walls for fun. Who else did he know? Jay, Ellie, Ellie's parents. All safe. The goth neighbors used to love him—no surprise there—but they were a thousand miles away. Nothing she could do to help them. Kirby also cared about Ellie's grandparents, cousins, uncles, and aunts. Did she have their numbers? She scrolled through her DM history and found a two-year-old conversation with Cousin Trevor. Although they used to be tight, Trevor's life became hectic after he married a teacher named Lenore Moore, moved to the Rio Grande Valley, and had a baby. The baby, now seven months old, had been born premature, almost dying twice in the neonatal intensive care unit. Little Gregory was doing well now, though. Right?

"Ma'am, do you need anything?" the concessions clerk asked, and it took Ellie a moment to accept that, at seventeen, she was now old enough to be called "Ma'am" by strangers.

"No, thanks," she said.

She needed the night to end without death. She needed to be overreacting. She needed Kirby's fit to be a fluke. But were they needs, or were they *wants*?

Did Jay need to break a cartoon heart on the Herotonic Bridge? He acted like it. Risked his life for it. Maybe, sometimes, wants felt like needs. Because the alternative hurt too bad.

A few minutes later, the post-movie crowd filled the lobby. Ellie left her bike propped against a table and found her parents near the bathrooms.

"Ellie, what the heck are you doing here?" her father asked. Luckily, he sounded more concerned than angry.

"You biked here?" her mother asked. "In the dark? Do you realize how dangerous that is, Ellie? What if a car hit you?"

"Your phone was off!" she said. "Plus, I have warning lights, and Kirby came with me." Ellie took a gulp of water from the drinking fountain. "Kirby freaked out. He was zipping through walls. The last time that happened, Grandpa . . . Hey, what's wrong?"

Her parents were glued to their smartphone screens. "Six missed calls," her mother said.

"Are most of them from your brother?" her father asked. "He called me, too."

"Did he leave a message, Mom? Dad?"

"Shh, Ellie, I'm listening to voicemail."

"What did Uncle want?" Ellie asked, and she felt goosebumps rising on her arms.

"I don't know, but he sounds terrible," her mother said. "I need to call him back."

The family exited the theater and congregated around their minivan. The nearby mountains perspired; soupy mist flavored every breath Ellie swallowed. She eavesdropped on one side of a conversation that became more frightening with every word. "How bad is it?" was followed with "What did the doctor say?" and "Is there any chance he'll wake up?" Then, Ellie's mother started shaking so hard that she almost dropped her phone. That's how she cried: no tears, but lots of shivering, like her sorrow was an earthquake, not a storm. By the time the call ended, they were alone, and Ellie was terrified.

"Trevor was in a serious car accident," her mother explained. She bowed her head, already mourning. "He's being treated at the Maria Northern Trauma Center. It . . . probably will not save his life."

"Cousin Trevor?" Ellie asked, rhetorically, because who else could it be?

"Yes."

"Mom," Ellie said. She sounded shrill. Desperate. "If he dies, I can—"

"Ellie," her mother cut her off. "No."

"But I—"

"You must never!" Raising her voice now. "You must *never*. All humans . . . all of us . . ."

". . . without exception," her father continued, because he was capable of calm speech; practicing veterinary medicine had not hardened his heart, but it taught him how to restrain signs of pain, "human ghosts are terrible things."

Ellie looked up to the sky. She saw an owl circling overhead.

⫸ TWO ⫷

I N HER DREAM that night, Ellie tried to cross the Herotonic railroad bridge, but it never seemed to end. The river was an ocean, the moon a yellow Owl eye. She called for Kirby. Instead, she summoned a blond, turtleneck-wearing cheerleader named Jay Ross. He blocked her path, smiling, like they were playing two-person Red Rover, Red Rover.

"C'mon, buddy," Ellie said. "Step aside. I'm not joking."

Jay pointed up. There, Ellie saw a single phrase painted on the highest horizontal beam: HIS LAST WILL AND TESTAMENT.

When she looked back down, Jay had vanished, and a thick, train-shaped mist rolled up the bridge, engulfing her. It smelled like wet dirt and motor oil. An obscure figure stood in the murk. She recognized his silhouette. "Trevor?" Ellie asked. "What are you doing here?"

"I'm dying, Cuz," he said. His voice gurgled like the river.

"No! That isn't fair."

"You're telling me." Trevor stepped closer, and details emerged. His face was swollen, broken, and bloody. Ellie turned away.

"It doesn't hurt anymore," he said. "Can I ask you for a favor?"

"Yes. Anything. What do you need?"

"A man named Abe Allerton murdered me." He pointed to his battered face. "Abe Allerton from Willowbee."

"Murder? Why?"

"That's what worries me, Cuz. I was trying to . . ." Trevor sank to his knees. "Getting weak. Ellie . . ."

"Trevor, fight it." Ellie tried to run to him, to hug him, but the fog was thick as molasses. "Who is Abe? Did you know him?"

"Barely," he said. "Met once before this happened. Parent-teacher conference. Two years ago. Listen."

She leaned forward. His voice was soft and tremulous, like an echo.

"Don't let Abe hurt my family," Trevor said.

"I promise."

"Thank you. Xastéyó."

In a moment of clarity, Ellie could see Trevor smiling, his young face uninjured. It was a sad smile but not a bitter one. Regretful, perhaps.

Before the dream ended, he was gone.

⫸ THREE ⫷

ELLIE AWOKE WELL before the alarm clock beeped. "I dreamed about the dead," she said. "What now?"

Kirby hopped off the bed. He'd been curled at her feet all night, entertained by who-knows-what. When ghosts fell asleep, they went back to the underworld, so he clearly didn't dream. Maybe Kirby contemplated squirrels and cheese for seven hours.

"Well, little guy?" she asked. "Is that what you did?"

His wagging poltergeist tail thumped against her desk: *thunk, thunk, thump.* Ellie concentrated on Kirby's shimmer, and his shape emerged, like an image popping from a hidden picture stereogram. Expressive, feathered tail. English springer spaniel face: black, with a wide white streak down from brow to nose. Soulful brown eyes.

"Let's see if anyone's awake." Ellie slipped into a white

T-shirt and denim overalls. They had threadbare patches over the knees. She enjoyed rollerblading as much as biking, and before Ellie wised up and purchased shin guards, the activity tore holes in all her jeans, leggings, and overalls. Her knees were still webbed by scars and dark patches. Ellie's skin was prone to hyperpigmentation; every scrape, scratch, and blemish left a deep brown impression for months.

As Ellie washed her face in the second-floor bathroom, her mind wandered to a frightening place. Most dreams were REM-stage fiction. Silly, scary, mundane, meaningless. Her conversation with Trevor felt different.

In fact, it reminded her of a story. One that chilled Ellie to the core.

As a young woman, Six-Great visited the southern Kunétai—the Rio Grande River—to investigate a series of disappearances. People were vanishing near its fertile estuary. At first, the locals blamed their misfortune on random mishaps. All manner of beasts and monsters lived in the Kunétai, but few were deadlier than the water itself, which could smother a powerful swimmer and fling the lifeless body into the sea. However, after eleven adults, four children, and a pack horse disappeared in one season, it seemed obvious that someone or *something* was intentionally causing harm.

When news of the mystery reached her, Six-Great was three hundred miles from the estuary. She traveled the distance by foot. Horses, skittish things, did not enjoy the company of ghosts, and her dogs could tote her supplies by sled. Even with their help, Six-Great was exhausted when she reached the river. Still a day away from the nearest Lipan band, she made camp near the riverbank and commanded her dogs to stay alert as she slept.

That night, she had a troubling dream. In it, a teen boy crawled from a black pool of water and said, "Are you the woman who kills monsters?"

"I am," she said.

The boy groaned. "I have the worst luck, Auntie," he said. "It just drowned me! Eugh! Not two minutes ago!"

"What?" she asked. "A gator?"

"Worse," he said. "It had the head of a man and the body of a fish. Be careful, Auntie. During the attack, something stung me in the water."

"Like a barb?" she asked. "Or the stingers of a jellyfish?"

"One of those. It made my limbs go numb. There's no time to rest. Hurry. You need to find the creature before it kills again."

Six-Great awoke in a state of panic. A person's last breath carried them to the underworld. Perhaps, with that breath, they could speak a last message. Whisper it into the ear of a receptive dreamer.

When Six-Great reached her destination, Lipan band was in a state of panic. Another person had gone missing.

A teenage boy.

There was no time for reverie. Ellie grabbed her mother's waterproof eyeliner pencil and used its freshly sharpened tip to scrawl "Abe Allerton from Willowbee" across her arm. Just in case.

Don't let Abe hurt my family.

On the makeup counter, her phone beeped, a text alert. She opened the messaging program and read:

JAY (9:31 A.M.) – Are you OK?

The message and its impeccable timing unnerved her. Was Jay prescient? He had a psychic auntie, but that didn't mean anything. The gift wasn't hereditary. It couldn't be passed on like blue eyes or large feet.

Her phone beeped again.

JAY (9:33 A.M.) – Did you make it home?

It took a moment for Ellie to remember that she forgot to send an "I'm still alive" update at the movie theater. Of course Jay was worried.

She responded:

EL (9:34 A.M.) – I'm home.
EL (9:34 A.M.) – Not OK.
JAY (9:34 A.M.) – ???
JAY (9:35 A.M.) – What's wrong?
JAY (9:35 A.M.) – Are your parents safe?
EL (9:35 A.M.) – Yes
EL (9:36 A.M.) – but
EL (9:36 A.M.) – I don't know.
EL (9:36 A.M.) – Gotta go.
EL: (9:36 A.M.) – Let's talk later.

JAY (9:37 A.M.) – Sure:)

JAY (9:37 A.M.) – Want a sundae?

That was his way of inviting her to meet at the mall, the only place in town with fresh ice cream. He wouldn't eat it from a cardboard box. Said it tasted like paper. Frankly, Ellie couldn't tell the difference.

EL (9:36 A.M.) – See you at 12.

After her sign-off, Ellie wrestled with knots in her hair. It was mid-back long, unlayered, and the kind of dark brown that looked black indoors. Ellie usually wore her hair loose, but today she wrapped it in a tight bun on the back of her head. She looked at her reflection, studied her face. The way it seemed fuller and more mature without hair cascading beside her cheeks and neck. Ellie hoped that she could get used to the new look. Hair should be cut to signify change or mourning—that was the Lipan way—and she felt both bearing down on her.

Ellie reached for a pair of scissors in the toiletry drawer, but she hesitated. No. Not yet. Maybe Trevor survived.

The stairs creaked as she descended to the ground floor. Although her family house was two stories high (sans the attic), it was narrow, as if squeezed. Thrift store paintings and framed photographs cluttered the limited wall space. Ellie paused at the staircase landing, her grip tightening on the wooden handrail. One of the hanging frames was blank. Her father must have removed the picture last night.

Ellie's elders often cautioned: when somebody dies young, it was dangerous to speak his name, see his face, or risk calling him back another way.

She touched the empty space where Trevor's smiling face used to be. The absence made her house feel subtly unwelcoming. It might as well be a stranger's home. Maybe, she'd woken up in an alternate universe, one so similar to hers it could only be distinguished by the people it lacked. "Goodbye," Ellie said. "Until . . ." She left the phrase unfinished. *Until we meet again.* Ellie didn't want to schedule that reunion too soon.

She trusted the wisdom of her parents and elders. Ellie had heard the dark and violent stories about human ghosts. They were rare and fleeting things that almost always left violence in their wake.

The thing was, she had never been able to understand why they were so terrible. Trevor loved his family and friends; how could death change that? How could anything from Trevor be cruel? It was inconceivable, and yet . . .

She withdrew her hand from the picture frame. Sometimes, the world was too mysterious for her liking; Ellie intended to change that someday.

In the kitchen, her father nursed a mug of coffee. "You're awake before noon?" he asked. "Did summer end while I was sleeping?" He smiled with his mouth, but his brown eyes seemed sad.

"Feels like it," Ellie said. "Where's Mom?"

"She took a dawn flight to McAllen."

"Is that because . . ." Ellie trailed off. Every word about the tragedy felt like a psychic paper cut, and too many stings would make her cry. There was nothing shameful about tears, but Ellie hated the way her face ached when she wept. The pain felt like a head cold. "When did it happen?"

"Last night," her father said. "Around two-thirty. He peacefully walked to the underworld. No struggle, no pain."

"No pain? You can't know that, Dad." Although Ellie spoke softly, he heard her. Must have. He no longer pretended to smile.

"Lenore needs help with Baby Gregory. That's why your mother left suddenly." He put his coffee on the counter and hugged Ellie. His wool vest tickled her chin. Ellie's father had to wear blue scrubs and a physician's lab coat at work, but during off-days, he broke out the cable-knit sweaters, tweed pants, and scratchy wool vests. "She has other duties. Your aunt and uncle are crushed with grief. They can't handle the burial preparations alone."

Oddly, thinking about Trevor's widow, infant son, and parents helped Ellie push through. She had a job to do: protect them from Abe Allerton. "Are the police investigating the crash?" she asked.

"I believe so."

"Let me make it easier. Abe Allerton killed him. Abe Allerton from a town called Willowbee."

Her father stepped back, perturbed. "Why do you believe that?"

"Cuz spoke to me in a dream. Told me who killed him. Same way that drowned boy told Six-Great-Grandmother about the river monster."

"I see." Judging by his furrowed brow, that was an exaggeration, at best. "Wait. What river monster are you referring to? Didn't she fight a few?"

"The one with a human face and poison scales. That's not important. Dad, I think Cuz reached out to me in between phases, after his last exhale but before his spirit went Below."

"It's possible. You and Six-Great are so much alike."

"You think so?" she asked.

"Sure. I never met the woman, obviously, but you're both remarkable ghost trainers. Intelligent and brave, too."

Ellie smiled faintly. "Thanks," she said, taking a glass from the cupboard and pouring herself some orange juice. She had no appetite for solid breakfast. "You know what this all means, though, right? Abe Allerton from Willowbee is a murderer, and he *cannot* hurt anybody else."

"Hm."

"Should I doubt myself? Can we really take that risk? Six-Great trusted her dream, and the decision probably saved lives."

"No. But . . ." Her father took a long sip of coffee. "As you slept, did Tre—I mean, did *your cousin* describe the murder?"

She shook her head. "We had so little time. Dad, he

looked terrible. Bleeding and broken. It must have been torture. Can we call somebody? What about a sheriff?"

"Give the police a few days," her father said. "Let them investigate."

"Will they, though?" She thumped her glass on the counter. Pulpy juice spilled over its rim and pooled between tiles. "Everyone thinks it was a car crash, right? Even Lenore!"

"Ah. Well. That doesn't surprise me." Her father adopted a dry tone, the kind he used to talk about clinical details from work. "Your cousin's injuries are consistent with trauma from a high-speed collision."

"He was driving fast? Where did it happen? A highway? Weren't there any witnesses?"

"No. A farmer found him along a wooded road. It was isolated. Not your cousin's usual route home. But he was alone in his damaged car."

"That's a big red flag. Tell the police he'd never speed like that without a good reason. Obviously Abe Allerton was chasing him." Yet that wasn't the obvious answer at all. In Ellie's dream, Trevor never mentioned a high-speed pursuit. He said Abe had murdered him. That required intent. What was the motive?

"Right now," Ellie's father said, "everybody is still wondering *what* happened, not *who* did it."

"The *what* and *who* are linked! So, let's use the *who* to find the *what*!"

"You aren't wrong." Ellie's father moved to the dining nook, a table and three wicker chairs. He unfolded a paper map of Texas and spread it over the crumb-freckled hardwood tabletop. The map resembled a wrinkled tablecloth interwoven by roads, rivers, and county lines.

"What's that for?" Ellie asked.

"Your mother needs a car, so we'll drive to the burial. I can leave the van with her and take a plane home."

"Will Mom be gone a long time?" Ellie's mother, Vivian (Ms. Bride to her students), taught high school math. The job might not be easy, but it came with one major perk: she had two months of summer vacation. "I can help her!"

"Are you sure? She wants to live with Lenore until things are settled. Might take weeks."

"I'm sure." She couldn't protect Trevor's family with an eight hundred-mile gulf between them.

"Thank you." Her father traced a path from North to South Texas. "This is our route."

"When do we leave?" Ellie asked.

"Two days." He leaned closer to the map, squinting, and pointed to a spot near the bottom of Texas. "What's that town name, Ellie? I'm not wearing glasses."

Ellie peered at the word above his fingertip. It was faint, as if printed incorrectly. "It says Willowbee. Dad . . ."

"I thought the name sounded familiar." He checked the map scale. "Willowbee is about thirty miles away from the elementary school, and ten miles away from the road."

"The road?" she asked.

"Where your cousin was found." He looked up. "I believe you, Ellie."

✙ FOUR ✙

THE FOOD COURT was packed with shoppers, but Ellie found an empty table near the pretzel kiosk. There, she nibbled on honey-roasted peanuts. Frustration did no wonders for her appetite. It filled her stomach like a boulder. Every honeyed bite tasted stale. Was that how Jay felt when he ate ice cream from a carton?

Ellie drummed her fingers on the tabletop and tried to redirect her thoughts from murder and grief. It was difficult to take her father's advice. To trust that police—strangers!—would give Trevor the justice he deserved. Especially after Trevor visited *her* dream. Entrusted *her* with his family's safety.

She hadn't cried about Trevor's death yet. Not much, anyway. A few tears had slipped down her cheeks as she biked to the mall, but the wind swiftly carried them away. When Kirby died, Ellie held his favorite squeak toy and wept on and off for hours. At the time, she didn't know if he'd return. Ghost-waking was a tricky technique, and not everybody excelled at it. Ellie's mother could only summon the dead in a state of deep meditation.

Maybe her dry-eyed spell was for the best. Crying helped blunt the edge of loss, and Ellie wanted her current pain to stay sharp. To prod her in the ribs until Trevor was avenged.

Hopefully, it happened through a police investigation that led to an arrest that resulted in a successful trial by jury and a murder conviction. However, the justice system was imperfect. Many crimes remained unsolved, especially violence against Natives. Plus, Trevor's death was so strange, magic might have been involved. That was a potential death blow against justice. Magic, as energy from another realm, corrupted and altered the fabric of reality. The defense for Abe Allerton could argue that any trace of magic at the crime scene negated his chance for a fair trial, since there was no way to trust the evidence beyond a reasonable doubt. Nine times out of ten, that argument worked for people with million-dollar lawyers. Strangely, it rarely worked for anyone else.

If the police failed, Ellie would have a busy summer vacation.

She sent a text: "Sitting near pretzel place. Bring your sundae." Ellie had to stay put, or she'd lose her spot. There were several food-laden people weaving between the tables, adrift and looking for a place to land. The tables were squeezed so close to each other that she could hear the conversation at the table beside her.

"Oh my God," a woman said. "Scarecrows?"

"Yes," a man said. "The kind with straw, but their eyes . . . they had *real human eyes*."

"Oh. My. God. I'll *never* drive through Iowa. How large was the corn field?"

"Who knows? We turned around after twenty-five miles. Gas was low, and I worried . . ."

"Yes?"

"The scarecrows. They were watching. If we broke down in that field, they might—"

"Hi, Ellie!" Jay said. Banana split in hand, he slid onto the empty seat in front of her. He wore a green polo, tan slacks, and bright white shoes. The outfit was definitely more his style than an all-black getup.

"Perfect timing," Ellie said. If she'd eavesdropped a moment longer, the scarecrow story might have given her the chills before her drive across Texas. Iowan farms had a reputation for strangeness, just like the prairie that once blanketed the Midwest.

"How are you?" Jay asked. His voice sounded gentler than usual. Concerned.

"Bad," she said.

"What happened?"

How could she answer that? Ellie didn't want his pity, kindness, or condolences. The prospect that somebody might comfort her was viscerally upsetting, although Ellie didn't know why.

"Somebody murdered my cousin," she said. "That's why Kirby had a fit last night."

"Wh—Trevor?"

"Careful. Don't say his name."

"I'm sorry." He reached across the table and squeezed her hand. She looked down, studying the differences between their entwined fingers. His nails were short and evenly trimmed. She'd painted hers neon green and filed them into points. "Is there anything I can do?"

She drew her hand away from his and drummed the table.

"The man who hurt him needs to pay," she said.

Jay said, without hesitation, "Let me help."

"Thank you." They ate quietly. She lingered on a honey-roasted peanut. He prodded his ice cream with a plastic spoon. It wasn't a companionable silence, Ellie realized. At least not to her. She felt awkward around her oldest friend. Maybe that's because they'd never had to deal with heavy stuff like murder before. Life's problems used to be graffiti mistakes and dogs afraid of googly-eyed skulls.

She missed that.

"What happened to the bridge heart?" Ellie asked.

"I . . . oh. Oh. Right. That. It's not a problem anymore. My sister cornered me last night. Ronnie knew I'd been up to something weird."

"Did the black clothing tip her off?"

He tilted his head in agreement. "She promised to keep the graffiti thing secret, but I guess boyfriends don't count, because now Al—that's Ronnie's guy—wants to climb the bridge in my place, like a stand-in."

"Can Al climb?"

"Probably. He's cursed." Jay cupped his mouth to hide it from eavesdropping lip readers. "The *vampire* curse."

"Whoa. That's uncommon." The United States tracked cursed individuals through Vampiric Citizen Centers. The VCCs provided yearly checkups to monitor curse progression. Once deleterious side effects crossed a "safe" threshold, the cursed were moved to a sanatorium until death. To avoid confinement, many vampires lived outside the US in more permissive countries.

"How'd they meet?" Ellie asked.

"During school. Ronnie and Al are both at North Herotonic."

"I need to talk to them before college application season," Ellie said. "Herotonic is on the top of my list."

He sat straighter, intrigued. "College? I thought you wanted to start that PI business."

"Well, I've been thinking . . ." If she wanted to be a paranormal investigator, a college degree wasn't strictly necessary. Ellie had researched options online. It was, after all, her top career goal. Her second goal was paleontologist, since she could always double-check her reconstructions with careful use of ghost dinosaurs. That said, although Ellie had summoned dogs, mosquitoes, butterflies, and mice from Below, she'd never attempted to wake up an extinct species. She had to practice that skill. Maybe the summer break would be a good time to start. "North Hero-tonic has a good invasive monster program and field-work opportunities," she continued. "Like, last semester, the ParAb department funded a trip to the panting caves out-side Austin."

"The panting caves? Those are dangerous. *Eat people* dangerous." He sounded more fascinated than afraid. It was the kind of reaction Ellie expected from Jay.

"See, that's the beauty of field trips," she said. "The cave uses tricks to attract prey. So, if you're prepared, it's no worse than a normal underground tunnel. That's why I want a degree. To learn from experienced PIs and build on their knowledge. The same way I learned Six-Great's secret. Like my mom always says, 'Don't reinvent the wheel.'"

"Saves a lot of time," he agreed. "I'm applying to Hero-tonic too, if my parents let me. They aren't happy about Al."

"Because of his curse?"

"Yeah. They offered to pay for his cure. He's only been vampiric for a couple years. Al refused, though. Said the ben-efits outweigh the drawbacks."

"Does he think it makes him immortal?" The average vampire lived ninety-two years. A decent lifespan, yes, but immortality? Not even close. As the curse fermented, its drawbacks multiplied. Sunscreen wouldn't always protect Al, and elderly vampires needed fresh blood; the bagged stuff turned their stomachs.

"I don't know." Jay seemed to realize that his ice cream was melting around the banana, because he shoveled a few soupy spoonfuls into his mouth before continuing. "That's probably why he's being so nice to me, though."

"Oh?"

"Yeah." Jay rested his chin on one hand and sighed. "I get where Al's coming from, but . . . it's awkward. Is he really a good man, or just faking it to get my approval? I don't enjoy feeling like a pawn."

"That's because you're a knight. They jump."

"Yeah! And can a pawn do this?" He half-stood, glanced over his shoulder, and then slowly sat again. "It's too crowded right now."

"Were you going to jump?" Ellie asked.

"Do a cartwheel."

"That would've been fun."

"Uh-huh." Another sigh, this one a bit less heartfelt. "I'm meeting Al at the bridge tomorrow. Sunset."

"Can I come?" Ellie asked. Why not?

"You want to?" Jay asked.

"What, worried I'll ruin the brotherly bonding?"

He straightened, dropping his spoon in the ice cream dish. "Brother? Al and Ronnie aren't married, you know."

"I assumed it was serious, since your parents offered a cure. That's expensive."

"Yeah," he said. "It's serious, but no *engagement*. They're both too young! Can you imagine getting married at twenty?"

"Me? Personally? I don't imagine getting married at all."

"Fair enough," he said. "Um. Ellie, I know you have more important things to deal with right now. Seriously, if—"

"I'll meet you at the bridge," Ellie interrupted. "We can't do anything about Allerton until I'm in South Texas."

"When are you leaving?" Jay asked.

"Thirty hours," she said. "I can barely stand the wait."

⇒⇒ FIVE ⇐⇐

L ATER, ELLIE AND JAY met near the skull-and-crossbones PCB warning sign. Under a sky lit by ripening sunlight, the Herotonic River glinted like quicksilver.

"You're early!" Ellie said. They were supposed to gather at sunset, but because the definition of "sunset" was unclear, she'd decided to play it safe and arrive before the color show began.

"I didn't want to make anyone wait," Jay said. He thrust his hands in his jean pockets. Tragically, his pants were so tight, he reached an impasse at the knuckles. "But I guess Al won't show until the sky is red."

"No worries," said a third person with a faint Minnesotan accent. "I use sunscreen. Plus, early birds eat toast, kid-dos." Ellie and Jay each whirled around so quickly they almost collided. A young man stood on a granite boulder near the riverside. He dressed like a retro greaser: leather biker jacket, white T-shirt, and slate jeans. His pale brow shone under pomade-slicked black hair. Opaque-looking eyeglasses completed the outfit, although Ellie suspected that they were more functional than fashionable. She also noticed a white film around his ears, evidence he was good for his word.

"Isn't it worms?" Jay asked, smiling. "Early birds get the worms?"

"Yeah, but birds prefer toast," Al said. "It's not a healthy choice, but when does that stop 'em? You ever see a goose turn down scraps of bread? They're self-destructive. Poor bastards. " He laughed, real loud, and Ellie wondered if Al always projected his voice like an opera singer. He might also be nervous. Hard to tell sometimes, especially with strangers.

"Yeah," she said. "I volunteered at a bird rehab center once. First thing they taught us: don't give the animals bread."

Al hopped off the boulder and approached, still grinning. Although his teeth were unusually white, the color of fresh snowfall or a news anchor's smile, they didn't seem sharp enough to pierce skin. Did he possess a hidden pair of needle-sharp second canines? Even newly cursed vampires had to consume more blood than solid food, and although they could purchase blood bags from private facilities, prepackaged supplies often ran low.

"Al, this is Ellie," Jay said. "Ellie, this is Al."

Ellie went for a handshake, but signals must have crossed, because Al stuck out his fist instead. It was the old fist bump vs. shake conundrum: if she didn't act decisively, the confusion would transform into a cringeworthy series of half-greetings and awkward laughter. Ellie grabbed his hand, the same way she folded "paper" over "rock" during a game of rock, paper, scissors, and shook it.

"I hear you're studying at Herotonic University," she said. "What major?"

"Chemistry," he said. "Same as Ronnie. We're both pre-med."

"I didn't know that," Jay said. "Ronnie says she wants to research . . ."

"Yeah. Biomedical research. We're going to start a private facility someday." He crossed his arms. "I don't want to bore you. Where's the heart?"

"Just a moment," Ellie said. "Can you climb?"

"Like a spider on a water spout." Al looked up. "No rain, so I'm good."

"Great," she said. "Where's the heart, Jay?"

"This way." Jay started toward the bridge. Again, his fingers burrowed into his pockets. As the trio crossed the metal walkway, Ellie and Jay clomped, tapping a techno beat against the walkway. Al made no such commotion with his feet, though he did chatter enough for all of them.

"Do you guys enjoy bowling?" he asked. "I want to start a team and compete in local tournaments."

"I think it's fun," Ellie said, "but that doesn't mean I'm

good at it. Although . . ." Perhaps she could train Kirby to stop her rolls from landing in the gutter. "Do the tourneys have prizes?"

"Trophies and gift cards," Al said. "Last year, the winners each took home fifty dollars for Jukebox Burger. Good stuff. They have seasoned sweet potato fries. What about you, Jay?"

"Bowling team? Um. No thanks. I'm busy. Cheer practice." Jay leaned against the bridge's safety railing and pointed at a beam over his head. "There it is. See?"

A gust whistled through the grand steel trusses and kicked ripples across the sunset-kissed river. Al and Jay switched places.

"What a view," Al said, and he inhaled deeply. "Eugh. Bad idea. Can you smell that? Rotting fish, sewer discharge, rust. I hate how spoiled the world has become." Al coughed, shuddering, and spat into the river. The spit blob was pink. Blood-tinted. Ellie wondered if his tears were bloody, too. "It's the running water," he explained. "Makes me sick. Don't know why. Something curse-related."

"What?" Jay asked, dismayed. "You don't have to do this. Seriously."

"It's no big deal," Al said. "Before the change, I used to feel pain all the time. A little congestion is fine." He shook a black spray-paint can—*clack, clack, clack*—and tilted his well-coiffured head in contemplation. "Okay. Go time." He hopped onto the beam and climbed its horizontal face.

"He really does look like a spider," Ellie said. "Four-legged one. So. Spider-Man."

"Or a lizard," Jay offered. "Somebody invented a paint that repels vampires. They can't cling to it. It's useful for preventing burglaries, I guess, but don't cursed people need to be welcome in a house?"

"Sort of." She lowered her voice. "They can enter any property, but if their welcome is revoked, the curse makes them sick. We shouldn't discuss that around Al, though. It might be a sensitive subject."

"Ah, sorry. I just—"

"You want me to put an *X* through it?" Al shouted. "An *X* for your ex?"

"No, a zigzag," Jay said. "Like a broken heart!"

"That's a bit pitiful, kiddo," Al said. "Are you sure?"

"Stop with the 'kiddo' stuff, okay?" Jay said. "You're just three years older than me."

"Force of habit." With a hiss of aerosolized paint, he inked a lightning bolt break into the heart. "It's what I call my little sisters."

"I'm not . . . What are you implying?" Jay called. "Ellie, ask him the question."

"Fine, fine," Ellie said. "Al, how serious are you and Ronnie?"

"Funny you should ask," Al said, "because I'm about to demonstrate." He started climbing. Within a minute, Al reached the highest horizontal beam on the Herotonic Bridge.

Over sixty feet above the river, the upper chord was the most prominent and dangerous canvas available.

"What's he doing?" Jay asked.

"Painting something? Writing? Hard to see." Ellie leaned farther over the rail. From her vantage point, she could barely see Al, much less the beam. "Definitely writing. Take my hand. I don't want to fall."

With Jay as an anchor, Ellie could lean far enough to read his message. She recited, "*R-O-N-N-I-E-W-I-L-L.* Ronnie, will . . . *Y-O-U.* You! Ronnie, will you—"

"Will you what?" Jay asked. "What? Is he writing an *M*?"

"Yes. Definitely *M*. Followed by an *A*. Wow. I can't believe he's proposing to your sister through graffiti. That's either adorable or awful, depending on her tastes."

"My parents will freak! Seriously! They'll stop paying for Ronnie's tuition! I have to stop him!" Jay helped Ellie back onto the bridge deck. Once she was safe, he climbed onto the lowest beam and began to inchworm up. His hands and knees dislodged flakes of rust. Unfortunately for mere mortals, the truss was shaped like an *X*. It was easy to climb the first half, but scaling the crisscross juncture ought not be attempted in skinny jeans.

"Cut it out," Ellie said. "Jay, seriously. You're going to fall! Have you ever heard the story of Icarus?"

"It's wider than a balance beam. I'll be fine!" Unfortunately, balance beams weren't steep and rusty. Jay's lower body slipped with a spray of oxidized metal. He dangled over the river. His feet were ten feet above Ellie's head.

"Damn it!" Ellie said. "Hang in there! Al, a little help, please?"

Al shouted something, but Ellie missed it, because Jay was slipping, and she had to catch him, and—

In her attempt to lean over the railing and catch Jay, Ellie fell. No time to call Kirby. Barely enough time for a scream! The river was thirty feet below her face. Twenty feet. Ten. With a tremendous, bubbly rush, her world became cold and dark. Her nose burned as water filled her sinus cavity. She kicked, trying to surface, fighting the weight of waterlogged jeans.

Denim was lead-heavy when it absorbed liquid. She wore pants to protect her legs from insect bites, but the extra fabric might drown her now.

Ellie's head popped above the river surface. As the downstream current drew her under the bridge, she breathed deeply and slowly, filling her lungs with buoyant air. The water was cool but not cold; she'd survived the fall, so escape should be easy. As Ellie cleared the shadow of the bridge, there was a splash. Seconds later, Jay bobbed up, coughing.

"You okay?" Ellie shouted. She had to shout. Her ears were muffled by water.

"Yes! Swim to shore! Diagonal!" He spat out water. "Hard to float! My pants are so heavy!"

"Mine too!"

"Like this!" Jay drew ahead with a powerful breaststroke.

Ellie tried to imitate him, but more water gushed up her nose, stinging like chili powder. She snorted with pain and transitioned to an old faithful doggy paddle. Kirby drifted beside her, swimming without disturbing the water, his body a hot-asphalt shimmer. "Having fun, boy?" she asked.

At least he seemed calm. That probably meant that PCBs and catfish were the biggest threats in the Herotonic. Then again, when the Kunétai creature attacked Six-Great, nobody—and that included her dogs—had been prepared.

Ellie felt dread building in her chest. What if the creature had friends? Poison-scaled, barb-tailed monster fish with human faces and a thirst for revenge? It wouldn't be the first time that Six-Great's enemies carried grudges across many human generations. And now Ellie was in the middle of a river, fighting the pull of her soggy jeans.

How did Six-Great survive the encounter at the Kunétai?

After Six-Great reached the southern Lipan band, she requested two things: a net large enough to ensnare a bison and something that belonged to the missing boy who visited her dream. A dozen women started weaving the net at once, and the boy's parents provided a pair of his knee-high boots.

"They were discarded near the riverbank," the father said. "As if . . ."

Six-Great said, "Xastéyó, Shela." And she asked her dogs to track the boy's scent. Even their paranormal sense of smell was confounded by the river. For three days, as the women wove her net, Six-Great traveled up and down the Kunétai, searching for any trace of body or monster.

On day four, her dogs found a hair tie near the bank. It was grimy and half-buried in drying mud. A knot of long, black hair was tangled around the strap. Six-Great put it deep within her satchel and returned to her hosts.

"We finished the net," the women said. "Do you need anything else?"

"Fresh meat," she told them. "Bait for the monster. Shech'oonii, did the missing boy tie back his hair?" In those days, most people wore their hair long and unrestrained.

"Only when he swims," one woman said. "In the lake, not the river. Our children never play there. We teach them caution!"

"Understood," Six-Great said. "So if he removed his boots and tied back his hair . . ."

"What?"

"He must have entered the water willingly."

The women protested. "Why would anybody do that?"

"I don't know," she said. "Yet. Thank you for the net. Ha'au. Right now, I must go foraging."

The following morning, Six-Great returned to the isolated bend where she found the hair tie. A hunter had provided her with a freshly slain buck. After thanking the animal for its sacrifice, she laid its heavy body near the river, so close that its hind legs dangled in the water. A copse of juniper trees grew nearby; Six-Great sat beneath them and waited. She played with her dogs to pass the time and made them toys from scraps of cloth and leather. She always carried a bundle of grinning dollies that rattled like gourds because they had dry mesquite pods in their bellies. The dogs never tired of fetch.

Six-Great wished she could be so easily entertained.

She waited.

And waited.

She waited until nightfall. Until her eyes burned with exhaustion. Until she fell asleep.

Until a scream woke her.

Briefly disoriented, Six-Great called for her dogs. They whined, confused but not defensive. Carefully, because scorpions and snakes hid in shadows, she maneuvered through the shrubs between the juniper copse and river. All that remained of the buck was an indentation in the grass. "Help me, Auntie!" somebody cried. "It won't let go!"

When Six-Great looked at the silver-ripple, moonlit surface of the Kunétai, she saw the missing boy. His face bobbed on the water, as if he floated with his head tilted back. "Please!" he repeated. Water spilled into his open mouth. With a gurgle, the boy slipped underwater.

"Hey!" Six-Great shouted. "I'm throwing a rope!" She unwound a cord from her dog sled and searched for a spot to cast the line. There were no signs of movement in the river; was he unconscious? How could he be conscious *at all*? Sometimes, people returned from the dead, but their body had to be in good condition. If they couldn't return their last breath to their lungs before rot set in, all hope was lost.

Six-Great hesitated on the bank. Why would the boy remove his boots, tie back his hair, and swim to his death?

"Is that how you lure victims into the river?" she shouted. "I know what you are, and it isn't human! That courageous boy spent his last moments in my dreams. He told me about you, creature. I hope you enjoyed the deer."

Ripples broke the river surface seconds before the monster jumped. It burst into the air, all ruby scales and black barbs; over ten feet long, the fish had two faces. The first was shaped like it belonged to a large river gar, and the second, which was roughly human-shaped and malleable as clay, protruded from the top of its head like a mask. Both faces laughed as the monster leapt, filling the air with shrill, discordant shrieks.

"It's a long river," the monster said, splashing down and swimming away. "You'll never see me again."

Six-Great's dogs began to howl, finally recognizing the danger. She raised a hand and commanded, "Quiet! We don't need to chase him."

She returned to the juniper trees and waited until dawn. Then, Six-Great gathered the woven net and traveled downriver. All day she walked, until she saw it: a great red body bobbing on the water's surface. Dead. She cast the net and scooped it from the Kunétai. With great caution, Six-Great dragged it to the middle of the desert and buried its body so deep, even burrowing badgers could not reach it.

She'd filled the deer with poisonous herbs. The monster died by a taste of its own medicine. But it was a monster, and they were harder to kill than humans. If she buried it near the river, a flood might draw it back into the Kunétai.

As Ellie thought about Six-Great, she glimpsed Jay's face bobbing on the Herotonic and wondered if the monster's bones still waited to be unearthed.

"Hey! You two! Grab a branch!" Al stood on the nearby bank. He'd pulled a sapling from the earth and now held it over the water. Jay and Ellie were swept toward its mane of thin branches. They each grabbed ahold and allowed Al to pull them ashore.

"Thanks," Ellie said. In the shallows, her legs scraped the river bottom and raised a murky cloud of silt. With a groan, she crawled onto the gravel and grass and sat beside Jay. "This will either give us superpowers or stomachaches," Ellie rasped. "Uck."

"What was that, you two?" Al said. "Does anyone need resuscitation? Nine-one-one?"

"We're okay," Jay said. "Are we?"

"Yeah," Ellie said. "Now that we're out of the water. I'd appreciate a towel, though. And a bottle of something that doesn't taste like goose turds and dead fish." She scrutinized the Herotonic. It seemed calm. Safe. That's what frightened her the most: danger hiding in plain sight.

"There's a gas station down the street," Al said. "Stay. I'll be back in five minutes."

Once Al left, Ellie wrenched her phone out of her soggy jeans. As she feared, the water had trashed it. "Black screen of death."

"Aw, no," Jay said. "Mine's waterproof, but . . ." He patted his jacket pockets. "It's also in the river."

Ellie wiggled her toes, cringing. Her socks were squishy. "On the bright side, the two-faced fish can now phone in a pizza order like the rest of us."

"The what?"

She shook her head. "Just . . . it's an old story."

"Ellie?" he asked.

"Yeah?"

"I'm really sorry."

"For what?"

"You tried to help, and this happened. I'll replace your phone."

"Appreciate that," she said. "But don't worry. I have a backup at home. There was a two-for-one deal from the phone company. My parents let me keep both, because Dad refuses to upgrade his eighty-year-old flip phone, and Mom always wants the newest models."

Her mind wandered to the fall. How it happened so quickly. How it hadn't been part of her plan. How she could have drowned because of a doodle on a bridge.

"Did I ever tell you about the howl incident?" she asked. "The one that happened in sixth grade?"

"Kirby destroyed your class, right?"

"Pretty much," she said. "He gave everyone nosebleeds, too. I'm glad you and I didn't share a homeroom."

"I'm not! That sounds exciting."

"You weren't there, Jay! You weren't there!" She wagged her finger. "Anyway, after I came home, *suspended*, Mom told me about the death of Icarus. It's an ancient Greek parable.

Icarus had this inventor for a father, Daedalus, who built functioning wings from wax and feathers. It was impressive engineering for the time. Daedalus warned him, 'Don't fly too high or too low.' Of course, Icarus didn't listen. He flew too close to the sun, and the wings melted, which sent him plummeting into the Mediterranean Sea, and—"

"Oh, sure, I know that story," Jay interrupted. "We learn about the ancient Greeks every year."

"That's what I figured, but you didn't get my two-faced fish joke, so I wanted to be safe."

"How does the parable relate to ghosts? Is there a sequel?"

"Not for Icarus. He stays dead."

"Aw."

"Mom told me, 'Don't be like Icarus, Ellie. Caution is our friend.' Because I was immature back then, I asked, 'Aren't we supposed to take risks?'"

"That's a good question," Jay said. "Not immature at all."

"Mom thought I was being—in her words—*obstinate*," Ellie said. "She was probably right, considering that I'd just been suspended. That's not important. What I'm trying to say is: this summer, investigating my cousin's murder, we might skirt the line between wise and unwise danger. It's hard to know that you're flying too high until the feathers start dropping."

"Don't worry. Everything will be okay," he said. "We're nothing like Icarus."

"Says the guy who just fell into a large body of water."

"Fell into a large body of water *and survived*."

Shyly, stars appeared one-by-one. As the dusk thickened, Jay held out his hand. "Look what I just learned," he said. A white, marble-sized globe of light blinked into existence and hovered over his palm. At first, Ellie mistook it for a firefly.

"Magic?" she asked. The light flickered, faltering.

"Yes." Jay's voice sounded strained. "It's a will-o'-the-wisp. Your family secret is way more powerful."

"My secret isn't magic, though. How are you doing that?"

"I'm descended from Lord Oberon." He lowered his hand, and the orb followed, as if bound to Jay by an invisible rod.

"You're serious!" Ellie slapped her knee; it made a soggy *thunk* sound. Oberon's line was known to have a stronger-than-typical knack for magic, although the reason for that trend was unknown, like many quirks of the alien dimension. "No kidding! You've mentioned it before. But . . . sorry . . . I thought, uh, the 'I'm descended from fae royalty' line is just something people say at parties to impress their friends. The same way everyone claims to have a Cherokee princess great-great-grandparent."

"To be fair," Jay said, "Oberon has a *lot* of distant descendants." The light winked out, and Jay dropped his hand. "After a while, though, all the magic gets diluted from our genes, or something. I'm probably the last light-maker in my line."

"Lucky for Kirby, my family secret is knowledge, not genetic," Ellie said.

"I've always meant to ask this: could you teach anyone—even me—how to wake up the dead?"

"Theoretically."

"Whoa."

"Generally, the secret is passed through eldest daughters when they come of age. Twelve, thirteen years old."

"Why's that?" Jay asked. "Why don't you teach more people?"

"It's dangerous. But . . . in the right hands, the secret can change the world. That's why it cannot be forgotten." As a breeze dried her face, Ellie said, "My six-great-grandmother once crushed an army of murderous invaders. She was twelve years old."

"How?"

"Six-Great woke up a thousand dead bison. Her ghost dogs herded them straight to the bad guy army. Flattened 'em." Ellie clapped. "Day saved. Guess what I did when I was twelve."

"You got your ears pierced?"

"No. I traumatized a room full of children and got suspended. Now, my victims egg my house every Halloween. Six-Great must think I'm pathetic."

"Hey. Don't say that. My grandma gave me a cookie when I learned how to tie my shoes. The point is . . . grandparents are easy to impress. Six-Great probably thinks you're the best."

"That makes me feel a little better." She looked at the bridge, thoughtful. Al's graffiti was still visible, though the black ink blended well with shadows. "Hah," Ellie said. "He actually wrote 'Ronnie, will you marry me?' on the

Herotonic Bridge. I hope there aren't other Ronnies in the city."

"What should I do?" Jay asked.

"Leave it. Our graffiti days are over."

"No argument here. Let's move to the sidewalk," Jay suggested. "The mosquitoes are gathering."

"Light our way, Baby Oberon."

The will-o'-the-wisp sparked in the air between them. It was bright enough, though barely, to navigate up the bank without tripping over a mica-glinting rock or empty beer can. Together, they climbed to high ground and waited for Al to return with towels. As Ellie and Jay watched the stars, Kirby tried to catch the will-o'-the-wisp. It slipped through his ghostly jaws.

Ellie's father was pacing on the porch when she returned home. "Why didn't you answer me?" he asked. "I've been calling all night!"

"My phone broke."

"Look at you. Covered in mud." He ushered her to the kitchen, ran warm water over a hand towel, and wiped grime from her face. In the well-lighted room, Ellie could see stress lines deepening on his brow.

"Sorry, Dad," she said. "It's a long story. Jay and I—"

"Of course he's involved."

"Hey, we didn't plan to fall in a river. It was an accident."

"The *river*, Elatsoe?!" He chucked the towel into the empty sink and left the kitchen in a scowling huff.

"I can explain! Dad, come on. Accidents happen." Ellie followed him to the living room. It was, more accurately, a living-room-slash-library, since every wall was lined with bookshelves. One shelf contained nonfiction, mostly medical reference books and biographies of great Indigenous people. Another shelf was filled with her mother's favorite genre: paperback fantasy. Another with her father's favorite genre: whodunits and crime thrillers. The fourth bookshelf, the largest one, had most of Ellie's comic book collection. She enjoyed indie titles and self-published series. They were more relatable, to her, than most popular superheroes.

"Accidents also kill," her father said.

"Are you referring to Cuz?" she asked. "He was murdered. I thought you believed me!"

"I'm referring to *you* in a *river*, Ellie." Her father pulled a comic book from the shelf. The cover depicted a brown woman wearing a billowing red cape. *Jupiter Jumper* #3, a stellar issue. "This is wish-fulfillment," he said. "Understand? It's not a guide to healthy living."

"I know."

"You don't act like it."

"I'm not wearing a cape, am I?"

"You're grounded."

"We're driving to the burial the day after tomorrow."

"You're grounded after the burial! Go take a shower. The Herotonic River is probably radioactive."

She almost protested. He didn't know what happened. She hadn't been the one taking the risk. She was trying to help Jay, that's all. He clearly needed it.

Yet, all things considered, a fight about responsibility was the last thing she or her father needed. "Okay," she said. "I'll rinse this mess off before the toxic waste makes me a super-powered villain." She removed her soggy shoes and headed for the staircase.

"Ellie?" her father called.

Ellie paused on the first step, turning. "Yes?"

"We will honor your cousin's last wishes," he said. "Together. As a family."

"As a family," she agreed.

⇒⇒ SIX ⇐⇐

THE THING ABOUT TEXAS: it's big. Some Texans will insist that it's the biggest state in the US of A, and although that isn't true, they're close enough. The drive from Texarkana to McAllen takes fourteen hours. Somebody can finish a road trip across New England—Maine to Connecticut—in less time. That said, Ellie enjoyed watching the world pass outside her window. She gazed at farm animals and great, gnarled trees amid corncob meadows. A rainbow of southern wildflowers bloomed alongside the road.

As her father listened to his favorite long-haul driving music (eighties rock), Ellie scrutinized her memories of Trevor. There were no clues, no warnings, that hinted at his violent death. If lives were books, his final chapter came too soon and belonged to a different genre.

At three years old, Ellie thought Trevor was old and wise.

He'd just gone through a growth spurt and was taller than her parents. Trevor used to pick her up and spin. Though he never went too quickly, Ellie felt like she was flying.

After Ellie learned how to read and type, Trevor tried to hook her on his favorite MMORPG, but she just wanted to read his comic books. He had so many; how did he afford them all? He explained that high school students could work part-time once they turned sixteen. "Sometimes I tutor kids," Trevor said. "If you ever need help with math, that's my best subject."

"Thanks, but I'm good at school," she said. "Can I borrow those?" Ellie pointed to a stack of *Mothman Detective* comics beside his lumpy beanbag chair.

"Ask your mom," he said. "They're really violent."

Her parents both said no. Instead, Ellie borrowed a copy of *Jupiter Jumper*.

Over a hundred issues of *Jupiter Jumper* later, fourteen-year-old Ellie visited Trevor in South Texas. She had not seen him since he moved to Kunétai, the Rio Grande, to be an elementary school teacher and father. When Ellie and Trevor greeted each other, she tried to shake his hand, and he laughed, and she wasn't nervous anymore. He introduced Ellie to his new wife, a woman named Lenore. Lenore had the kind of streaked, layered hair that required maintenance every six weeks, and she smelled like gardenias. The perfume was subtle enough that Ellie only noticed it when Lenore hugged her.

Because Trevor and Lenore both worked as teachers during the school year, they had a quick, purely legal wedding in the spring, with a family wedding and honeymoon planned for summer vacation. "Where are you going?" Ellie asked.

"First, we're visiting my great-grandparents in Guadalajara," Lenore said. "They won't be able to fly up here for the marriage ceremony."

"That's sweet of you," Ellie said. "Where are you going after that?"

"Across the Atlantic. England, France, Spain." Lenore counted the countries on her fingers, highlighting long French-tip nails.

Trevor said, "The Apache invade back!"

"Don't make that joke when we're traveling," Lenore said. "Some people won't understand."

"You think it's funny, though, right?"

"No! And it's not even true."

According to Ellie's mother, who was a library of family knowledge (including gossip), that was a common point of contention between them. Lenore, who was a mix of Spanish and unknown ancestry, wasn't Native, but Trevor figured marriage could change that. After all, their children would be Lipan, and culture was the most important part of belonging. That's what he always said. But Lenore had her own culture, her own experiences. It was one of those complex, deeply personal matters of identity with no one-size-fits-all answer, and Ellie wasn't looking forward to a rehash of old arguments. To change the subject, she demonstrated all the tricks Kirby knew. Appear. Disappear. Heel. Sit, stay, roll over, play dead-dead. Track. Listen. Levitate object.

"He is *so* much cleverer than my momma's Pom!" Lenore said, trying to pet the shimmering air. Kirby leaned against her hand, basking in her praise.

"Someday, I can teach your oldest kid how to wake the dead," Ellie offered. "I don't plan to have my own."

"No, no, no," Lenore said. "My hypothetical babies won't learn ghost secrets. Death is a natural end point."

Ellie pet Kirby, too. It felt odd, like trying to press two positive magnetic poles together. Her hand met some resistance, but it was almost intangible. Nothing like warm, silky fur.

"Mom felt the same way when she taught me," Ellie said. "She's still afraid. We never wake up humans, though. Just animals."

"Death is death. No offense, Kirby. You're perfect, perrito."

Ellie didn't try to convince Lenore further. It wasn't her place.

The next day, Ellie and Trevor went hiking at a National Park near sacred mountains. At first, they passed several other people; it was a pleasant spring day, sunny and just breezy enough to feel refreshing, the perfect weather for a jog or stroll. But the trail had numerous offshoots, some less traveled than others, and Ellie picked the most overgrown path. She and Trevor were looking for rare birds: warblers, kingfishers, thrashers. Gemstone feathers of red, green, and yellow. The animals shied away from crowded places.

"I want to walk here every day," Trevor said. Quietly, to spare the birds a fright.

"Why don't you?" she asked.

"There isn't time, Cuz, and it's sweltering by summer. Maybe when I retire."

"When's that?"

"Fifty years from now, if I'm lucky."

He stopped suddenly and looked at his feet. The trail, formerly narrow and overgrown, had petered out. Was it ever a park trail at all? Maybe they took a wrong turn and followed deer tracks. Trevor took a map from his cargo shorts and unfolded it. "We went this way," he said, pointing to a tangle of brightly colored lines on a cartoon forest. "Took the blue route. We should be here. Where's the path?"

"Is it time to send a flare?" Ellie wasn't scared yet. She had a fully charged phone, carried a water Thermos, and could rely on Kirby to howl for help. She did not consider that where they were now, the park had bad reception, water went fast in hot environments, and Kirby's howl was more likely to scare away hikers than draw them near.

"Let's turn back," Trevor said. "I haven't seen a bird lately. It's like they're hiding." He was right. The forest was quiet. When did the leaves stop rustling? Ellie felt like she was wearing earmuffs. Even Trevor's voice sounded muffled.

As they retraced their steps, a single hiker rounded the bend to greet them. The elderly man was stooped so low, his silver hair brushed the leafy trail, almost like a veil.

"Excuse me," Trevor said. "Are we on the blue trail? I seem to be . . . oh, damn!"

Trevor leapt between Ellie and the hiker, his arms spread, like a human shield. Had a black bear broken through the bushes? "What's wrong?" Ellie asked.

"Run," he said. "Ellie, go!"

"Where? We're lost!"

The hiker straightened from his stoop, rising and rising until he loomed over Trevor. His gray hair shivered and jumped, as if tickled by an invisible, static-charged balloon. To Ellie, the strands resembled antennae or snake tongues. Tasting, considering, searching for prey. The hiker had no mouth, nose, eyes, or ears. Nevertheless, his blank face followed Ellie and Trevor as they scrambled back.

"Can your dog attack?" Trevor asked.

"I don't know! He's just a pet! What's happening?"

"Ancient evil. It's the Leech."

"But Six-Great killed him!"

She remembered a story, one of many about her six-great-grandmother's exploits. Her mother shared it years ago.

"Once," her mother had explained, "a monster climbed from Below and made his home inside the swamp. Like roots, his hair spread through the water and muck; it climbed trees, wrapped around their branches, and slithered between furrows in their bark. It covered the swamp with a mycelium black skin, absorbing the land's vitality. Many heroes tried to slay the Leech, but they were encumbered by mud, wrapped—as if by spider web—in loathsome hair, and devoured. For centuries, the Leech flourished, made strong by blood. At last, a hurricane loosened his grip on Earth, and Six-Great-Grandmother cut off his cursed hair. Hope that the Leech will stay Below."

"She tried to kill me," the Leech said. "Yes." Its voice hummed like wasp wings. Because the Leech spoke Lipan, not English, Ellie struggled to understand it. She spent more time training Kirby than learning her language, something that constantly frustrated her mother. "I have enough strength for revenge," the Leech said. "You smell like the one who wronged me." Its writhing gray hair coiled around twigs and snapped them into wood chips.

"Old one," Trevor said, "I have bad news. Your hair is now whiter than sheep wool. You're dying. I could end you today with a needle. Or this." He flourished a Swiss Army knife. Its two-inch carving blade was sharp, as if never used. Trevor was more likely to need its pliers, nail file, or screwdriver.

"Is that right?" the Leech asked. Its hair swarmed more quickly. "Show me."

Even if the Leech was dying, Ellie doubted that she and Trevor would escape with a wee knife. The Leech's thirst for revenge had been strong enough to anchor it to Earth for centuries. How dangerous would its last death throes be? How could Trevor stab it with anything if he could not get past the swarm of fishing line-fine hair, each strand sharper than needles and hungrier than mosquitoes . . .

Suddenly inspired, Ellie reached beyond the earth, ran

her consciousness through the sea of dead beneath the park, and woke them by the thousands: every mosquito that had perished there. She and Trevor wore heavy-duty repellent; would that work on ghosts, too? Ellie hoped so. She also hoped that dead mosquitoes—the females, anyway—still hungered for blood.

She heard them humming, saw the air shimmer from ground to canopy, felt pinpricks on her arms. Blood was drawn from her, ruby red droplets shivering against her skin and zipping away, carried by invisible bellies. But the repellent mostly worked, because she and Trevor were only nipped a dozen times each, if that, whereas the Leech was writhing, its hair entangled by clumps of semi-solid ghosts, its body covered in a shell of trembling red droplets.

Trevor took Ellie's hand and ran. Later, after they reached the ranger's station and reported their brush with death, Trevor said, "That was amazing, Ellie. You're a freaking superhero."

"Hah. No. Come on. I'm no Six-Great."

"Not yet," he said. "You will be."

"Maybe by the time you retire," she said, laughing, embarrassed and proud and still a little frightened, because the monster had taken her by surprise, and now she didn't know when or if she could feel safe.

"Way before then," Trevor said.

The park was evacuated for a week. During that time, all the ghost mosquitoes fell asleep, returning to the underworld Below. Rangers found a tangle of gray hair on the blue trail. It took a while, but the Leech was finally dead. Ellie had finished Six-Great's task.

It should have been a proud moment, but Ellie also felt profoundly sad. The Leech was the last of its kind. The monsters of her ancestors had been replaced by different threats. Invasive creatures, foreign curses, cruel magics, and alchemies. Vampires were the new big bloodsuckers.

Trevor, however, was overjoyed. "I'll talk to Lenore," he said. "Convince her that our hypothetical children need to learn your secret. Incredible!"

That was the last time that Ellie and Trevor chilled together, and the memory brought unshed tears to Ellie's eyes because her Cuz would never retire now. Would never get another high score at the arcade or text Ellie cat pictures or wear a cheesy alphabet-embroidered vest on the first day of school to make his students cringe. She couldn't save him.

She could, however, protect his family. That's what Trevor believed, anyway. Guess he really meant it when he called Ellie a hero.

⇛ SEVEN ⇚

WITH NINE HOURS of road trip behind her, Ellie saw a billboard along the highway: ROCK SHOP TRUCK STOP! MUSEUM! EXIT TWO MILES. "Do we need gas?" she asked.

"The tank is half full," her father said. That was a yes. He never let the needle drop below a quarter. Even less than half made him anxious. Whenever Ellie teased him about this habit, her father related a cautionary tale that usually involved a friend of a friend who perished because they weren't prepared for the worst-case scenario.

"We can drive a long way on half a tank," Ellie mused. She really enjoyed his stories.

"Sometimes, you need to drive more than a 'long way,' Ellie," he said. "Remember the Brown-Johnsons? Your old babysitters?"

"Yes?"

"Their neighbor's boss took a wrong turn in Iowa. He drove through a field of corn that never seemed to end. When the gas ran out after one hundred miles . . . cursed scarecrows got him. They put a feed bag over his head and tied him to a post. The man barely escaped with his life. If only he had a full tank of gas," Ellie's father shook his head. "It's better to be safe than sorry."

"How did he escape at all?"

"Eh. I don't know. Probably wriggled free and lit the crops on fire with a matchbook hidden in his shoe."

"I'll keep that in mind." Judging by the gossip Ellie had overheard in the mall earlier that week, evil scarecrows were becoming a pest. Probably spreading with fields of monoculture corn and soy crops. The formerly diverse scary stories of the prairie were being replaced by repetitive encounters with straw-filled bodies and dead, button eyes.

Fortunately, although Ellie and her father had passed farmland during the drive to South Texas, it was all rather ordinary. "Can we refuel at the Rock Shop Truck Stop?" she asked. "I want to check if there are fossils for sale."

"Sure," her father said. He yawned and rolled his shoulders. "I hope they have coffee, too."

"Dad, are you tired? I can take over for a couple hours." As of January, Ellie had a driver's license. She hated the license itself, because her ID photo was an unflattering combination of a half-smile and half-blink, but it did enable her to drive a bona fide motor vehicle. Not that she had the chance very often. Car accidents killed or injured more teens than any other cause, including curses and slippery bathroom floors. Therefore, until she graduated from high school, Ellie could not drive alone, parents' orders.

Did it count if her father was sleeping in the passenger seat? Apparently not, because he said, "No, no. I'll just take a quick nap in the parking lot."

"You'll burn up, Dad."

"It's not that bad anymore. I can park in the shade and lower the windows."

"Cool, cool, but Kirby comes with me. I'm not leaving any dog in a hot car."

"I wouldn't have it any other way." He exited the highway. Ahead, a truck stop broke the monotony of middle-of-nowhere, Texas. A warehouse-sized building with a flat roof was surrounded by gas pumps and concrete. Her father pulled into a parking spot in front of the building. "We can get gas on the way out," he said. "Do you need fossil money?"

Never one to turn down free cash, Ellie said, "Yes, please!" He gave her twenty dollars and reclined his seat. "Buy me a cup of joe, if they have it."

"Joe? Never took you for a cannibal, Dad."

"Oh, c'mon, let me have a little old-man slang. And—"

"You aren't old!" she interjected.

He raised his eyebrows, folding wave-shaped creases into his forehead. "Thanks. And more importantly, cannibalism is no joke, honey. Even talking about it might invite . . . trouble . . ." He trailed off.

"Dad. We're Apache. Wendigo is a monster for the northerners."

"Easy, Ellie. Better safe than sorry."

"Got it. Cup of joe, hold the human. Thanks for the fossil cash!" She jogged off before he could start a long, unnerving story about a friend of a friend who encountered the Wendigo. There'd be plenty of time for that in the second half of the drive.

The rock museum entrance led to a typical gas station convenience store. It had candy, beef jerky, soda, cigarettes, and other amenities for needy drivers. There was a sign over the checkout counter that advertised "ROCKS & MUSEUM THROUGH BACK. ASK FOR HELP." Ellie approached the cashier, a middle-aged white woman with a heart-shaped face and pink-rimmed glasses. "Do you have lots of fossils?" Ellie asked the woman.

"We do. Fossils, insects in amber, and minerals. Museum is five dollars."

"Thanks! That sounds perfect. Are there megalodon teeth or *T. rex* footprints?"

"The first one sounds familiar. Well?" The woman held out a hand. Amusingly, her fingers were tipped by sharp acrylic nails. They were almost as pointy as velociraptor claws, which suited the museum well.

"Awesome." Ellie forked over the twenty and received a crinkled five and ten in change. Lincoln and Hamilton were certainly easier on the eyes than Indian Killer Jackson. Not that she was particularly thrilled to see any early president.

As Ellie walked to the museum entrance—a door behind the counter—the cashier cleared her throat: *ahem!*

"Um, yes?" Ellie asked.

The woman pointed to a screen beside the cash register; it projected gray security footage from the museum interior. At first, Ellie was puzzled. She couldn't see anything interesting. Just empty rows between display cases. In fact, she was the only guest at the moment.

Ah. That must be the point. The woman wanted her to know: *I have my eyes on you, delinquent.*

"What?" Ellie asked. "Do I need to sign a release form to be on your TV show?"

The woman didn't respond—didn't even smile or frown—so Ellie pushed ahead, determined to enjoy the damn rocks. She could ignore the rude interaction; that woman was a stranger, one of billions. Ellie would never see her again. As her father always said, "Bad vibes are water off a duck's back. As you know, duck feathers are coated with hydrophobic oils that repel water. It's crucial for their survival."

The duck feather routine got wearisome, though. Ellie had brushed off more rudeness than she could quantify. Why did strangers take one look at her and think, *This person is no good?* Some of them probably treated all youth like potential troublemakers. That didn't explain why, when she and Jay went to the local mall, loss prevention agents and security guards only followed Ellie around department stores.

Ellie called Kirby to her side. She touched his shimmering

brow, and he affectionately leaned into her hand. Kirby may not have a cold wet nose or silky fur anymore, but his love for pats and scritches had survived death. "Good boy," she whispered. "Good, good boy."

The museum was an open space with rows of glass display cases. Ellie felt the camera's gaze on her back as she approached the first case. It was filled with samples of fool's gold and rainbow-glinting peacock ore. Two of her favorite minerals. She didn't care that they cost nickels. They were beautiful.

As she leaned over the case, admiring each sample, Ellie wondered if her posture was too threatening. Maybe she should fold her hands behind her back to prove that she wouldn't smash the display case and run off with enough mineral loot to buy a hamburger from McDonald's. How long should she linger? Too quick, and she'd seem antsy. Too slow, and she'd seem covetous. Where were those cameras, anyway? No, don't look. That might seem suspicious, too. Ellie didn't want to look suspicious. But most of all, she didn't want to seem bothered. Because why should Ellie moderate her behavior because of some mean woman? Why should she care about the opinions of a stranger?

Why did she care?

Her phone rang. Ellie had assigned personalized ringtones to all her family and friends; this ring was an energetic melody that reminded her of rah-rah cheer songs. She glanced at the screen. It read: "CALL FROM JAY."

She answered, "What's up, Baby Oberon?"

"Again? Hah. Is that my new name?"

"It depends. Do you love it or hate it? Can't be ambivalent about a nickname."

"I like it, but don't drop the second part."

"You are, like, ten millionth in line for the throne of black roses?" Ellie asked. "Doesn't that make you some kind of royalty?"

"Not at all," he said. "All I have is the power to make light. And not a lot of light, either. I can barely read a book with it."

"Can your sister do magic too?" Ellie asked.

"No. She doesn't practice like me, though."

"Why not?" Ellie asked. "Is she worried about destabilizing reality? Pretty sure that's not gonna happen with parlor tricks."

"Ronnie says that cell phones make more light than twentieth-generation wisps, so there's no point in wasting time on parlor tricks. Plus, she's worried about the environmental impact of magic use. She can step through fairy rings, but that's not actually a power. Still. Creating a little blip of light is way less damaging to the environment than ring transport. It's like comparing the CO_2 emissions of a motorized scooter to those of a whole airplane."

"Y'all lucky," Ellie said. "I'd give up my bike to travel between Austin and New York City in a millisecond. It's not like I hate driving across Texas with my dad, but after hour six, my butt starts to fall asleep, and the whole road trip loses its charm."

Simply put, fairy rings were portals powered by

fae-realm magic and composed of fungi and flowers. There were Ring Transport Centers in most major cities. Ellie couldn't use the rings, however, because all portal travel had to be approved and facilitated by fairy folk, and fairies didn't like "strangers." Strangers, in their opinion, constituted any-body without familial ties to at least one interdimensional person, commonly known as "fae." That wasn't Ellie. Every time she had to pay for an expensive airline ticket or miss a field trip, her disdain for the otherworldly snobs increased. It seemed cruel that humanoids from a different realm could discriminate against her—and others—on her own home-land. The "fair" in "fairy" didn't stand for justice, however, and they didn't care about any rules but their own.

"Sorry," Jay said. "I wish I could help. There's a loophole, you know."

"Is it marriage?"

"Maybe."

"I'd rather spend hours in a hot car, but thanks anyway." She winked, which, in retrospect, was a waste of energy. "What's up?"

"I just wanted to check on you," Jay said. "Are your lungs okay? You didn't inhale any river water, right? This guy I know told me about something called secondary drowning. Which . . . okay, so, it's a fatal condition that can happen up to a day after you get water in your lungs. Are you having trouble breathing? Does your chest hurt?"

"Nah. Don't worry. I feel great."

"Um, okay. Be mindful about your oxygen intake."

"If I stop breathing oxygen, I'll let you know."

"Thanks," he said, in a genuine way that made Ellie feel guilty about her use of sarcasm. "How's the drive?"

"We're taking a short break. I found a fossil shop. If they have something small and harmless, it'd be nice to practice waking up prehistoric ghosts. Keep my mind occupied."

"Can you do that? I mean. Can you wake up extinct creatures?"

"Definitely," she said. "My grandmother found a woolly mammoth tusk ages ago. It took, like, four decades, but the mammoth is now her best friend. She doesn't need a car anymore. She just rides the mammoth to town when she needs groceries."

"Are all your ancestors basically superheroes?"

"Yeah," she said. "We live in the shadow of Six-Great, though. She had a better resume than most tall-tale characters."

"That's a glass-half-empty mindset. You're an intergenerational team! Her shadow and your shadow are the same thing. Growing with time, soon eclipsing us all!"

"Thanks, Jay." She smiled; Ellie wished they'd connected by video chat so he could appreciate how much he'd cheered her up.

"Ellie . . ." He trailed off.

"Uh-huh? What's up?"

"What else can I do to help?"

She considered his question. Ellie did not know whether the police, based on Trevor's autopsy results, would pursue a homicide investigation. As a person in a glass-half-empty mood, she suspected that the coroner would take one look at his injuries and write "accidental" on his death certificate. They might try to confirm the cause of death with a psychic, since psychic visions weren't magic; like ghosts, they originated naturally, and could therefore be used in a court of law, much like expert testimony. However, police psychics were notoriously unreliable. It was difficult to have detailed visions on demand and easy to mistake imagination for the truth. Still, Ellie had promised to give the police a chance to react.

That didn't mean she couldn't start harmless information gathering.

"Actually, yes," Ellie said. "How well can you research?"

"Very well," Jay said. "Ronnie can lend me her student password to the Herotonic University digital library. They have books, newspaper archives, articles. Lots of stuff."

"Google is your best friend for this task, I figure. We should learn more about Abe Allerton, the murderer. What kind of man is he?"

"A-b-e A-l-l-e-r-t-o-n?" Jay asked. "Is that how you spell it?"

"Hopefully. Try alternate spellings if that one doesn't work." She leaned against a wall and idly looked at a chest-high, violet-tinted geode beside her. If she squinted, it resembled a mouth with jagged crystal teeth. Before Ellie understood how geodes formed, she thought they were monster fossils. Imprints of ancient faces frozen in rage or yawning hunger.

"Abe Allerton," Jay repeated. "He's from Willowbee, Texas, right?"

"Uh-huh."

"Do you know anything else about Abe?"

"He has a son who used to be in Tr—in my cousin's third-grade class. Two years ago. Other than that? Abe is a stranger. I can't even guess his motive."

"I'll do my best. Cyberstalking is easy, really. Everyone's online somewhere."

"Except my grandmother," Ellie said. "Eh. Never mind. I forgot about the viral video. Somebody filmed her during a grocery run. The mammoth was invisible, so it looked like she was levitating ten feet above the ground."

"Can you forward me that link?"

"Sure. Oh, and give me another call when you're finished with research. I'll be on the road until late tonight. Actually, we're passing through Willowbee around nine. So if you can pin down information before then . . ."

"Fingers crossed," he said. "Be safe."

"You too. Jay, we don't know how dangerous Abe is. Don't draw his attention. Just do a basic search, okay?"

"Don't worry about me," he said. "Talk to you soon."

As the call ended, Ellie stepped into a new row of display cases, and there it was: the fossil collection. Spiral ammonite shells, pocked coral, fanlike crinoids, and trilobites with delicate spines. There were shark teeth, too, but none came from a megalodon.

No matter. Ellie wanted to start small, anyway. Her

grandmother did not make the jump from dog ghosts to mammoth ghosts overnight; she'd practiced on Cambrian cockroaches and puppy-sized dinos. The Earth's old dead napped below a Mount Everest of younger souls. It helped to have a connection—a body imprint, tooth or shell or bone, preserved as rock—if you wanted to wake them.

Ellie lingered over each object, grasping for their ghosts. It became apparent that sight alone could not connect her to them; she needed to hold the fossils, feel their shape and size. She went to the gift store, a dimly lit room with several shelves of polished rocks, minerals, and fossils. Ellie chose a ten-dollar trilobite. The inch-long arthropod was trapped in a chip of limestone, but most of its body had been exposed and polished.

At the register, Ellie asked, "Do you know the species of this trilobite?"

The gift store cashier, a teenage version of the woman up front (perhaps they were mother and daughter), shrugged. "Not sure. How many species are there?"

"Over twenty thousand," Ellie said. "According to your exhibit."

"I haven't visited the museum," the cashier admitted. "This is just a summer job, and I'm not into rocks. Ten dollars, please."

After the exchange of cash and change, Ellie asked, "Can I get a receipt?"

"Why? We don't allow returns."

"I know. Still need one, though."

"Ahhh. Right." The girl scribbled an itemized list on a Post-it note. "Here. This'll have to do. Have a good day."

"You too!"

Back in the convenience store, Ellie filled a Styrofoam cup with lukewarm coffee and carried it to the checkout counter. "Just this," she said.

"Drink costs one dollar," the beehive-haired cashier informed her. "Twenty-five cents extra if you want dairy creamer."

"No creamer."

"Did you pay for that fossil?"

"Sure did." Ellie stuck the Post-it note to a one-dollar bill, slapped them both on the counter, and walked away.

Water off a duck's back.

⇜ EIGHT ⇝

W HEN ELLIE AND HER father were ten miles from
Willowbee, Jay called back.

Ellie had spent the past hour staring out her window,
daydreaming about the shadows alongside I-35. If she concentrated, Ellie could feel her consciousness brush countless
others; they were ghosts in the underworld Below. She wondered if she could wake them all up. How long would they
play in the dark until they drifted off to sleep again? Could
she entice the wild ghosts to follow her to Trevor's grave like
a funeral procession? Would their little parade frighten Abe
Allerton from Willowbee so much, he'd confess everything
about his crime to the police?

Like many daydreams, hers were unrealistic. Of course
wild animals wouldn't follow her. Ellie could no sooner command a dead doe than a living one. And in the case of the

dead doe, it had the capability to tap into massively dangerous paranormal strength. Ellie pulled her consciousness away
from the dozing dead. She didn't want to risk an accidental
stampede. Instead, she ran her fingers over the trilobite,
memorizing its segments and shape.

Her phone played the familiar cheery tune. "You're just
in time," Ellie said, answering Jay's call. "I'm nine minutes
from Willowbee. What did you find?"

"Tons. I'll text you images later. Long story short, Abe
Allerton is a family man, a Boy Scout leader, and he lives on
the fringe of Willowbee. I even know his exact address,
because he hosts charity events every month. Like, according to this public announcement, the Willowbee bicentennial
celebration will be in his *mansion* this summer. Everyone's
invited. There's a lawn party and a masquerade ball. He's
giving away a free trip to Hawaii."

"Uh. Whoa."

"Plus, based on reviews from Rate-a-Doc.com, his
patients love him. Ellie, I have to ask something touchy . . ."

She braced herself for the question: *Are you sure Abe is a
murderer? He seems like a first-rate guy.*

"Go ahead," Ellie said.

"Are you sure you're safe? Abraham Allerton is . . .
well . . . he's rich and connected. Remember those charity
events I mentioned?"

"Yes. What about them?"

"He also hosts the Holiday Policeman's Ball. Profits go

to needy children. I'm not saying the police are in cahoots with a murderer, but—"

"I get it. Local law enforcement knows Dr. Allerton, and they probably like him. I need more proof. *Any* proof, besides a dream."

"I wish I could help, but his online presence is sparkly clean. I can't find a single negative article. Like . . . one person gave him four out of five stars on Rate-a-Doc, but she only subtracted points because—and I quote—'Dr. Allerton is often busy, so it's difficult to schedule appointments.' That's hardly a bad thing."

"Ugh." She rolled her fingers against the window pane, thoughtful. "How about this: text me his address. My dad can drive past the mansion and let us scope it out."

"What was that, Ellie?" her father asked, pointedly lowering the radio volume.

"Don't eavesdrop, Dad!"

"I'll send it," Jay said. "Promise you won't get hurt?"

"Fortunately, due to parental supervision, I won't have the *chance* to do anything risky. Anyway. I appreciate it. You've already helped a lot."

After hanging up, Ellie took the GPS from its window mount. "Ellie," her father said, with the stern I-so-do-not-have-time-for-this tone he used on misbehaving puppies at work.

"I'm just plotting a quick detour in Willowbee. My friend found Abe Allerton's address."

"Legally?"

"Completely. What, you think I know hackers?"

"Don't all kids these days?"

"I can't tell if you're being serious or not."

Ellie's phone beeped. An address popped into her messages: "19 Rose Road."

"Ah, here it is, Dad. I can't make you drive anywhere, but . . . you promised. Remember? We'll honor certain last wishes together. As a family."

"If it's fast," he said. "No getting out of the car."

"That's fine with me!" She punched the address into the GPS and turned up the radio, blasting his eighties rock. Her father promptly lowered the volume to a respectable level.

"Don't want to announce our presence with Bonnie Tyler," he said.

They took the next exit and started driving through a strip of undeveloped country, a buffer between Willowbee and the hustle-bustle traffic on I-35. Alone on the two-lane road, her father turned on the brights. They were in a flat, prickly corner of Texas. Cacti, shrubs, and mesquite trees flanked the minivan, and tracts of grazing land were delineated by barbed wire fences. In the distance, Ellie saw a white rectangle. It appeared to be a sign of some kind. She could not make out its message yet.

Kirby barked once, sharply—an alert. He'd been riding in the back seat, a content shimmer. Kirby always traveled well. As a living English springer spaniel, he'd press his nose against the window and enjoy the view. He probably did the same as a ghost, but it was difficult to tell without his breath fogging the window.

"What is it, boy?" Ellie asked. She loosened her seatbelt and looked behind her. "Dad, did you hear that?"

"Kirby barked?"

"Yes. He's not supposed to make sounds unless . . ."

"Hm?"

"Unless he senses danger."

Willowbee was the kind of town that announced itself. As they neared the sign, Ellie read the cutesy-quaint slogan written in a whimsical, curling font: WILLOWBEE, TEXAS. POPULATION = JUST ENOUGH! The word *Texas* looked new, as if fresh paint had been applied over graffiti. Ellie wondered what the paint was hiding.

There was a symbol on the back of the sign, a plump, snakelike creature with squiggles radiating from its body.

"That must be their high school football mascot," her father said, but he sounded uncertain.

The van skirted downtown Willowbee, a few blocks of well-maintained brick and wood buildings. Ellie saw a church, a shopping plaza, and a spired town hall. Outside the cozy library, a sign announced: HAPPY 200th BIRTHDAY, WILLOWBEE! VISIT OUR HISTORY EXHIBIT TODAY! Tourists probably visited the town for a taste of old-fashioned Americana. The town architecture was unusual for the region; it seemed inspired by colonial New England.

Beyond the shopping district was a neighborhood of two-story wooden houses with too-green, freshly cut grass lawns. South Texas was naturally a dry, yellowish country during the best summers. That year, a drought had aggravated matters. In some cities, people barely had enough to drink. The lush grass of Willowbee must take daily watering. It had wealth.

They passed a stretch of sprawling ranches. There were no animals on the fields so late at night, but Kirby's shimmer pressed against the window, intrigued by something Ellie could not see. Maybe he smelled horses and longhorns sleeping in their stables. Was that why he'd barked earlier?

"In one quarter mile, you will arrive at your destination," the GPS said. Ellie saw a bubble of light on the horizon.

"That's it," she said. "It must be."

"I'll try to get closer, but the driveway seems to be gated," her father replied. Indeed, there was a heavy iron gate blocking the turnoff into the property. From their vantage point along the road, they could now see the fabulously symmetrical Georgian-style brick mansion, complete with marble columns, a half-dozen chimneys, and the kind of green, wooded acreage that belonged in the Pacific Northwest. The lawn was speckled by white polka-dots, the heads of round mushrooms. Didn't mushrooms usually sprout in moist environments? Exactly how much water did Dr. Allerton waste on his grass every day? Oaks and firs blocked most of the mansion's side wings; Ellie could not estimate how many rooms it contained, but she wouldn't be surprised if there were twenty. "Are all doctors that rich?" she asked.

"Animal doctors sure as hell aren't," her father sniped. "Christ. Who needs that much house? What a waste."

The air buzzed. Rumbled. "Dad, I think Kirby is growling. We need to get out of here."

"You don't need to tell me twice." Her father hit the gas and accelerated up the street. Soon, the Allerton mansion was just a faint glow in the rearview mirror. They did not speak again, however, until they merged onto the highway and put several miles between their voices and Willowbee.

"Why did he do it?" Ellie said, softly. "I don't understand."

"There won't be a good reason," her father said. Sometime during the five-second stakeout, he'd cut the radio. Neither of them felt like turning it back on.

"You believe Allerton is a murderer?" Ellie asked.

"I . . . believe in you, Ellie, and your dream."

"Thanks, Dad. I'll try my best."

How did Trevor, a public school teacher with drought-tolerant plants in his tiny duplex yard, become involved with Mr. Moneybags in the first place? Their only connection seemed to be a child. During the dream, Trevor said, "Met once before this happened. Parent-teacher conference. Two years ago . . ."

Ellie blinked back tears, thinking of her cousin's final words and the way he slipped away like mist.

Trevor taught third grade. That meant the unnamed student would probably be ten or eleven years old now. Did he share the surname Allerton? Possibly. Some research couldn't be conducted online.

It was customary to bury the dead with their treasured possessions. Ellie hoped that Trevor did not take his teaching materials to the earth. They might be the best initial lead she had.

⇜❯❯❯ NINE ❮❮❮⇝

TREVOR AND LENORE bought a three-bedroom starter house when Baby Gregory was born. They chose a child-friendly neighborhood with a low speed limit and ample sidewalks. Although everyone kept bars on their windows, the area had almost no violent crime thanks to a vigorous neighborhood-watch program. It also bordered a playground, an elementary school, and a dog park.

Ellie and her father arrived at the house just after 10:00 P.M. They parked on a gravel driveway, unloaded their luggage, and knocked on the door.

"What should I say?" Ellie whispered.

"Say?"

"To Lenore."

"Offer your condolences."

"Do they really help?"

"Yes. More than saying nothing."

Ellie's mother, Vivian, opened the door. She wore a T-shirt and old, comfortable jeans. "Come in," Vivian said. "Don't thump around. The baby is sleeping. So is Lenore. Goodness knows, they both need rest."

They gathered in the guest room; it was unfurnished except for a cot and queen-sized air mattress on the carpeted floor. Most of the house smelled like a nursery, but the guest room still had its new-house smell: fresh paint and carpet cleaner. Sterile, closer to a hotel room than a home.

"Get ready for bed, Ellie," her mother said. "You'll use the cot. It's memory foam. Fancy stuff."

Obliging, Ellie brushed her teeth in the half bathroom. After grimacing at a couple painful blemishes along her jawline, she opened the mirrored cabinet, looking for a clear spot to stow her toiletries. There, on the lowest shelf, was a tangle of Trevor's black hair in the plastic teeth of a comb.

"Oh . . . no. No." His hair—*so much hair*—could not remain in the house after Trevor was buried. Too dangerous. He might be drawn, like iron to a magnet, back home.

He would be a terrible thing. Just rage, sorrow, keen intelligence, and vindictiveness. Unlike an animal, he would know that he was dead; the awareness would allow him to fully exploit his supernatural abilities. If Trevor returned, he could tear the neighborhood apart like a hurricane with hatred at its core.

Ellie rummaged through the bathroom cabinets until she

found one of Lenore's empty travel makeup bags. Gingerly, she dropped the comb into the bag and zipped it shut.

In the guest room, Ellie sat on her cot and skimmed the data Jay sent. It fell into three categories:

1) Allerton's medical accomplishments, including his online patient ratings.
2) Articles about his charitable work.
3) Miscellaneous references to Abe Allerton, predominantly from the *Willowbee Times* online.

She pulled a spiral notebook from her backpack and thumbed to a blank page.

"What are you doing, Ellie?" her mother asked; her father was already snoring on the air mattress.

"Taking notes." Ellie glanced at the chest of drawers against the far wall. The makeup bag was tucked in the lowest drawer, hidden under a folded bedsheet. "I found some of his hair," she said. "What should we do?"

"His . . . oh." Vivian held out one hand, fingers flexed slightly. "I'll take care of it. Thank you."

"Will you bury it?"

"The less you know, the better."

Ellie stood, crossed the room, and reached into the lowest drawer; she delicately handed the makeup bag to her mother. Vivian accepted the bag without looking down. As if, much like gazing into the sun, the sight would hurt her.

"Alright," she said. "We'll talk tomorrow. I want to know all about your dream. By the way?"

"Yes?" Ellie asked.

"Your father told me about the river incident."

"*Pfft*. Mom, Jay was the one who climbed the bridge. I tried to stop him."

"Good to know," her mother said, and Ellie's explanation must have sufficed, because Vivian promptly turned off the light.

"Guess I'll take these notes tomorrow," Ellie said. "Thaaanks, Mom."

Settling into post-road-trip exhaustion, a state of aching eyes and muscles, Ellie pulled her cotton bedsheet to her chin. Kirby curled atop the foot of her bed; luckily, as a ghost, he didn't shed all over and fill the air with allergens. Baby Gregory had sensitive lungs.

Her phone beeped. Another message. *Leave it alone*, Ellie thought. *You can't jump at every text.* But she was curious.

Jay had sent the message. "Abe (blue shirt) with mayor!!! The mayor TATTOOED Abe for charity. It looks awful. XD XD XD." He accompanied the message with two pictures from an article. The first showed a man's lower back, which was marked by a shaky signature in black ink, the mayor's name. The next picture depicted two men standing in a garden. Ellie zoomed into Allerton's face. Glared at his square jaw, blue eyes, and baseball cap. He had the kind of face that she associated with department-store clothing ads. Conventionally attractive, mature, and forgettable.

That said, his smile gave her chills. It looked genuine. Like he was having fun with a good friend, and it was sick.

"Enjoy it while you can, asshole," she whispered. "I'll wipe that smile off your face."

Ellie bid Jay goodnight and locked her phone.

Later, as she bobbed on the surface of unconsciousness, a floorboard creaked in the hallway. Ellie snapped awake, listening. She heard muffled footsteps, a door creaking. Lenore probably just needed to use the bathroom.

Ellie's phone beeped. It had received a text from Lenore. The message read:

AWAKE?

Ellie responded: "Yes. R u ok?"

A moment passed. The floorboard creaked again. Lenore messaged:

COME 2 KITCHEN PLS. ALONE.

After a moment's hesitation, Ellie slipped off her cot, tiptoed past her snoring parents, and left the guest room. The kitchen was down the hall; light spilled from its entrance. "Hello?" she asked. "I'm here . . ."

Ellie turned into the kitchen. Fluorescent light assailed her sleep-widened pupils, and she had to squint until they contracted. There, against a counter, leaned Lenore.

She wore jeans and a black sweatshirt with its hood raised.

Her long hair, a brown-to-blond ombré with black roots, tumbled over her chest in stringy, tangled waves. Uncombed, unwashed, because who had time to spare as a new mother and widow? Lenore's face was tilted down, amplifying the shadows beneath her large brown eyes. "When did you arrive, Ellie?" she asked. Her voice sounded raw and deep.

"Hours ago. You were sleeping. I . . . my condolences. I don't . . . don't know what to say."

"It's okay. Come here, honey." Lenore spread her arms, and Ellie fell into the hug. For a moment, they simply embraced. Lenore felt warm and soft. Comforting. Ellie felt guilty; shouldn't she be comforting Lenore, instead of the other way around?

That's when Ellie noticed that something was off. Lenore was the kind of woman who dressed in both fabric and fragrances. Usually, her hugs carried the embrace of gardenias, with a hint of coconut or citrus. That night, instead of her usual gardenias-scented hug, with a hint of coconut or citrus, she smelled like neutral soap, the kind that came in a bar and was advertised as "fresh-scented."

It was vaguely disconcerting.

"Here," Lenore said, handing Ellie a velvet-wrapped parcel. "He wanted you to have this."

Gingerly, Ellie unwrapped Trevor's Swiss Army knife. "He used to carry this during hikes," she said. "Every hike. Even little ones in Grandma's yard. Just in case." She held it tightly. "I'll always carry it, too."

"That's Trevor," Lenore said. "Prepared for just about anything. It didn't help him in the end."

"I'm sorry," Ellie said.

Lenore sagged against the kitchen counter, allowing the fake marble block to carry some of her weight. "What now?" she wondered. "How will I do this alone?" She spread her arms wide, as if gesturing to the universe and everything in it.

"You aren't alone."

Lenore's expression softened. "Yeah?"

"I promise," Ellie said. "If you need anything, just ask."

For a quiet moment, Lenore stared at the spice rack against the wall, lost in thought. Then, she took Ellie by the hand. "I want to show you something," Lenore said. Gently, she pulled toward the door that linked the kitchen to the garage.

"Wait, are we going outside?" Ellie asked. "It's midnight. What about Gregory?"

"Your mother has a baby monitor." Lenore turned, smiling. It was the littlest, saddest smile Ellie had ever seen. "Are you afraid of the dark, ghost raiser?"

"Sometimes. What do you want to show me?"

"Where it happened." A bloated tear slipped down Lenore's left cheek. "Where he died. You need to see."

"Oh. Hey. We should wait until sunrise, right?" Ellie tried to pull away, but Lenore's grip tightened.

"It doesn't make sense. Why would he park in the middle of nowhere? What happened? You need to see the spot. It's this straight road in the woods. A mile from his usual route. What. Happened. What happened?"

"I don't know, Lenore." Ellie shook her head. "But going there in the middle of the night won't explain anything. Later. I promise."

"Just . . . just come with me. Maybe you can . . . maybe you can bring him back."

"What? No! I can't!"

"You said you'd do anything for me!"

"That's too dangerous, Lenore!" Sharp nails pinched Ellie's skin.

"Teach me how to do it, then! Please? Ellie . . . this is agony."

"It doesn't work that way. Dogs are different from people, okay? If I tried . . . I'd only bring back his anger. He's happy. I promise. When he said goodbye, all his pain went away, and he smiled, and—"

"He said goodbye to you?" Lenore finally released Ellie. "I never had the chance. The last thing I said to him was, 'Do you want soup for dinner?' Freaking *soup*. Just give me one last conversation! I don't care if he's angry as long as it's him!"

Vivian must have heard them arguing, because she darted into the kitchen wearing a bath robe and cotton pajamas. "Ellie, please return to the guest room!" she said. "Lenore, honey, he's gone . . ."

Before the situation could get worse, Ellie escaped into the hall. From his nursery, Gregory was crying, his distress a shrill staccato. Her sleepy father was leaning over Gregory's crib, making soothing sounds. Ellie retreated to the guest room and, alone, shut the door. It was a flimsy barrier against the ruckus.

How could anybody expect Ellie to sleep while the bereaved mother and child wept outside her door? Their voices seeped through the walls. The house vibrated with grief.

The guest room window overlooked a fenced-in backyard. Ellie opened the window, slid aside the security bars, and climbed outside. Her movement activated a motion-sensitive light on the back porch wall. Against the house, white lawn chairs surrounded a plastic picnic table. Desert flowers grew in planters along the yard's edge.

She reclined on one of the lawn chairs, closed her eyes, and pulled the trilobite from her pocket, rolling it in her hand. By now, Ellie could mentally visualize its hammer-shaped head, spiny and ridged thorax, and the raised axial lobe that ran down its body. How did it spend its final days? As an arthropod, a scavenger, it probably fed on bacteria and organic scraps. Scuttling across the sea floor, glutting itself before larger predators descended.

It died peacefully, Ellie decided. Just slipped away, settled in the sediment, its body buried and transformed into stone over geologic time. In the underworld, the place of dreams, it continued scuttling, for what else could a trilobite do? She reached out, parting the ghost of an ancient sea. *Come back. Wake up.*

Ellie felt a tickle on her arm. An animal crawling from her elbow to her shoulder. She opened her eyes and glimpsed a flash of shiny exoskeleton. An impression of the trilobite's ghost. However, it had been dreaming so long, its drowsiness lingered. The trilobite shimmered, faded, and slipped back to the underworld.

But for a moment, she'd brushed a little soul that had lived on Earth five hundred million years ago. What else could she accomplish?

"She's asleep," Vivian said. "You can come inside."

Ellie turned; she'd been so preoccupied by the trilobite, she had not heard the back door open. "Not yet. I'm having a trilobite party, Mom."

Vivian sat in the chair beside Ellie. "Sometimes, people lash out when they're in pain. Because they don't know what else they can do."

"I know. Want to see my friend?" She passed the fossil to her mother. Vivian held the trilobite into the porch light.

"Millions of years," Ellie said. "I can't get over that. How can anything exist more than a few millennia without getting bored?"

"Trilobites are easy to entertain," Vivian said. "I guess."

"What about more complex things? Like Grandma's mammoth. Does she ever seem . . . bored? Like a caged tiger pacing back and forth in the zoo?"

"Not that I've noticed. Boredom is for the living." She frowned with her forehead, eyebrows crinkling. "That doesn't mean other emotions disappear. The mammoth can get upset. I've seen her lash out."

A mournful cry lifted from the park nearby. It was high-pitched and trembled with canid vibrato. Ellie waited for more howls to join the first; that's what packs did. They sang together to communicate and commiserate.

But the coyote in the park was alone. After a minute, its voice faded, swallowed by the chirps of midsummer bugs.

"Did Six-Great ever wake up prehistoric animals?" she asked.

"I haven't heard any story about it," Vivian said, "but she definitely knew about them."

"Yeah?"

"Actually, it's a funny story."

Ellie leaned forward, propping her chin on her hands. "Go ooooon."

"This chasm appeared in the middle of the wilderness. And by appeared, I mean . . . overnight, a hole opened in the earth, and it had no bottom. At least, none anyone could see. When the news reached your six-great-grandmother, she said, 'I need to investigate. It may be dangerous.'

"'Okay. Sure,' her husband said. 'I'll go, too.' He knew that he could not convince Six-Great to stay away from danger. She was stubborn and very concerned about the safety of other people, even strangers. One of her flaws, in my opinion. It made her impulsive. Usually, Six-Great didn't use horses during her journeys because they were frightened by her ghost pack. But she made an exception that time because it was a quick trip. Plus, her husband was a skilled rider. One of the best, actually.

"The chasm was in a region that had many known caves. People avoided them, for the most part. They were filled with guano and the bones of ancient mammals. Poor, magnificent animals that died in darkness, often after a debilitating fall. In death, their bones served as warnings. Stay away. These caves are dangerous.

"When she reached the site, however, Six-Great was surprised to see a crowd of people, mostly young men, around the chasm. It was a perfectly circular hole with a diameter about five feet wide. The length of two arms. The vegetation had been manually cleared around it to stop accidental falls. A savory scent wafted from the hole, one that reminded Six-Great of cooked meat.

"'I expected something larger,' she said. 'What is the trouble? Caves are not uncommon.'

"'Sister,' one of the young men said, 'listen.' He threw a pebble into the chasm. It never clattered against a rocky floor.

"'Maybe the landing is padded by soil,' Six-Great said. 'Have you tried measuring its depth with rope?'

"He nodded. 'Yes. We lowered it almost all the way, and then something tugged it out of our hands! Our new plan is to ignite a bundle of dry grass and wood and throw it down. The illumination will help us decide how to proceed.'

"Six-Great's husband, normally content to let others speak, said, 'No. Do not use fire.'

"'Why not, Brother?' the man asked.

"'Because something is living down there. It may get hurt.'

"For a while, everyone discussed the matter. They did not want to risk harming the person living in the chasm, but they were worried by its strangeness. The meat-like smell was also concerning. Had something fallen and died?

"At last, one of the young men volunteered to descend the chasm. 'You can lower me with rope,' he said, 'I'll carry a torch and a weapon. If the person is peaceful, they will not attack. If they are injured, I can bring them to the surface and call a healer. If they are dangerous, I'll shout and . . .' He kicked the air. '. . . fight!'

"Everyone agreed that his plan was the best they had. As the locals constructed a sturdy harness, Six-Great and her husband took the horses to a nearby stream to drink. It was a fifteen-minute hike away from the strange chasm.

"'What do you think?' her husband asked. 'Is it a wise idea to send somebody down there?'

"'I don't know. The smell concerns me. It's not the scent of a fresh kill or a rotten one. It's cooked meat.'

"As the horses drank the fresh, cool water, a coyote woman approached. She was in her human guise, but even disguised, coyotes cannot hide their yellow eyes. They use sunglasses these days. Even at night. There's so many electric lights, it's easy to see, especially with coyote eyes."

"What about colored contact lenses?" Ellie asked.

"I don't think they fit right—unless there's a company that manufactures contacts for coyotes. Which may exist, actually. I wouldn't know." Vivian shrugged. "In the old days, animal people didn't need to hide. Six-Great greeted the coyote woman like family. 'Hello, Sister,' she said. 'Can we help you?'

"The coyote woman circled the horses like they were a

marvel. 'I've never ridden one of these before,' she said. 'How fast do they go?'

"Six-Great's husband considered the question. 'They could outrun a bear,' he said. Grizzly bears are disturbingly fast, as you know. If you ever see one, it's safer to curl up in a little ball than turn your back and—"

"I don't need to curl up in a ball. Kirby would protect me."

"It's safe to have a backup plan. He might not always be with you."

"He *will*. But my backup plan is another ghost dog."

Judging by her deadpan stare, Vivian was unimpressed.

"What happened next?" Ellie prompted.

"The coyote woman asked, 'Can you give me a ride? I want to go far away.'

"'Yes,' Six-Great's husband said, 'after we finish our business here.'

"'What business? Watering your animals? They seem content.'

"'A deep hole opened in the earth,' Six-Great explained. 'We need to understand how it formed so quickly.'

"'Oh, that!' the coyote woman said. 'Stay away from it. The hole is not dangerous. Just annoying.'

"'Do you know what lives down there?' Six-Great asked.

"'Yeah,' she said. 'My father.'

"After the coyote woman vented—she was understandably annoyed by her dad's recent behavior—Six-Great and her husband returned to the pit. They moved quickly, but it was too late! The young man had descended and was at the mercy of a prankster who used the cave system for sneaking and hiding. Normally, that deep, narrow pit was hidden by a boulder, but the prankster had roasted a deer underground, believing that the caves were large enough to safely absorb the smoke. That plan flopped. So, he had moved the boulder to ventilate the area before the bats got pissed.

"The moment Six-Great reached the pit, there was a cry of fear from the depths. 'Pull me up!' the young man shouted. 'It's a monster! Hurry!'

"Everyone hoisted him out of the hole. He was unharmed but shaken, trembling like a skinny-dipper in the winter. 'We disturbed the ancient dead!' he said. 'They demand gifts of food for our insolence!'

"'Dead don't eat,' Six-Great said. 'Calm down. What did the monster look like?'

"'It was covered in white spikes and had a skull head!'

"'Send me down there,' she insisted. 'I want to see it for myself.'

"The young men tried to convince her that it was too dangerous. 'You may anger him,' they said. 'Let us send food instead.'

"Six-Great's husband laughed at that. 'Save your resources,' he said. 'And while you're at it, save your breath. You might as well tell the sun to rise in the North. What are you doing, my wife?'

"Six-Great delicately held two prickly-pear fruits. 'He wants food,' she explained. 'I'll give him the gift he deserves.'

"After she scraped the spikes off one fruit, Six-Great slipped into the harness, and the young men lowered her into the pit. The sunlight above her head became a little circle of light. When Six-Great felt the ground beneath her feet—it was soft and spongy, like a pile of dirt and leaves—she lit her torch.

"'Come out, monster!' she called. 'I have an offering for you.'

"'Ooooooo! Woooo! Woooo!' came an eerie response. I bet it sounded a lot like that lonely coyote howling in the park. 'Put my food on the ground and leave!'

"The coyote man stepped into the flickering light, and for a moment, Six-Great mistook him for something intimidating: pearly white spikes jutted from his stooped back and arms. His yellow eyes glinted, doglike, as they reflected fire through the white bison skull he wore as a mask.

"'Here,' she said, offering him the fruit without the prickles. She'd been impressed by his costume. It must have taken hours to collect a dozen stalagmites and fasten them to his body.

"The coyote plucked the fruit from her hand, sniffed it thoughtfully, and then withdrew into the shadows. 'Send more meat,' he said. But . . . obviously, he didn't speak English. Or Lipan. Animal people use a language that needs no translation.

"'You roasted a whole deer,' Six-Great said.

"'And? So what? Monsters have big appetites.'

"'I'll grant you the big appetite, Coyote.' She wagged her torch in his direction. 'I haven't shared your secret . . . yet. If you keep trying to frighten humans, that's gonna change, and you can forget about using these caves. Understand?'

"Coyote whipped off his bison skull mask and flung it against a stone wall. 'How did you know?' he asked.

"'I've met plenty of monsters, and you aren't even *close*.'

"From afar, there was a rhythmic clatter, like dry sticks snapping against each other: *clck, clck, clck*. The cave system was a maze of passages and chambers, so Six-Great could not pin down its source. She swung her torch side-to-side. 'More tricks, Coyote?'

"'Always,' he said, 'but that isn't one of them.' He lowered the fruit and tilted his head, as if listening. 'Uh-oh.'

"The clatters were drowned by a multitude of rustlings and squeaks. A flood of bats burst from every passage, rushing around Six-Great. She could feel wings whispering against her arms as they disturbed the air with powerful, rapid flaps. The animals were packed so tight, it was impossible to see her hand in front of her face, as if the darkness of the cave had been manifested in thousands of fuzzy little bodies. The bats shot up the vertical chasm, and within a minute, they'd all escaped the cave. 'It's too early,' Six-Great said. 'They shouldn't be awake until evening.'

"'Coyote!' said a high-pitched voice. 'You are no longer welcome in these caves!'

"Deep within the largest passage to her right, Six-Great saw a hint of movement. She stepped forward, with her torch held out, and lit a bat person. The bat wore many beaded necklaces, some dangling below her belly, others clasped tightly around her throat. The beads were made from the strangest stones Six-Great had ever seen. Minerals of all textures and colors. One resembled a leaf's imprint embedded in rock.

"'Why not?' Coyote demanded. 'I've always been good to you folks.'

"'You defaced our home,' she said. 'The spikes on your back took millennia to grow. Drop by drop, the earth layered each stalagmite with the salt in her tears. And you harvested them for a prank?'

"'There are so many!' Coyote said. 'I only took . . . what is this? Six? Seven?' He turned around, as if expecting Six-Great to count each stalagmite pinned to his back. By the way, there were nine.

"'There are so many,' the bat woman repeated. 'An excuse to do as you please, regardless of the impact. Gather your belongings and get out before the warriors wake.' She struck the cave wall with a type of mallet and turned her back.

"'Grandmother,' Six-Great said. 'Forgive me for intruding. May I ask you a question?'

"'You may,' the bat woman said. 'And forgive me if I yawn. It's the time, not the company.'

"'Of course.' Six-Great nodded at the stones around the elder's neck. 'I've seen rocks like that before. Stone leaves, shells, and creatures. What are they? How did they form?'

"'Over time,' the bat woman said. 'More time than it takes to grow a stalagmite.' She smiled, revealing tiny white teeth. Nothing like the kind vampire bats have. I'm sure that she was a free-tailed bat person. They're everywhere in the south."

"So cute!" Ellie said. "They always look like they're smiling."

"You're right," Vivian agreed. "With her always-smiling

mouth, the bat woman said, 'When you live as we do, you learn a great deal about time. It's like living in the underworld—ghosts are everywhere, teaching us about fragility and extinction. Do you know what that is?'

"'No,' Six-Great said.

"'Absolute death. Nothing remains but shapes in the ground.' The bat woman held up her leaf fossil, thrusting it in Coyote's direction. 'There were once *so many* of these, too.'

"'There's still leaves in the trees,' he said, snorting.

"'Billions. Trillions. None of them are like mine.'

"With that, the bat yawned, stretched her winged arms, and shuffled away.

"'I advise that you listen to her,' Six-Great said.

"'*Pssssht*. Bats. They're hypocrites. You oughta see what some of these caves are filled with.' He threw the fruit skin on the ground, wriggled out of his stalagmite suit, and scampered into the darkness. With that, Six-Great returned to the surface and informed the onlookers that the terrible monster was no longer a threat. 'The bats defeated it,' she said.

"During the return trip home, the coyote woman rode on Six-Great's horse. She spent a few weeks with Six-Great, mostly chilling with the dogs. All the dogs, alive and dead. Then, without a goodbye, she was gone. That's how some people live. Planktos."

"Plankton?" Ellie asked.

"No. Planktos. It means . . . drifting, I think."

"What's the Lipan word for drifting?"

Vivian shook her head. "If we had a word for that, it's been lost."

"Are there really any left?" Ellie asked. "I mean people. Coyote people, bat people, bear people. I've never met one."

"Their numbers and strength reflect the health of their species," she said. "I really doubt coyotes and bats are in trouble. They've flourished in the new normal. You won't see them very often, though. They're too good at hiding in plain sight. Pretending to be something else to get by. Kind of like our people did after Civil War. Actually, have you ever learned about the panting caves near Austin?"

"Sure! They eat spelunkers! The Herotonic University ParAb department studied them last year. Didn't the History Channel do a documentary on their mysteries, too? I tried to watch, but the reenactments were too awkward. Couldn't sit through more than a couple minutes."

"I have it on good authority," Vivian said, "that the whole thing is a ruse. The bat people who live in them don't want to be troubled."

"Wait. Are you saying they pretend to be monsters to scare away humans? As in *exactly* what the trickster Coyote did?"

"With much more finesse."

"Still!" Ellie looked at her trilobite wistfully. "I want to meet them."

"Someday," Vivian promised. "When the world is less frightening, they'll stop hiding."

Ellie snorted. "Might as well ask the sun to rise in the North," she said.

⇜ TEN ⇝

THE CORONER DETERMINED that Trevor's death had been an "accident—no investigation pending." Ellie was not surprised, but the ruling still felt like a punch to the gut. How could anyone determine cause of death under such odd circumstances?

No matter. Death certificates could be changed. Once Ellie and her family finished her own investigation, Trevor's cause of death would be "homicide."

After a closed-casket funeral service, Trevor was buried in a sacred place with his most personal belongings. Only elders and close family saw him to the earth. Later, Ellie's parents hosted a public wake at a park outside the city. There, Trevor's friends, coworkers, students, and extended family could gather and celebrate his life.

Former students dominated the wake. The black-clad

children draped every bench like some dreary tablecloth. They picked at cookies and lemon bars, sniffling. Ellie realized that many, especially the youngest generation, had never been to a funeral before. The luckiest had no personal experience with death. Others had lost a grandparent or great-grandparent, somebody who died peacefully after a long life, as was right and just.

Most of the adults stood in chattering clusters. Regularly, the groups broke apart and re-formed with different members, much like a typical dinner party. Herself in a solitary mood, Ellie watched the gathering from an ant-free spot under a mesquite tree. She drank a cup of strawberry punch. Slivers of ice bobbed on the pink liquid, melting double time in the summer heat. How did Lenore handle the parade of condolences and hugs? How did anybody? Ellie was afraid she'd start crying if another stranger commented, "He was a good man."

Beyond the crowd, a Mercedes-Benz pulled into the parking lot. Its paint shone like polished onyx. The luxury vehicle stuck out like a sore thumb among the more modest cars that belonged to Trevor's circle. That's what first caught Ellie's attention. Made her suspicious.

Television crime dramas liked the refrain: *they always return to the scene of the crime.* This wasn't a crime scene, but perhaps . . .

The car door popped open, and a tall man stepped outside. His black suit was a far cry from golf-course casual, but Ellie recognized him anyway.

Abe Allerton was at Trevor's wake.

Ellie dumped her remaining punch on the grass, crumpled the plastic cup, and jogged toward the parking lot. She had no plan; did she need one? Yes, of course. She couldn't just punch Dr. Allerton in the face, key his new car, and accuse him of murder. That would land her in a heap of trouble and endanger her family. Dr. Allerton didn't know that anybody suspected him yet.

Just be cool, Ellie thought. *Say hello. Play nice. Dig for clues. Make sure that the doctor isn't here to kill Lenore, or something.*

She suspected that Dr. Allerton would not cause trouble around dozens of witnesses. Then again, most people wouldn't kill an innocent man, either. Ellie was prepared to use Kirby's Big Howl if the situation called for a fight. Plus, the family-friend woolly mammoth could charge Dr. Allerton's car and prevent his escape. Unfortunately, Ellie's grandmother was old-school; that meant Grandmother never attended wakes. It wasn't right, in her opinion, to speak so freely about the new dead. Although Ellie had commanded the woolly mammoth before, her grandmother had always been nearby, supervising. How would the big animal behave without her beloved master? Ellie didn't want to chance a negative reaction. Grandmother had warned her that there were three places she should never summon something larger than an elephant: crowded places, confined places, and noisy places.

That said, it did amuse Ellie to imagine the Mercedes-Benz crunching under an invisible mammoth butt.

Dr. Allerton must have noticed Ellie's approach, because he lowered his sunglasses and peered over the silver frames. Ellie relaxed her stance, shoulders dropping and fists uncurling. After tossing the empty cup in a mixed-material recycling can, she smiled. Too wide, at first; it was a wake, not a birthday party. *Act natural, Ellie.* "Hi," she said. "This is a private event, um . . ."

"Abe. My sincere condolences. I'm here to pay respects." He smiled the right way: sympathetic, bittersweet. Was it genuine? No. Couldn't be. He just knew how to act, unlike some people.

"Sorry," Ellie said. "You're just so, um . . . well, I bet that suit costs more than every other suit in the park combined."

He shook his head, his eyes crinkling with (fake, surely) compassion. "We all express grief differently. Mister Reyes taught my son two years ago."

"Where is your kid?"

"With his mother. We're separated." He clasped his hands. "What a tragedy."

"Are we . . . still talking about your divorce?"

"No," Dr. Allerton said. "That was amicable. This. This is a tragedy. Although we met only briefly, Mister Reyes made an impression. He was an intelligent, passionate man, and he genuinely cared about his students."

Ellie's eyes burned; she could not maintain her faux-pleasant expression. "Yes. He was. He's always cared about . . . about other people."

"Are you family?"

"A cousin."

Dr. Allerton reached out, as if offering a side-hug, but Ellie jerked back. Kirby barked once, a warning.

"Sorry. I should have asked," Dr. Allerton said. He looked around, searching for the mysterious dog. At least he didn't have keen ghost-detecting powers; Kirby was at Ellie's side, a vague shimmer that blended in with the hot air rising over the asphalt parking lot.

"It's fine," she said. "What's your son's name? Some of Cuz's students signed a card."

"Brett." Dr. Allerton pursed his lips and bowed his head, the figure of commiseration. "Where is Mister Reyes buried? Brett could not be here today—summer camp is wrapping up—but he wants to visit the grave later and say goodbye."

"It's a secret," Ellie said.

Dr. Allerton looked up, and his sympathetic smile tightened. Was he anxious? Angry? "Secret?" he asked.

"That's our way," she explained.

"Brett is very upset. Mister Reyes was his favorite teacher. Maybe an exception can be made?" He looked over her shoulder, regarding a cluster of Trevor's extended family, probably wondering whether they'd be more helpful than Ellie.

"Do you want to insult our elders?" Ellie asked. "Because that's how it's done."

"Ah," he said. "I forgot. You're . . . Native American?"

"Lipan Apache." Ellie answered. "Has anyone . . . told you how my cousin died?"

Allerton nodded, a subtle movement. She wished she

could look into his eyes. There was a reason poker players wore sunglasses. They protected bluffers, liars.

"He had an accident," Allerton said, softly. "Is that right?"

"I wish I'd been there when it happened. Could have helped. Somehow." She rubbed her nose on her sleeve. "I'm here now. Pleasure to meet you."

"Mm-hm." He frowned and pointed at her side. "Sorry, do you see that glimmer in the air?"

"It's my dog. Appear, Kirby." Ellie felt a tingle of satisfaction when Dr. Allerton stepped back, startled. Kirby looked solid, though his edges crackled now and then, as if projected by a faulty lens.

"Ghost pet," Allerton said. "How did you manage that?"

"Old family secret."

He chuckled. "Oh, dear. I know *all* about those."

Allerton's laughter was gentle, polite. Ellie had to step back and collect herself, because another minute of good-natured conversation with a happy Dr. Allerton might make her projectile vomit all over his expensive suit.

"I gotta go," she said.

"Be well."

"Oh. Abe?"

"Hm?"

"That's a new car, isn't it? What happened to your old one?"

"Strange question," he said.

"My friend is in the market for a reliable used vehicle."

"Sorry," Dr. Allerton said, "but I'm not selling. Goodbye."

More like: *Nice try.*

As Dr. Allerton made a beeline for the snack table, Ellie paced around his car. It still had a temporary license tag on the rear window, with the dealership name—Mercedes-Benz of Mary County—beneath the numeric ID. The car wasn't just new, it was fresh off the lot. Did Dr. Allerton lose his previous car in the same accident that killed Trevor?

Ellie's father approached her. He had a hesitantly worried expression, as if anticipating the worst but hoping for the best. "Who is that?" he asked, looking in Dr. Allerton's direction. "It's not . . ."

"It's the doctor."

"*The* doctor? Murder doctor?"

"Yeah."

"You talked to him? What does he want?" Ellie's father put an arm around her, as if a hug could deflect the world's evil.

"I dunno. Maybe he enjoys our misery. It's messed up, but so is murder." She watched Dr. Allerton a moment. The murderer sipped his lemonade slowly, as if drinking fine wine. "There is one thing," Ellie said. "Dad, he asked for the location of the burial grounds."

"He *what*? Why?"

"His son, Brett, wants to visit the grave." Ellie shook her head. "That's the story, anyway."

"You don't believe him."

"I don't. When I told Dr. Allerton that nobody can see the grave, he looked downright *scared*. Like he needs the visit more than his kid does."

"All the more reason to keep it secret." Ellie's father started walking toward Dr. Allerton. "That man needs to leave. If he stays any longer, somebody might talk."

"Wait!" Ellie grabbed her father's hand. "Be sneaky."

"Of course. Give me some credit. I've read hundreds of spy novels. *Hundreds*."

Without further ado, her father crossed the park and introduced himself to Dr. Allerton with a handshake. Although Ellie could not hear their conversation, her father must have put his spy skills to good use, because within minutes, Allerton returned to the Mercedes-Benz. With a spray of gravel, the car reversed and sped from the parking lot. Clearly, Dr. Allerton did not care about speeding tickets. Why should he? A few hundred dollars was pocket change to men like him.

"He's going to crash that pretty new car," Ellie said. "What do you think, Kirby?"

Kirby, still visible, rolled over and sunned his belly.

⤜ ELEVEN ⤛

ELLIE WAS PORING over Abe Allerton's glowing Rate-a-Doc reviews when she heard the news.

"Lenore called," Ellie's mother said. "Chloe Alamor is passing through town. She volunteered to check Trevor's accident site for residual traumatic energy."

"Chloe Alamor!" Ellie whistled, impressed. "Why does that name sound *really* familiar? Doesn't she have a reality TV show? *Hollywood Crime Scene Psychic* or something?"

"The very one."

"Why her?"

"She has family here, I think. After your cousin's death was ruled accidental, Lenore and I . . . well, we've been protesting. We even tried to get the news interested. I explained how uncharacteristic it was for your cousin to be speeding down a wooded road. The reporter didn't bite, but Chloe must have heard about us through the grapevine."

"You don't sound too enthusiastic, Mom."

Vivian smiled in her tight-lipped, make-an-effort-to-seem-cheery way. "I'm keeping an open mind," she said. "Psychic testimony alone doesn't hold up in court, but if Chloe points a finger at Abe Allerton, the police might look into him and use her to strengthen their case. Maybe."

"They haven't already? I thought you were going to send an anonymous tip."

"I did. Just . . . anonymous tips aren't compelling unless there's good reason to pursue them." She patted Ellie's head. They were sitting side-by-side in the backyard lawn chairs. Lenore had taken Gregory to visit his maternal grandparents, and Ellie's father flew home that morning. His patients— mostly dogs and cats, though he also treated birds, small mammals, and reptiles—needed him.

"I understand," Ellie said. "Can we watch the psychic do her thing?"

"Yes. Family is welcome, and Lenore wants our support. Your aunt and uncle won't be there. Too painful."

"Chloe won't film this for TV, right?"

"Right," Vivian said. "I'm going to make supper, Ellie. Let me know if you find anything interesting."

As soon as her mother went inside the house, Ellie called Jay. The phone only rang once before he answered. Had he been waiting for her call?

"Hi!" he said. "How's it going?"

"Not well enough. I've been reading all Dr. Allerton's reviews on Rate-a-Doc. They're ridiculous. Listen to this one . . ." She glanced at the tablet in her lap and read, "'After my son was diagnosed with glioblastoma, we visited five oncologists, and none could slow its growth. My friend recommended Dr. Allerton. I was skeptical, but he saved my son. There is NO trace of the tumor left! Dr. Allerton works miracles!'"

"I remember that one," Jay said. "Every other person calls him a miracle worker. Makes you wonder if it's true. Think he can heal with magic? Touch somebody and cure them?"

"Jay. No healer is that powerful. Even with magic."

"Maybe he's the first."

"If that's the case, why doesn't he tell everybody? 'Hey, I can instantly make cancer disappear.' Wouldn't that be amazing news? World-changing!"

"Hm. Well, it's weird. I dunno."

"Guess what else is weird."

"Anglerfish?"

"Uh . . ." Ellie realized that she was smiling. Smiling during a phone conversation was just as awkward as winking—what was the point?—but the expression felt pleasant. "Besides that," she continued, "I have weird news. A psychic is going to visit the murder spot tomorrow. Chloe Alamor. You know her?"

"Alamor. Like *L'Amore*? The name sounds familiar. Really familiar. I don't know anything about psychics, though. Except for my aunt Bell."

"Chloe found that missing Girl Scout troop, the one that got lost in the Appalachian Mountains. I'm looking at her biography now." Ellie scrolled through information on her tablet browser. "Twenty-one missing-person cases cracked. Assisted on twelve murders. Highest-rated reality TV show on the Psy101 channel. If she can't help us, I don't know who can."

"Ellie. Um. Not to be a wet blanket, but . . ."

"Go on."

"Like I said, my aunt has the gift. It's not that great. The stuff she senses—when she senses anything at all—is really vague. She'll pick up lingering feelings, you know? Like sorrow or envy. Sometimes, she hears whispers, phrases that barely make sense 'cause they're soft as a heartbeat. The only exception to that is when she has a strong personal investment in . . . whatever the vision's about, you know?"

"Oh." Ellie's smile fell. "I doubt Chloe has much of a personal attachment to my family. We need more than subtle feelings."

"Fingers crossed. My aunt isn't a *celebrity* psychic. Chloe Alamor may save the day."

"I hope so."

There was a pause. Ellie thought she heard birds cheeping on the other end of the call. Jay must be outside. Either that, or he was watching a nature documentary.

"Hey," Ellie said. "Did Ronnie see the proposal?"

"Not yet. She's doing an internship at the university. When she comes home next week, um. Al probably has something planned."

"Let me know how that works out."

"Will do!" Jay said. "Can you call me after the psychic reading?"

"Sure. You're basically my partner in a buddy-cop movie. Everything I learn, you learn, and vice versa."

"Which one of us is the funny guy?"

Ellie considered the question. "Neither," she said. "But I'll laugh when Abe Allerton is locked up. The ultimate punchline."

That night, Ellie fell asleep on her memory-foam cot and awoke in the shade of a juniper tree, her head pillowed by a cloud of white mushrooms. Nearby, a sluggish river bisected the landscape. Ellie's mouth was so dry, she could not speak. With no other option, she walked barefoot to the water's edge, the hems of her pajama pants becoming stiff and dark with mud. She cupped her hands and knelt to drink.

There was movement in the impossibly deep water. Trevor's face peering at her from the depths. He reached for Ellie, his fingertips nearly brushing the boundary between water and air. Trevor's lips moved: *Help me.* He was trapped below.

Yes. Ellie wanted to take her cousin's hand and pull him into the warmth. But she couldn't! Because that wasn't Trevor. No. It was a monster with Trevor's face.

"I'm sorry," she said, and crawled backward up the bank,

only stopping when her spine pressed against the juniper trunk.

The river boiled with the monster's rage.

Ellie.

ELLIE!

This time, Ellie actually woke up; Lenore loomed over her. "Wha . . . huh?" Ellie asked. "How long have you been watching me?"

Lenore stepped away from the cot. "Get up," she said. "It's time to meet Chloe Alamor."

After a breakfast of migas and orange juice, Ellie and Lenore drove to the site of Trevor's death in grim silence, chased by the rising sun. When they turned onto the narrow, wooded road, they had to maneuver around a three-person camera crew and a souped-up black RV. Lenore parked on the shoulder and stared out the window, as if watching a movie she didn't much enjoy. "This is where the farmer found Trevor," she said.

"It's so isolated," Ellie said. The dirt road was flanked by thorny desert willow, mesquite, and calico bush. The small, drought-resistant trees and shrubs thrived in the Rio Grande Valley. They had thick, waxy leaves and pale, woody branches. Between them grew tangles of flowering wild plants, the kind that fed butterflies in the spring and early summer. Some of the vegetation was damaged, as if crushed under tires in an accident.

"I'm sorry," Lenore said. "About that night. It was wrong to shout at you. To demand impossible things."

"No worries," Ellie said. "When I first heard about the tragedy, I . . . I wanted to bring him back, too."

"It isn't fair," Lenore said. She dabbed her eyes with a handkerchief. Since Trevor died, Lenore had not worn her usual plum-colored lipstick, wingtip eyeliner, full-coverage foundation, and golden highlighter. She looked like a different person. Not unrecognizable; if Ellie saw photographs of Lenore-with-makeup and Lenore-without-makeup side-by-side, she'd recognize them as the same person (or identical siblings). However, like her perfumes, Lenore was the kind of woman who poured her personality and artistry into her makeup. Ellie wondered if the creative spark would ever return.

"We're the only people here," Ellie said. "Besides Chloe's equipment van. There's no traffic."

"It's a back road," Lenore said, " that leads nowhere. Just a few houses and farms."

Ellie and Lenore watched the camera crew, two men and one woman, hammer red stakes into the ground, cordoning off the spot where Trevor's car had been found. They set up an expensive-looking tripod and camera outside the ring. "Is this being filmed?" Ellie asked. "I thought . . ."

Lenore nodded once, curtly. "Yes, but not for a TV show. Chloe records all her work. It's better than trusting memory."

"Where is she, by the way?"

"Probably still in her RV." Lenore hid her face behind her hands, like somebody playing a game of peekaboo who never intended to reappear. "This was a bad idea," she said through her hands. "I'm not ready. I should have stayed with Gregory and let your mother handle the . . . the *circus*."

"I'm sorry, Lenore," Ellie said. "Maybe you should wait here till you're feeling better? If it's filmed, you won't miss anything. I'll talk to Chloe."

"Thank you," Lenore said, peeking over her fingers.

Ellie tried to look reassuring as she unbuckled and stepped from the car. Warm, wildflower-scented air washed over her. She waved at the camera crew and walked along the wide shoulder, stopping at the edge of the staked-off ring. "I'm Ellie Bride," she said. "Are y'all working for Chloe Alamor?"

"That's right," said the youngest crew member, a thirty-something man in a checkered shirt. He wiped his sweaty brow with the back of his hand. "We were expecting a woman named Lenore Reyes."

"She's waiting in her car, where it's cool. Lenore might come out once Chloe arrives. It'll be soon, right?"

As if summoned, the RV side door popped open, and the TV psychic entered the scene. Chloe Alamor wore a blue dress, sunglasses, and a polka-dot infinity scarf. The scarf was draped over her bare shoulders, protecting them from the sun. She had the kind of pale, freckle-dusted skin that probably burned more quickly than it tanned.

"This is the spot," Chloe said with a deep, rich voice. It quaked with emotion. "I can feel it."

"What do you feel?" Ellie asked. The camera was already rolling; the checkered-shirt man turned it toward Chloe, capturing the psychic's first impressions. Chloe walked slowly, every step deliberate. Dry twigs cracked beneath her red pumps. Her chin was tilted upward, and her arms were spread. To Ellie, Chloe resembled a tightrope walker.

"A terrible energy," Chloe said. "A screaming secret. Who are you?" Smelling of strong rosemary perfume, she stopped beside Ellie. Her large, sorrowful eyes were semi-visible through the sunglasses, although the black-tinted glass obscured their color.

"The victim's cousin," Ellie said.

"Be at peace, my dear," Chloe murmured. "I'm Mistress Alamor. Where is his widow, Lenore? Could she be here?"

"Yes. Do you need her?"

"Please. Her presence will help clarify the message Trevor has left us."

"Oh? How does that work?"

Chloe removed her sunglasses. She had vividly violet eyes; she probably wore special-effect contact lenses. Ellie was always tempted by them at Halloween, but they cost a small fortune, and she preferred to spend her allowance on comic books.

"My gift resembles other senses," Chloe said. "When somebody visualizes the world with sight, light goes through the eyes and is processed by the brain. With the gift, I absorb and interpret impressions that powerful moments leave behind."

"In this comparison," Ellie ventured, "Lenore is like sixth-sense reading glasses?"

"Exactly. Because of your connection to Trevor, so are you."

Although Ellie flinched when Chloe spoke Trevor's name,

she could not expect everyone—or even most people—to observe Lipan death rituals. Fortunately, for all the caution they took, it still normally required a serious insult to rouse a human ghost, one reason why Dr. Allerton should never learn the location of Trevor's body. There were few more serious blasphemies than a murderer stomping around the grave of his victim.

Ellie waved at Lenore's parked car. After a moment, Lenore opened the driver-side door and slid outside with markedly less enthusiasm than Chloe Alamor.

"Please don't film me," Lenore said. She turned her face to the side, as if hiding from paparazzi. Ellie noticed that Lenore's eyes were wet.

"I'll keep the focus on Mistress Alamor," the cameraman promised. "Are we ready?"

Chloe held up her hands, bidding everyone to be silent. Only the birds and insects continued chatting. "You have invited me to witness something intimate," Chloe said. "For that, I am humbled."

"Invited?" Ellie asked. "Didn't you contact us first?"

"I volunteered my gift," she said, looking pointedly at the camera, "but would not be here today without an explicit invitation and acceptance. That's for the record."

"Yes," Lenore agreed. "You have my permission to continue."

Chloe walked onto the patch of tire-flattened dirt and brush where Trevor's car had been found. "Stand in quiet contemplation," she said, "of your loved one."

Lenore bowed her head. In contrast, Chloe closed her eyes and leaned back, as if basking in the sun. Ellie watched them both, afraid to blink. The camera might be running, but it couldn't capture everything.

Ellie hadn't watched a full episode of *Hollywood Crime Scene Psychic* before, but she'd brushed up on clips of Chloe Alamor in action. Every psychic reading was different. Sometimes, Chloe swayed and related her observations in a singsong voice. Other times she shuddered violently, screamed, and collapsed, overwhelmed by the energy at the crime scene.

That day, at Trevor's accident site, Chloe went very still. Perhaps she had turned to stone. No: as a breeze rustled the mesquite leaves around them, Chloe's mouth began to move. Ellie couldn't tell if she was miming words or gasping like a fish out of water.

Ellie leaned closer to the psychic, trying to read her lips. They seemed to repeat the same word over and over. *Anger? Ate her?*

"Danger!" Chloe cried. Her panicked shriek sent everybody, including the cameraman, scrambling back a couple steps. Ellie readied herself to lead Kirby into battle.

"What do you mean?" Lenore asked.

"I see everything," Chloe said. The psychic collapsed to her knees and clutched the ground, as if trying to dig her own grave. "Trevor is driving home. It's dark outside, and he's troubled. There's so much work to do."

"Right," Lenore said. "The first day of summer school was coming, and he needed to finish lesson plans—"

"Lesson plans! Yes! They dominate his thoughts! Until . . . what's that?!" Chloe pointed at the street, trembling with intense emotion. The cameraman turned to film empty air. "There's a woman in the road!" Chloe cried. "Staggering . . . bloody . . . injured! Trevor tries to brake! But the car is not responding. Something is—"

"A woman?" Ellie asked. "Are you sure?"

"Yes. Oh!" Chloe swayed, as if resisting a swoon. "There's something terribly wrong. She's not human. She's not even alive!"

"Wait a second," Ellie said. "I don't think—"

"Quiet, please!" Chloe said. "No more disruptions. I can't . . . can't stand this much longer. I am assailed by the ghost's bitterness and rage! She . . . she died in a car accident, such a violent event, and she wants the world to know her misery. To feel her pain."

"You mean . . ." Lenore could not finish, but her question was clear.

"Yes," Chloe said. "The car accelerates. Trevor cannot make it stop. He swerves off the road, and—"

"Um," Ellie said, "sorry to interrupt again, but none of that happened."

Chloe stood, crossed her arms, and treated Ellie to an affably exasperated smile. "Ghosts are real, love," Chloe said.

"Oh, I *know* that," Ellie said. "I also know that my cousin wasn't killed by a ghost. Anyway, what was he doing on this nowhere road to begin with?"

"I'm not here to defend my gift. Believe me or don't."

Chloe snapped her fingers, and the crew started packing up the stakes, camera, and tripod. "Lenore, my sincere condolences for your loss. I can put you in contact with a poltergeist specialist, if needed."

"I know one already," Lenore said. Her face was inscrutably blank. "Thank you, Mistress Alamor."

"It's my pleasure." Chloe put her sunglasses back on. "If you need a copy of the tape for legal proceedings—life insurance claim, cause of death determination, lawsuits, anything—please give me a call. Here's my card." She handed a midnight blue business card to Lenore.

"How did you learn about our loss?" Ellie asked. "Family in the area?"

"Mm-hm," Chloe said. "My nephew. Excuse me. Gotta go. I have a meeting in another county, and this road desperately needs spiritual cleansing. Don't linger."

As Chloe Alamor and her crew puttered away in their RV, Ellie asked, "You don't believe her, do you?"

"No," Lenore said. "This was a waste of time. A joke."

"Makes you wonder . . ."

"Wonder? No. I understand what happened. Mistress Alamor didn't sense anything. She's a scammer. My parents warned me about them. I just . . . I was hoping for a miracle today."

"Me too." Ellie shook her head. "I feel like we're missing something. What?"

Five hours later, as Ellie looked over Rate-a-Doc reviews for the third time, the answer came to her. There was a reason the name "Alamor" had sounded so familiar to both Jay and her. It wasn't just because of the reality TV show, which Jay hadn't even seen.

One of Dr. Allerton's glowing reviews came from a man named Justin Alamor.

Ellie called Jay. He answered with a "Hey, what's up?"

"A conspiracy! That's what's up. You were right. Dr. Allerton has connections in high places."

"Uh-oh."

"According to this website, the doctor treated a man named Justin Alamor."

"Huh! Is Justin related to Chloe?"

"I'd wager yes. Their surname isn't common like 'Smith' or 'Brown.' There must be a family link."

"So Chloe Alamor, Hollywood Psychic, knows Dr. Allerton?"

"Knows him and owes him. I suspect that Allerton pressured Chloe to contact Lenore and lie about my cousin's death."

"Why?"

"Probably 'cause my family isn't satisfied with the whole 'accident' story. We're causing a fuss."

"So Chloe Alamor swoops in, blames a wandering ghost, and hopes that her convenient explanation will satisfy you?"

"As if we're that gullible. Hey, Jay."

"Yes?"

"Can I borrow your psychic aunt?"

⇒≫⟶ TWELVE ⟵≪⇐

FAIRY RINGS WERE fickle things. They had to be the right size and shape (a perfect circle with a 5.16-foot diameter, the length of Fairy Queen Titania's hair), and be composed of mushrooms belonging to one of six specific fungus genera. Furthermore, ring travel was strictly regulated within the United States for reasons related to national security. Designated travelers had to purchase transportation passes at official Ring Transport Centers, and if they failed to appear at their appropriate destination, they were declared "missing in transit" and promptly retrieved by ring agents. Nobody wanted a repeat of the island incident: in the nineties, five twelve-year-old boys who'd wanted to see a baseball game in Chicago somehow landed on an abandoned man-made island in the middle of the Pacific, a former military site that was slowly crumbling into the ocean. It took six days to find them, and by the time the rescuers arrived, only four of the boys were still alive.

Jay and his auntie had plenty of ring travel experience, so their trip was quick and uneventful. Ellie met them in McAllen, the nearest city with a Ring Center. Jay, with his white T-shirt, pink Bermuda shorts, and flip-flops, had dressed for the heat wave. In contrast, his aunt wore a knitted sweater and ankle-length skirt. Her eyes were magnified by round glasses with copper frames. "Thanks for coming so quickly!" Ellie said, running up to the pair. "I really appreciate it."

"Aunt Bell," Jay said, "this is my friend Ellie."

"Good to meet you, but I wish the circumstances were better," Aunt Bell said, extending a plump hand. As Ellie shook it, she was surprised by how soft, dry, and cool Bell's skin felt. Particularly since it was high noon, sweltering, and sunny.

"Are you hungry?" Jay asked. "We haven't eaten lunch yet."

"They make good tacos up the street," Ellie suggested.

"You're driving?" Aunt Bell asked. "How long have you had a license?"

"Six months, Auntie," Ellie said, "and I've never had trouble. Not even a parking ticket!"

To emphasize her driving proficiency, Ellie chose a parallel-parking spot outside the taco shop, even though there were plenty of easy-peasy pull-in spots available. "How's that?" she asked. "I'm just an inch from the curb."

"There's no need to show off, dear," Aunt Bell said. "I'm not impressed by razzle-dazzle."

"You're much different than Chloe Alamor," Ellie said. "She was forty percent razzle, forty percent dazzle, and twenty percent terrible liar. She blamed my cousin's death on a wandering ghost."

"I've seen her show," Aunt Bell said, grinning. "Ridiculous stories are par the course."

They settled into a booth and ordered lunch. Despite Ellie's objections, Aunt Bell paid for everything. Ellie and Jay sat side-by-side, their elbows brushing each time Jay spoke. He was the kind of person who emphasized his words with expansive hand gestures. Thus, as he described Trevor's murder, he seemed to parry invisible foes. "We know it was murder," he concluded, "but there's no obvious motive or method."

"Let's see what I can do about that," Aunt Bell said. "How far is the road?"

"Forty minutes," Ellie said. "Sorry. There isn't a closer Ring Transport Center."

"I made a playlist for the trip," Jay said. "It's mostly NPR podcasts. Do you prefer slice-of-life storytelling or news?"

"Stories," Aunt Bell said. "Jay, don't talk with your mouth full."

He swallowed a bite of vegetarian meat-substitute taco before responding, "Sorry. I was trying to be efficient."

They refilled their soda cups for the road and started the long drive. Although Jay sat in the back seat, Aunt Bell gladly filled the role of "backseat driver," warning Ellie whenever they approached a stop sign or traffic light. Ellie thanked her each time; she'd been raised to respect her elders, no matter how difficult the task became.

Her patience was tested when Aunt Bell hollered, "Slow down!" Ellie was driving past a strip mall, but she didn't see any crosswalk or stop sign; nevertheless, she slammed on the brakes, rapidly decelerating from forty to twenty.

"What is it?" she asked.

"I saw a girl running toward the street. She wasn't paying attention."

At that instant, a mother and daughter exited a boutique at the end of the strip mall. The child's free arm was in a cast, and bruises purpled the skin below her eyes.

"That's her," Aunt Bell said. "Oh no. Poor darling. She's already been in an accident."

"That's creepy," Ellie said. "Do you often see the past?"

"No. Not like that. Not so . . . suddenly and powerfully. It's strange." Aunt Bell removed her glasses and vigorously wiped their lenses with her sleeve.

"You're extra psychic today," Jay said. "Isn't that good?"

"We'll see," Aunt Bell said. "But I need to focus on your cousin's death, Miss Ellie, and block all unrelated noise." She closed her eyes. "There. No more visions."

Forty-three minutes later, Ellie pulled onto the lonely road where Trevor died. "This is it," she said. "They found his car up ahead."

Jay hopped out of the minivan and opened the door. He

assisted his auntie as she slid off her seat and onto the dusty shoulder. By that point, Ellie was already standing beside the spot where Trevor had been found. She kicked a clump of dirt that Chloe Alamor, in the throes of psychic theatrics, had pulled from the earth.

"Ah," Aunt Bell said. "The residual energy is faint, dispersing, but . . . yes . . . I feel intense concern." She closed her eyes and leaned against a nearby mesquite tree. "Somebody is speaking. I hear a question. 'Sir, are you okay? Sir?'" Aunt Bell's voice deepened and adopted a southern twang.

"You sound just like the farmer who found my cousin," Ellie said. "He was at the wake." Ellie frowned. "Do you hear anyone else? Another man, maybe?" Dr. Allerton did not speak with a Texan accent. She wondered if he'd been raised somewhere else.

"No," Aunt Bell said. "There are whispers in the air, but those could belong to anyone. Dear, I don't think the accident happened here. There's no . . ." She opened her eyes, pushed away from the tree, and waved a hand through the air, as if swatting an annoying fly. ". . . no sudden *change*. No impact, no flash of pain. No violence."

"But he was found here," Ellie said, "in his car. By that farmer you just channeled. You really feel nothing else? Nothing?"

Aunt Bell shook her head.

"So your cousin must have been hurt somewhere else," Jay reasoned, "and then moved."

Ellie considered the possibility. "I'd been wondering why

Cuz was driving here in the first place," she said. "It makes no sense. He shouldn't be near this road. Unless you're right. Unless he and his car were towed or driven here by somebody else. Why, though? What was Allerton trying to hide?"

Whatever the case, Ellie was confident that the real crime happened somewhere else. That scenario also explained why Trevor had been found unbuckled with no sign of accident-related seatbelt bruising, even though he was Mr. Safety First when it came to crossing the road or riding in a motorized vehicle. The last time Ellie shared a car with him, Trevor wouldn't even cruise through the parking lot before she was strapped in. "You'll be going five miles per hour," Ellie had complained. "Do we really need the extra security?"

"What if my students saw us driving without a seatbelt?" he'd asked. "They'd never accept lessons from a hypocrite! Anyway, a truck could careen around the corner and hit us like a battering ram."

"Can you, um, track down the accident site with your gift?" Ellie asked. She hoped that, to a woman like Aunt Bell, the traumatic incident resembled a tornado siren or lighthouse beam.

"I'm sorry," Aunt Bell said, "but no. I need to be close. Especially since days have passed since his murder."

"Your cousin was returning from work, right?" Jay asked. "Do you know his usual route home?"

"Oh, yeah!" Ellie said. "Yeah, I do! That's brilliant."

Jay covered his face with one hand and brushed away her

compliment with the other, feigning modest embarrassment. "Aw," he said. "Thanks."

They drove to the elementary school, a gray building with a fenced-in playground. Although a couple cars—most likely belonging to administrators or teachers—were parked outside the school, it seemed otherwise deserted. Summer school ran from morning until noon.

"What do you feel, Auntie?" Ellie asked.

Aunt Bell closed her eyes. After a minute, she reported, "This place reeks of emotional highs and lows, but there's no sign of grievous physical pain."

"Okay," Ellie said. "Must have happened somewhere else. I need your help with directions, Jay. There should be a map back there somewhere."

"A *paper* map?" He sounded incredulous.

"My dad likes to be prepared. What would you do if all the GPS satellites dropped from the sky?"

"Hide in my basement," Jay said. "That sounds terrifying!"

"Me too, I guess," Ellie admitted.

She heard paper rustling; in the rearview mirror, Ellie watched Jay struggle to unfold a humongous map of southern Texas. It soon concealed him.

"Tell me the quickest route between here and King Street," she said.

"Got it." He lowered the map. "I think I'll use my phone for this, since the satellites are still working."

His smartphone intoned, "Turn left on Fullerton Avenue."

"If the robot handles directions, you can be lookout," Ellie said. "If you see anything weird, like skid marks on the road or blood stains, let me know."

Ellie drove at an unhurried pace. She wanted to give Aunt Bell ample time to process the metaphysical surroundings. They had just crossed a covered bridge when Jay pressed his face against the window. "Look!" he said. "Those plants are messed up, and there's a tire skid leading straight for them!"

Ellie glanced out the passenger-side window. Several bushes were in disarray, their branches snapped, their roots unearthed, as if they'd been crushed by a bison or a car. Since bison were all but extinct in Texas, the car scenario seemed more likely. Ellie immediately parked on the dirt shoulder. "Kids, be careful when you get out," Aunt Bell said. To the right, the land dropped into a steep-sided valley.

"Yes, Auntie," Ellie said, disembarking. She walked around the car and inspected the roadside foliage. Up close, she could see a trail of crushed bushes and weeds. The trail ran down the valley and ended at a tall, broad tree with a foot-wide gash on its trunk.

"This is it!" Ellie said. "It must be!" She started into the valley, her feet triggering a mini avalanche of sandy dirt.

"Don't go too far!" Aunt Bell called, her voice taut with anxiety. "We don't know who owns the land! Could be somebody who is champing at the bit for a chance to shoot trespassers."

"Keep watch, Kirby," Ellie commanded. If a stranger came too close, Kirby would howl. "Watch, boy. *Watch.*"

At the tree, Ellie observed that its bark-stripped gash oozed sap. She took out her phone and started filming. Chloe Alamor had been right about one thing: video evidence was persuasive in court. "We just crossed the bridge on Derby Street," Ellie said, "going east. I'm no tree expert, but the sap is semi-solid. See? Not super fresh, not super old. Looks like a heavy object caused this damage between one and two weeks ago." She turned around, recording Jay and Aunt Bell as they cautiously descended.

"It's two-fifteen in the afternoon," Ellie continued narrating. "Before our psychic does a reading, I will look for evidence around the apparent point of impact." She crouched and inspected the trunk. There were red flecks clinging to its bark and trapped in beads of sap. "Aha! Paint residue."

"What's that?" Jay called. "Did you say something?" He and Bell were halfway down the valley slope; Jay steadied his aunt by the elbow.

"Paint!" Ellie shouted. "Oh! Also glass!" She turned the camera to the ground and nudged aside a dead leaf with her tennis shoe. The move fully exposed a jagged fragment of clear material. It glinted in the sun, lovely as a quartz shard. Ellie poked it with a twig because she didn't want to leave a fingerprint on its flat surface. It was a sturdy, transparent breed of plastic, the kind used in vehicle head lamps. She wondered if a forensic expert could identify a vehicle make and model based on the physical and chemical properties of its head lamp cover.

"Whoo," Jay said. "What a miserable climb." He put his

hands on his knees and leaned over, as if fighting a side stitch. Beside him, Aunt Bell brushed off her skirt, barely fazed.

"Better than a bridge trestle, though," Ellie said. "Less dangerous, too."

"I wouldn't know." Jay looked pointedly at his aunt. "I've never climbed anything higher than a jungle gym."

"Aaaaanyway," Ellie said. "This is what police need. *Physical* evidence!" She swept her phone camera side-to-side, capturing details for later scrutiny. She was hesitant to walk around too much, afraid that her footsteps might destroy something that linked Dr. Allerton to the accident site. A strand of hair, a drop of blood. A fiber from his designer slacks.

Ellie was pulled from her thoughts by fingers on her upper arm. Aunt Bell grasped her tightly. The older woman swayed.

"Auntie, are you alright?" Ellie asked.

"Pain . . ." Aunt Bell drew her eyebrows closer together and pursed her lips, an expression of intense discomfort. "Two people suffered here."

"Wha—oh!" Ellie made eye contact with Jay. He seemed torn between fascination and worry.

"What else do you sense?" he asked.

Aunt Bell cocked her head, thoughtful. For a moment, the valley was silent, except for the twittering of summer birds. Jay started filming, too, as if aware that he had a better view of the psychic reading.

"I hear . . ." Aunt Bell trailed off.

When she spoke again, her cadence was deeper and more youthful. "Damn! Are you alright? Don't move. Help is coming. I'll call . . . What are . . . No! Stop!"

Aunt Bell screamed, a quick burst of anguish.

"That's my cousin's voice," Ellie said.

⇒ THIRTEEN ⇐

As Ellie returned to Lenore's house, she tried to glean Trevor's last moments by mulling over each sentence.

Are you alright? Don't move. (Was Trevor speaking to Dr. Allerton, or somebody else? A witness? An accomplice?)

Help is coming. I'll call... (Who did Trevor want to call?)

No! Stop! (Why did he sound so frightened? What did Dr. Allerton do to him?)

The final scream of pain seemed self-explanatory.

By the time she pulled into Lenore's short driveway, Ellie had come to one conclusion: she needed to see the call record on Trevor's old phone. She hoped that it was still accessible. Few things were more personal than a smartphone, so it was probably interred with Trevor during his traditional burial. Sure, their ancient ancestors hadn't owned pocket-sized computers, but tradition accommodated the adaptable nature of humankind. Trevor had carried the images, names, and conversations of his loved ones on that phone. It was linked to his social media accounts, his favorite music and podcasts, his high scores in Tetris and Pac Man, and myriad other stuff. It deserved to be with him.

Inside the house, Lenore, Baby Gregory, and Ellie's mother were lounging in the living room. An episode of *Sesame Street* played on the wall-mounted television. Gregory seemed more interested in his plastic geometry toys. He stacked spheres on pyramids on cubes and laughed as the ramshackle tower collapsed.

"You've been gone a long time," Ellie's mother said.

"I had to return Jay and his aunt to the Ring Transport Center." Ellie sat beside Gregory and kissed his fuzzy head. Her dark braid dangled in front of his face like a fishing lure. He kneaded it between his tiny hands, puzzled by its woven texture. Ellie finally pulled away when Gregory tried to eat the paintbrush-puffy tip of her braid.

"Did the psychic detect anything useful?" Lenore asked.

Ellie hesitated. She had planned to tell her parents everything, but what about Lenore? Was it really a good idea to spill the beans about the accident site, the physical evidence, and Trevor's chilling last words? What if Lenore did something rash? She had already begged Ellie to wake the dead.

Perhaps, deep down, that's what Ellie wanted. "We need to check Cuz's phone, but first, I have a video you need to see," she said. "It's disturbing. Should I move Gregory to his playroom?"

"Yes," Lenore said. "I don't know how much babies understand, really, but his life will be hard enough without extra trauma."

Ellie passed her phone to her mother. "Press play and the video will start."

"Thank you," Vivian said.

In Gregory's room, there was a rocking chair near the crib; Ellie sat on it and cradled the baby in her lap. He wiggled and kicked until she started to rock. The motion seemed to calm him.

"Kirby, appear," Ellie said. "Appear, boy." Kirby blinked into visibility near the doorway. He trotted closer, his tail wagging sedately, and tried to rest his head on her knees. With every backward swing, Ellie's legs passed through his head. She felt slight resistance, as if pressing against a gust of wind.

"See the dog?" Ellie asked. Gregory uttered a curious shriek and reached for Kirby's ear. At the same time, Kirby tried to lick his hand. Neither was successful.

"I'm never lonely," Ellie said. "That's my favorite part of the ghost secret. My best friend is always nearby. I just have to reach for him. Right, Kirby? Is that right? Is it? Are you here? Yes, you are!" His ears perked up, and his tail wagged more quickly. "I do miss his fur," she said. "Good for hugs and pets. He used to like it when I scratched his forehead."

Gregory rolled onto his stomach and tried to crawl onto Kirby. "You don't want to fall," Ellie said, pulling him back from the edge of her knees. "Someday, I'll tell you about Icarus. He was Greek."

She heard raised voices in the living room. Angry voices.

"I think they finished the video, Greg. Should we play with Kirby a little longer?"

"Eeee-eeeh!" Gregory squealed.

"Honey, can you come here?" Ellie's mother shouted.

"We've been overruled." Ellie stood. "Let's go."

In the living room, Lenore paced between the sofa and the dark television. "Ellie," Lenore said, "Trevor's phone is in the basement. I boxed it with his teaching materials."

"You didn't bury the phone with him?" Ellie asked, surprised.

"No. Like I said. It's in the basement. Out of sight. Why? Can't I keep some things to remember him by?" The tense, I'm-in-no-mood-for-this edge in her tone discouraged Ellie from explaining.

"Sorry. I was just surprised. Be right back." She put Gregory next to his geometry blocks and speed-walked to the basement. The wooden stairs creaked as Ellie descended into a dim, cool room. Plastic storage bins stacked three high lined the cement walls. Most of the containers had labels like "Old Clothes," "College Books," and "Kitchen." It did not take Ellie long to notice the seven twenty-gallon bins, all labeled "Trevor," piled in the middle of the basement. They resembled a monolithic island. The labels were written in Lenore's unique style, each letter tilted forty-five degrees to the right, as if toppling over.

Ellie hefted a "Trevor" bin from the stack and lowered it to the ground with a grunt. It must have weighed forty pounds. When she cracked the lid and peeked inside, Ellie saw stacks of papers. She riffled through them, looking for the phone. Most were old lesson plans, grade books, and notes. A packet of brightly colored tessellations was buried at the bottom.

Ellie found the phone in the second bin. It was tucked alongside Trevor's laptop, a vinyl record player, and dozens of Sharpie-labeled CDs. Out of curiosity, she peeked into a third bin. It was filled to the brim with binders.

Mysterious, black, unmarked binders.

Ellie glanced behind her shoulder. She was alone, except for Kirby. "The binders might have clues," she said. Kirby sniffed a cobweb in the corner, noncommittal. Taking that as encouragement, Ellie pulled out a binder; it was four inches thick and heavier than a dictionary. She opened it.

"Oh, Cuz," Ellie said, smiling sadly. "You nerd."

The binder was filled with plastic-protected, alphabetized comic books. As she browsed the titles, Ellie recognized several issues that she had borrowed years ago: *Down Underworld* #1-5, *Fade to Jack* #9-10, *Jupiter Jumper* (as many as she could manage), and the complete run of *Sous-chef PI*.

"Did you find the phone?" her mother called, at the head of the basement stairs.

"Yes," Ellie shouted back. "I'm on my way. Just need to repack some stuff."

As Ellie put the binders back into their plastic crypt, her chest tightened with regret. Perhaps someday Gregory would wander downstairs and find them.

If he didn't, she'd introduce him to comic books on Trevor's behalf.

Upstairs, because the cell phone had run out of power, Lenore plugged it into the wall. "I checked outgoing calls last week," she said. "There was nothing. Did I miss something?"

"All we know," Ellie said, "is that he *wanted* to call for help."

A red light on the phone indicated that it had enough battery life to function. The three women gathered around its bright screen, and Lenore clicked on a phone-shaped icon that loaded a "history" page. The final recorded call was a five-minute conversation with Lenore at 6:00 P.M.

"I remember that," Lenore said. "It's the last time we spoke."

"Did he sound upset?" Ellie asked. "Or say anything unusual?"

"Not really. Just annoyed about working overtime. They don't pay teachers enough."

"If we believe that Aunt Bell is legit," Ellie said, "and I do—"

"I believe her too," Vivian interrupted. "Unlike Chloe Alamor, Aunt Bell has no reason to lie."

"That's right," Ellie said. "Based on her psychic reading, Cuz was attacked before he could dial nine-one-one. The attack happened fast."

"He was so close," Lenore said. "Three numbers away from survival."

"Maybe not," Ellie said. "I suspect that Dr. Abe Allerton has friends in high places. Nine-one-one might be a direct line to the murderer's allies."

"EMTs? Police?" Lenore laughed. It was a hollow, mirthless sound. "Who can we trust?"

"Can't trust anybody near Willowbee, that's for sure," Ellie said.

"Willowbee isn't the only town in Texas," Vivian said. "I'm going to contact Bruce and Mathilda. Family friends. They work for Dallas PD." She looked at Ellie. "Nobody jump the gun until they respond. We agreed that you wouldn't go vigilante, honey. This Aunt Bell business is borderline."

"Mom, I told you about her yesterday."

"I didn't know that you'd poke around a car-crash site at the bottom of a gully."

"At least she found something," Lenore said. "At least she's *trying*."

A pause. Ellie looked from Lenore to her mother, unsure who'd break the silence first.

"It's time for supper, isn't it?" Vivian asked. "I made casserole."

"I'm not hungry," Lenore said. "Maybe later."

"Give me double portions," Ellie said, hoping to make peace. Plus, she loved that casserole.

After scarfing down two helpings of elbow noodles in cream-of-mushroom sauce, Ellie returned to the basement to rummage through Trevor's teaching materials. Four of the seven bins were school-related. They contained a variety of art projects, papers, and attendance books. As Ellie worked, Kirby curled at her feet, blinking in and out of visibility, an anxious habit. Ellie wondered if he could sense the unhappiness around him. Anger. Grief. Helpless despair. What did the poor dog think? Was he concerned about his humans?

She pulled the trilobite fossil from her pocket and sent its ghost scuttling across the cement basement floor. Kirby looked up, intrigued. "You can't play with it," Ellie said. "Sorry, boy."

He was a friendly, social dog, eager to play with any species that moved. Unfortunately, Ellie didn't know how destructive a startled trilobite ghost could be.

"If I go to Herotonic University," she told Kirby, "I'll find a sibling for you. A Chihuahua from the pound." Most university dorms had strict no-pet policies. However, since Herotonic was local, Ellie could continue living at home.

"Maybe you'd prefer a pack of ghosts," she mused. Her family line included hundreds of domesticated animals, beginning with Six-Great's pack of thirty heroic ghost hounds. Sometimes, when Ellie called for Kirby, she sensed a friendly, exuberant presence behind him. A whisper of barks and wagging tails. As if the dogs of her ancestors heard her voice and recognized its timbre. Only fear stopped Ellie from calling them too. She worried that something else—something dangerous—might follow. Animal and human souls shared the vast underworld. Domesticated animals probably lived near their masters. If Six-Great's dogs went missing, would her ghost try to find them?

Ellie didn't want to find out.

"We'll have a farm someday," Ellie said, "with ten dogs from the pound. How do you feel about goats? Cats? Cows? We need chickens for fresh eggs."

Kirby's tail wagged; it always wagged when she smiled at him.

"Someday," Ellie said.

After the trilobite returned to the underworld, Ellie sorted the teaching materials by year. She isolated the two-year-old pile for further scrutiny. It might contain something from Dr. Allerton's son, Brett. The kid wasn't a murder suspect, but maybe Brett's schoolwork hinted at illegal activities, dark magic, or *anything* that would tarnish his father's reputation as an angelic, charity-funding, miracle-working doctor.

Ellie started her search with a stack of "brainstorm webs," interconnected bubbles with phrases that, presumably, inspired the student. Regretfully, they didn't inspire a breakthrough in Ellie's investigation. Brett's web contained phrases such as "invention," "virtual reality," "choose-your-own-adventure," "4-D," and "static shocks."

"Clever," she said. If nothing else, a VR game that

electrocuted its players would be extremely motivational. Ellie placed the document in a special "Brett" stack and continued her research. As the stack grew, Ellie felt wearier but no wiser. Based on a job aspiration assignment (Brett wanted to be a doctor who worked with cybernetics), the kid idolized his father.

Nearing the end of her material, she skimmed through illustrated biographies. With titles like "Harriet Tubman" and "Sarah Winnemucca," they seemed to be about US heroes. Ellie found Brett's booklet at the bottom of the collection. At first, she thought that Brett had glued a portrait of his father on the cover. But no. The name below the portrait was "Nathaniel Grace," not "Abraham Allerton." Plus, the man in the painting wore old-fashioned clothes. With his tall, wide-brimmed hat and bib-like collar, Nathaniel Grace looked like a Puritan colonist. He'd fit in a group picture of the Massachusetts Bay Colony.

Ellie wasn't familiar with Nathaniel Grace, and that bothered her. She aced all her classes, including history. Therefore, although she held the typical US history textbook in contempt (none acknowledged her heroic six-great-grandmother or, for that matter, any Lipan Apache person), Ellie could regurgitate its contents by heart. Nathaniel Grace had not appeared in any of her course materials. Who was he? Some distant Allerton relative?

She opened the ten-page booklet and saw Brett's youthfully sloppy handwriting over a hand-drawn picture of a church. Ellie read: "My top American hero is Nathaniel

Grace. In 1702 A.D. Nathaniel Grace and his wife Joan Grace came to the New World because they wanted freedom of religion. They built a church in Massachusetts. It made the other Pilgrims afraid."

"Who is down there?" Ellie's mother called from the head of the staircase.

"Just me, Mom!"

"Have you seen Lenore? Spoken to her?"

"No!" Ellie put down the booklet. "Not since before supper!"

"That's bad. Her car is gone, and she won't answer the phone."

"Damn!" Ellie thundered upstairs, followed by an invisible Kirby. Her mother wore yellow pajamas and soft slippers. Judging by Vivian's wet hair, she had been in the shower. Was that when Lenore slipped away, unheard?

"Did you call her parents?" Ellie asked. "She might be visiting."

"Not yet. Gregory is in his crib, though. Why would she leave him behind?"

"It's late?"

"She would have told me. Asked me to babysit. Something is wrong."

"Oh, no."

"Ellie. What is it?"

"You don't think . . ."

"She wouldn't!"

It dawned on them simultaneously: Lenore absolutely *would* confront Dr. Allerton.

"We have to stop her," Vivian said. "I'll set up the car seat. You find directions to the mansion. What is she thinking?"

"Probably 'Nobody kills my husband and survives to brag about it'? I understand the sentiment, but Lenore is going to get killed, too."

"Hurry, Ellie!"

Gregory didn't appreciate the early wake-up, but his wails calmed once he'd been buckled into his cozy car seat, a rear-facing variety with cartoon ducks on its fabric lining. Ellie tried to call Lenore five times during the drive to Willowbee. Each attempt went directly to voicemail. "Lenore either turned her phone off, or it ran out of power," she said. "I don't know which is worse."

"Do you see her?" Vivian asked. She pulled up next to the iron gate outside the Allerton mansion. All the front-facing windows shone like rectangles of golden sunlight. Despite the late hour, the forested grounds bustled with activity; Ellie noticed figures milling between the trees, their faces obscured by dimness. They resembled shadow puppets. Some of the human silhouettes were indistinguishable from the forest until they moved.

"She isn't here," Vivian said, sounding at once surprised and relieved.

"Not yet, anyway. Want me to call her parents again and update them?"

"In a moment." Vivian stared at the manor grounds, no doubt puzzled by its activity too. "Are those people?"

"He throws a lot of parties," Ellie said. "Like, there's a masquerade in a week. I don't what the heck this is, though. Hide-and-seek after dark? Want to knock on the gate and ask if they've seen a young woman?"

Vivian shook her head. Since they'd left the house, her hair had dried into damp strings. The pointed tips swayed side-to-side in front of her chest and around her shoulders. Ellie thought of pendulums. Time ticking forward beat by beat to an inevitable conclusion. Would she and her mother find Lenore before the morning?

It occurred to her, then, that Trevor would be extremely disappointed to learn that Ellie, Vivian, and his infant son were idling outside a murderer's house because Lenore was missing. Trevor never asked for vengeance. He wanted his family to be safe. "Mom," she said. "I screwed up."

"This isn't your fault." Vivian tapped her fingers against the steering wheel. "Where would Lenore go? Maybe . . . hm . . . there's a nearby Waffle Hut that's open late. She enjoys waffles, right?"

"Who doesn't?"

There was another possibility, of course. One Ellie didn't want to consider.

The grave.

"Me too," Vivian said. "Please be there, Lenore. *Please.*" She put her hand on the gear shift, but before she could reverse and turn around, a tall, pale man stepped behind the car and spread his arms.

Ellie first saw his face reflected in the rearview mirror; his eyes sparked, reflecting the van's taillights like a pair of cat eyes. *Vampire*, she thought. She hoped that he was harmless, like Al.

"What the—excuse me! Can we help you?" her mother shouted, cracking the window so her voice would carry outside the car. If the vampire had an ounce of power, he could hear their heartbeats and breaths without difficulty. A pane of glass would not impede him from eavesdropping on their conversation.

Anxiously, Ellie again looked out the window. The figures in the forest were all standing still, like stone statues or—and this thought chilled her blood—department-store mannequins. She wondered if they were vampires too. That would explain why they didn't carry flashlights. It didn't, however, explain why they were lurking around Dr. Allerton's property like the creepiest alternatives to garden gnomes.

The cursed man behind them gave a chipper wave and jogged up to the driver's side window. He leaned over, going eye-to-eye with Ellie's mother. He had a contemporary haircut, trimmed tight around his ears and messy on the top. His lips and cheeks had the feverish blush of a well-fed vampire.

"I was fixin' to ask you the same thing, ma'am," he said. "Are you ladies lost? Town's that way." He pointed down the street.

"Thank you," Vivian said. "Actually, we were turning around until—"

"Cute baby," he interrupted, and the tip of his red, sharp tongue flicked across his lips. Ellie couldn't decide if he was being theatrically sinister to frighten them off, or if his curse was so deep-rooted, he could not suppress the expression of terrible hunger.

Vivian rolled up the window, rapped the glass with her knuckles, and reversed. She made a quick, tight U-turn. Half-obscured by the car-exhaust fog, the vampire raised his hand. Was he waving goodbye or reaching for them?

Once the mansion was a quarter mile behind them, Ellie felt safe speaking again. They were alone on the dark road. "Cute baby?" she asked. "What the hell? We should have—"

With a tremendous *thunk*, the minivan roof bent inward, as if something heavy had landed over Ellie's head. She cried out, startled, "What is that?"

"We were followed," Vivian said, slowing from forty to twenty-five. "Protect the baby!"

Ellie unbuckled and climbed into the back seat. There, she draped her arm over Gregory. He clutched her sleeve and shrieked happily.

"Get off my car!" Vivian shouted, smacking the felt-coated roof. The interloper knocked twice in response.

"Kirby, destroy!" Ellie shouted. "Get him, boy!"

Kirby whined and huddled against the floor. Usually, he saved his aggression for people who hurt Ellie. When Ellie was nine, a kid named Sam shoved her against a tree, and

Kirby started barking like a Baskerville Hound, his teeth bared. If Sam hadn't run away, the old springer spaniel might have torn him a new one. That said, Kirby wasn't trained to attack car-surfing vampires.

"This is your last warning!" Vivian shouted. "Leave us alone!"

An upside-down face peeked through the windshield. Unsurprisingly, the baby-threatening creep from Dr. Allerton's mansion had chased them. He mouthed the word *good* and pulled back a fist, poised to break the glass with his bare knuckles.

"This is my home, my people's home!" Vivian shouted. "You aren't welcome along the Kunétai! You aren't welcome in my home!'" She slammed the brakes, and the vampire flew off the car and tumbled down the cement road. He stood, pinned by the headlights.

"What was that?" he shouted. He grinned, like Vivian had made a joke. For a moment, Ellie wondered if her mother had made a mistake. Nothing happened.

Until the grin faltered.

"What have you done?" the vampire asked. "I feel like . . . no. This is a public road. You have no rights over it. None!" He staggered forward and swiped a fist at the van, but his movements were so sluggish, it didn't make a dent. Vivian rolled down her window and leaned outside, while Ellie watched the spectacle from the back seat.

"What has she done?" the vampire cried. "What has she done? I'm dying!" He started to bleed. From his tear ducts, his nose, his ears. He bled from his pores, and the pink sweat smoked, as if evaporating. It smelled like unseasoned meat.

"You might survive," Vivian said, "but not here. We're Lipan Apache."

"So?" he screeched, spraying red spittle. Ruby flecks peppered the windshield. "Is that like . . . magical?"

"No. Christ. We're Indigenous to the southern US and northern Mexico. Really, you've never heard of us?"

"I know what Apaches were—"

"*Were?* This land is still our home, and Euro-vamps can't occupy a home when they're unwelcome."

"I pay taxes! It's a public road, bitch!"

"You don't pay taxes to my people," Vivian said. "I hope you came here alone. I'm not afraid to banish all your friends."

As the vampire's hair began to fall out, he wailed, "I don't believe it! I don't believe it!"

"What you *believe* means nothing," Vivian said. "If you want a chance to live, start running north. Don't stop till you're off our land."

"How large is Apache land?" he asked, backing away from the minivan.

"Before colonization," Vivian said, "we were a cyclical people, moving with the seasons. Our home is vast."

With a sickly poof of mist, the vampire shifted to bat form, a skill that only the oldest, strongest curses produced. Curses that had developed for a century, at minimum. He zipped and zigzagged through the sky, like a pinball with wings, and eventually vanished with distance.

"I'm surprised he didn't know about our power over him," Ellie said.

"Not many people do," Vivian said. "Probably 'cause it raises uncomfortable facts about dispossession and colonization."

"Why did he attack us? Did Allerton send him?"

"I don't think so. He came alone." A contemplative moment passed. Baby Gregory gurgled and laughed. Vivian continued, "Sometimes, the vampire curse makes it difficult to restrain violent impulses. Especially old curses. Considering his bat trick, I'm surprised that he had any control at all. We . . . need to find Lenore." She pressed the accelerator. Ellie remained in the back seat with the baby, just in case.

"What are all those vampires doing on Dr. Allerton's lawn, though?" Ellie asked, chewing on her thumbnail. "None of this makes any sense."

"It will. There's an explanation. Must be. Something simple. One wretched secret that explains everything. Occam's razor."

When they stopped at a red light, a black SUV pulled up behind them. It had local plates and an innocent-looking driver, but Ellie, concerned that Dr. Allerton sent a friend to tail them, watched the stranger's blurry reflection in the rearview mirror until the light turned green. The SUV followed them a minute longer before turning onto a side road.

"It'll hurt," Vivian said.

"What will, Mom?"

"The secret. Learning the secret. It will hurt, because I

can't think of anything . . ." Her grip on the steering wheel tightened, flexing. "I can't think of anything worth his death."

"Me either."

"When I was a new teacher, one of my students lost his father during a robbery."

"God," Ellie said. "I'm sorry."

"Me too. The kid's father was a good man. I met him during a basketball game at the high school. He worked two jobs. Had to. His family needed every cent."

"What happened?"

"Two guys robbed the twenty-four-hour convenience store that employed him at night. It was a little roadside operation that sold junk food, amenities, and gas. The robbers wanted money, cigarettes, and beef jerky. He emptied the cash register, gave them everything they asked for, but one robber shot him anyway."

"That's terrible."

"The two made off with four hundred dollars, Marlboros, and ten bags of dried meat. I remember a news reporter saying, 'They killed a man for just four hundred dollars.' And I thought that the word 'just' was completely unnecessary. No amount of money would make the crime less heinous. I don't care if there was four billion dollars in that register, Ellie."

"How'd the kid manage after his father died? That . . . that's just . . ." Sometimes, it occurred to Ellie that her parents would not live forever, but she always crammed the thought into a neglected pocket of her brain before it could blossom into full-blown horror.

"With great difficulty," Vivian said. "He took a couple weeks off to mourn, and when he returned to school, his friends were supportive. Initially. After a while, he withdrew, or maybe they did. People cope with tragedy in different ways. That's important, Ellie. There's no one right method of grieving. He . . . how do I explain the way loss changed him? Besides the way his grades dropped. Besides the fair-weather friends he lost. I noticed a change in his eyes. Like he now viewed the world as the place that stole his father."

"Where is he now?"

"I don't know. Somewhere kinder, I hope."

A neon yellow WAFFLES ALL DAY sign beckoned them into a nearly empty parking lot outside a diner. As if on cue, Ellie's phone rang. She checked the caller ID. "It's Lenore!" she said, answering. "Hello?"

"Hi, Ellie. Sorry to miss your calls. I lost reception."

"Where are you?"

"Visiting Trevor."

"At this hour? Why didn't you say something? We were worried! Mom and I thought you took a pitchfork to the Allerton mansion!"

"Just how reckless do you think I am?"

"I take the Fifth. Are . . . are you home?"

"Not yet. Twenty minutes. See you there?"

"Sure. I guess waffles are out of the question."

"Waffles?"

"Ah, nevermind. Have a safe drive."

"You too," Lenore said.

After the call ended, Ellie turned to her mother. "Lenore was visiting the burial site."

"I see. That's worrisome."

"Less worrisome than a one-on-one confrontation with the doctor, though."

"Is it?"

Ellie's phone chimed once. She had a message, but it wasn't from Lenore. Jay had sent the following:

JAY (11:12 P.M.) – How'd you like to be my date to a fancy party at ABE ALLERTON'S MANSION? We should crash the masquerade together.

JAY (11:13 P.M.) – Platonic date.

JAY (11:13 P.M.) – For investigation.

JAY (11:14 P.M.) – Also fun.

JAY (11:15 P.M.) – Did I make things weird?

She hurriedly texted a reply:

EL (11:16 P.M.) – No weirder than usual.

EL (11:17 P.M.) – Maybe we should avoid the party tho. Maybe. Mansion is dangerous. Vampires. Tell u more later.

"What was that?" Vivian asked.

"Jay. He wants to crash Dr. Allerton's party next week. It's open to the public. It's a charity event to celebrate Willowbee's bicentennial."

"Bicentennial? Two hundred years? That's older than the state of Texas."

"Huh! True enough. Weird."

"More than weird. I've never heard of Willowbee before. An old town like that? We should know about it. Before Texas became a state . . . before the US government slaughtered us . . . our tribe helped the settlers. We traded goods. Protected their cities—Houston, for instance—as lookouts. We never had any business with Willowbee. *Never*. How can that be?"

"It can't be," Ellie said. "What the hell is going on?"

Perhaps Trevor's death was entwined with a greater, stranger mystery than Ellie could have anticipated.

⟫⟫⟫ FOURTEEN ⟪⟪⟪

"I T'S JUST A LIBRARY," Ellie said. "Mom, please?"

"A library in a creepy town."

"I'll ask Jay to come with me."

"Why is this necessary?"

"To research the history of Willowbee. There's a bicentennial exhibit in the—"

The front door opened with a rattle and click. Ellie and her mother had been waiting for Lenore to return, and now they both slipped into expectant silence. Lenore stepped into her living room. Her hands were grimy. Dirt clung to her long nails.

"Welcome back," Vivian said. "Gregory is in his crib."

"Thanks for watching him." Lenore smiled. "I'm going to bed, too. There's work in the morning. As they say: no rest for the wicked."

"Um," Ellie said, "were you . . ."

"Yes?" Lenore prompted, pausing in the arched hallway. She did not turn around.

"Were you digging?" Ellie asked. "Digging a hole in the *burial ground*?"

"Yes. I was." With that, Lenore proceeded to her bedroom.

"She won't manage to wake him up," Vivian murmured. "No matter how hard she tries."

"Are you sure?" Ellie whispered.

"Almost certain. It would have happened by now. I hope."

"You hope."

Despite all of the warnings Ellie had heard her whole life, the fact remained: waking up a human ghost was like getting struck by lightning. Extremely unlikely but dangerous enough that precautions had to be respected. When it came to attracting electricity during a thunderstorm, there were ways to improve the odds. Fly an aluminum kite. Stand under a tall tree. Wave a metal pole at the tumultuous clouds. Likewise, if somebody wanted to wake up a ghost, they could repeat the deceased's name, disturb their burial ground, or otherwise meddle with the dead person's body, possessions, home, or family. Nothing was guaranteed, however. Folks stood under trees every day, rain and shine, without becoming a conduit for a billion volts of electricity. Similarly, although Lenore had disturbed the earth over Trevor's body, that didn't ensure that his ghost would pay a visit.

Even a one-in-a-million chance was too high for Ellie's comfort.

"I thought Lenore understood," Ellie said, "that he won't come back the same."

"Hm." Vivian stared at the blank television screen, as if enthralled by its void. "Maybe she does understand."

"That's not reassuring! His ghost could kill us all!"

"Lenore probably believes that he'll kill Dr. Allerton instead." Vivian twisted side-to-side until her back made a cracking sound. "It's been a long day. I'll speak to her tomorrow. Are you going to bed, too?"

"In a bit," Ellie said. "Or I might never sleep again, because it'd be dangerous to drop my guard for a second."

"That's why you have Kirby."

"Stay vigilant, pup." Kirby was curled on the sofa, a doughnut-shaped heat-mirage shimmer. As a living dog, he'd had a memory-foam doggy bed that was more comfortable than any La-Z-Boy recliner. Nevertheless, every time Ellie and her parents went on a family outing, they'd return to white and black fur on the sofa.

It didn't matter anymore; Kirby had no fur to shed, no dirt on his paws, no flaking dander or wet tongue. He could sleep on her supper for all she cared.

Once Vivian left the room, Ellie sat down beside Kirby. "One more thing before we rest." She unfolded Brett Allerton's Nathaniel Grace biography and flipped to page two. It depicted the same hand-drawn church that was on page one, but in this drawing, the bell tower was engulfed by orange flames.

Brett had written: "People hurt things that frighten them. Other colonists lit the church on fire. Nathaniel Grace burned inside it. All his body burned, but his wife Joan rescued him."

On page three, the illustration showed a tombstone with the name *Joan* chiseled into its face. No caption or paragraph accompanied the image.

The grayscale portrait of Nathaniel was glued to page four. Brett had drawn a clownish smile over his stern line of a mouth. "Nathaniel Grace learned a lesson from the fire. He made friends with other Pilgrims by hurting the people who frightened them more than he did."

Page five continued, with a picture of a boxy building, "Nathaniel Grace made a hospital with the money he earned. He saved many lives."

On page six, the single building had multiplied into ten identical buildings. They'd been drawn using a fine-tipped pen, with windows the size of pencil erasers. Brett only had room for one sentence: "He saves lives everywhere."

The final page displayed an anatomically accurate drawing of a leech. It belonged in a biology textbook, not a historical biography. Brett concluded: "Nathaniel Grace is a great American because he saved the lives of many people like presidents and war heroes. Without him, the country would not be the same and there would be no Willowbee. He founded the town to be a good home."

Ellie felt a hint of understanding and a prickle of confusion, as if all the threads of evidence were entwining, woven, her mind a loom—but she couldn't see the pattern she was spinning. Nathaniel Grace could heal and hurt, much like Dr. Allerton. Were they linked? Did they sprout from the same family tree? They looked like twins, and she could think of no better reason why Brett would write about Nathaniel, a man too obscure for the footnotes in Ellie's AP history book.

She felt a jolt of déjà vu. Ellie often resented the scholastic erasure of her six-great-grandmother and other Native people. Did Brett feel the same way about Nathaniel Grace?

It wasn't the same. As a child, Six-Great saved hundreds of people from an invading army. She fought blood-sucking monsters and developed a method to raise the dead. Six-Great was an undisputed hero, while Nathaniel Grace seemingly founded hospitals with blood money. How else could Ellie interpret the statement, "He made friends with other Pilgrims by hurting the people who frightened them more than he did"? Particularly because she knew exactly who frightened colonists the most.

"Okay. I'm going to. Um." Ellie tucked the pamphlet in her jacket pocket. "I'm going to sleep. Heel, Kirby."

That night, Ellie dreamed about Abe Allerton; he wore sloppy clown makeup and a tall, wide-brimmed hat. "What's your secret?" Ellie asked. "Did you hear me?"

Dr. Allerton opened his large mouth, and an avalanche of wriggling leeches tumbled out. They hit the ground with soggy *plop-plip-plops* and screamed like infants until Ellie woke up, her brow wet with sweat. For a dizzying moment, she feared that dreams and reality had fused, because the leeches' screams reverberated through the house. But it was only Gregory crying.

"Me too, baby," she muttered. "Me too."

FIFTEEN

EAGER TO LEARN more about the mysteries of Willowbee, Ellie texted Jay at sunrise. Unsurprisingly, it
took a couple hours for him to respond.

> EL (6:50 A.M.) – Jay can u visit the Willowbee library with me?
>
> JAY (9:36 A.M.) – Not today. :(Family troubles.
>
> EL (9:37 A.M.) – What's wrong??
>
> JAY (9:38 A.M.) – Ronnie said yes.
>
> EL (9:38 A.M.) – Uh-oh.
>
> EL (9:39 A.M.) – I mean congrats!! Send her my good wishes.
>
> EL (9:40 A.M.) – Do your parents know?
>
> JAY (9:42 A.M.) – Yeah. D: They're angry. I gotta be family peacemaker.
>
> EL (9:42 A.M.) – It's not fair of them to put u in the middle.

JAY (9:43 A.M.) – No worries, Ellie. Library tomorrow?

EL (9:43 A.M.) – See you then.

EL (9:45 A.M.) – In the meantime, I gotta tell you about my BRUSH WITH EVIL last night.

After describing the vampire attack (and reassuring Jay that she, her mother, and Gregory were alright), Ellie slipped into plastic flip-flops and stepped outside. She needed a break from bad dreams and dark thoughts. A walk might help.

Kirby in tow, Ellie meandered through the neighborhood until she came upon the park. It was mostly empty, although two kids lounged on a yellow slide. As Ellie passed, they scampered across the playground and started climbing a rope ladder, as if afraid to be caught slacking off during playtime. The sun speckled Ellie's brown forearms with pinprick-sized freckles. They always came out before she burned. She rubbed her arms, as if brushing the sunlight away, and relaxed on the farthest bench.

Ellie hadn't brought the trilobite fossil, but she knew its shape and personality by heart. She called its hologram-dense body from the ether. As a child, when Ellie daydreamed about dinosaurs, they seemed mythological. In a distant way, Young Ellie understood that prehistoric animals came from the same planet as humans. Breathed the same air, saw the same sun and moon. Now, it still surprised her how familiar the trilobite ghost was. Its appearance and behavior reminded her of horseshoe crabs, lobsters, roaches, and many other beasties that shared her slice of time. Why not? After all, they were kin. The similarities among earthlings, dead or alive, outnumbered their differences.

Ellie wanted to meet every species on the tree of life. Witness the ghosts of its oldest branches. Velociraptors. Giant sloths. Megalodon sharks.

As Ellie watched the trilobite scuttle over a clump of yellow grass, she heard a whisper of sound. She concentrated, and the sound swelled, louder and multitudinous, as if an army of trilobites swarmed under her feet, crawling on the memory of a deep seafloor.

Ellie jumped off the bench and backed away from the park, concentrating on anything but ghosts, but she could still hear the trilobites swarming. Did she accidentally wake them up? *How?* That had never happened before! Luckily, nobody else seemed to notice the ruckus. Not the middle-aged jogger with a sweatband around his forehead. Not the woman checking her mail or the family having a barbecue on their front lawn.

In fact, nobody seemed to notice Ellie. The jogger, mail-checker, and barbecue eaters didn't even glance in her direction. That might not be unusual elsewhere, but in Lenore's friendly neighborhood, Ellie couldn't walk down the street without hearing "Hello!" or "Hola, buenos días" once or twice.

The trilobites streamed from the gutters along the street like ants evacuating a flooded hive. They spread, invading the sidewalks and yards. Ellie eyed the neighbors, waiting for a reaction. A gasp. A scream. Anything.

Nothing.

Because she spent so much time around Kirby, Ellie was more sensitive to ghosts than the average person. The neighbors should sense *something*, though. The trilobites were visible, audible, swarming entities.

"Everyone stay calm!" she announced. "They're harmless. Won't hurt a fly! Ghosts fall asleep quickly! Well. Most do. These will!"

Again, the neighbors ignored her. As she walked forward, parting the trilobite sea with each step, she felt like a ghost herself. It was terrifying. "Can you hear me?" Ellie shouted. "Anybody?" Her voice had a weird, attenuated quality, like when she spoke underwater in a swimming pool. The air resisted her movements, thick as water. She struggled onward; she had to reach Lenore's house! Her mother could help!

The trilobites flowed over Ellie's feet and climbed her legs. They weren't afraid of the human anymore. She could barely stand, much less attack. "Shoo!" Ellie tried to shake them off her pants, but her kicks were too slow. She plucked one from her knee, but two others took its place. There were probably more trilobites in the underworld than stars in the sky. They'd had millions of years to breed and die. With that thought, Ellie staggered.

Before her knees hit the ground, a sharp, anxious bark rang out. The trilobites tumbled away from Ellie, as if their little bodies had been thrown off by a hurricane-strength wind. Evidently, Kirby's weaponized howl worked on ghosts, too. That might come in handy someday, especially if Ellie investigated violent hauntings.

"Kirby," she said, "good boy!" He floated beside her, as if caught in a sluggish current. His tail wagged in slow motion, and he was visible, though she had not asked him to appear. Overhead, all the fire leeched from the sun, and it shone more timidly than the moon. The neighborhood was cast in a blue haze. Mesquite trees resembled branching coral, and the cacti were wrinkled brain coral heads. It seemed that Ellie had not only raised extinct arthropods; she had woken up the whole ancient ocean.

Before Ellie could panic, something drifted between her and the sun. Until the figure moved, she mistook it for a fish-shaped blimp. No. It was an immense ghost.

And there were others.

Above her head swam the biggest pod of whales she'd ever seen, and she'd watched a lot of nature documentaries. Blue whales, humpbacks, sperm whales, and species she could not identify floated together, sharing a pod. Some were so high, they seemed to skirt the edge of the atmosphere.

At the scale of evolutionary time, cetaceans were new. This wasn't an ancient ocean; it was every ocean since the beginning of time.

Ellie was submerged in the sea of the dead.

⟫⟫⟫ SIXTEEN ⟪⟪⟪

THE WHALES BEGAN to sing. Their ancient voices harmo-
nized, swelling in volume and number until Ellie's
teeth ached. As if she could escape the whalesong by hiding,
Ellie dove for cover. For an uncomfortably long moment, she
floated two feet above the ground (and twenty feet under a
humpback's belly). She kicked her feet so hard, one flip-flop
launched off. The motion propelled her behind a clump of
branching coral. Ellie held up her hand; her red-painted nails
looked black. Red light waves were quickly absorbed by
water; that's why the ocean looked blue. The neighborhood
was rapidly transforming into a strange version of Atlantis.

She took a deep breath, grateful for the life-sustaining
oxygen that filled her lungs. Ellie's chest felt corset-bound-
tight, as if pounds of water squeezed her body. It was
an alienating and uncomfortable sensation. Ellie enjoyed

snorkeling, but she'd always refused to try scuba diving. Yes, it would be fun to see shipwrecks and swim with basking sharks, but humans weren't made to survive in the ocean's cold depths. She didn't trust a wetsuit, a mask, and a pair of gas tanks to keep her alive.

Kirby happily paddled circles around her head. With a soft exhalation of worry, she grabbed him by the scruff and tugged him behind the coral. Ellie didn't know whether ghosts could eat each other, but she didn't want to tempt the carnivorous whales with her vaguely seal-shaped best friend. "Good boy," she whispered. Gradually, the pod passed them and swam into the distant gloom.

Out of the whales' shadows, Ellie had a chance to focus on sensations beyond fear. For example, Kirby's neck felt soft. It felt like *fur*. Ellie threw her arms around him and gave him a firmly affectionate hug. "How'd you get a body?" she asked. "You're solid again!"

Sometimes, Ellie dreamed that Kirby never died. That he could still coat the furniture with fur and warm her toes when he slept at the foot of her bed. This wasn't a dream, though. She could tell the difference. Consciousness was a sensory banquet compared to the worlds that her mind invented.

Now, Ellie didn't just wonder whether ghosts could *eat* each other. Could they hug each other too? Was she dead? Horror welled in her chest, but she pushed it down and tried to think logically. If she had died, she would be with family, not trilobites and sharks. Trevor, Six-Great-Grandmother, and everyone in between would guide her to their homeland in the country of ghosts.

Ellie cautiously peeked around the coral. The street had dissolved into a field of brown silt. She was afraid to swim up toward the light, just in case that action dropped her in midair when—if?!—the world returned to normal. She clung to Kirby like he was a life raft.

"If I brought us here," she said, "I can . . . find a way home." The ocean felt so heavy. So cold. She remembered plunging into the Herotonic River. Struggling to breathe and stay afloat. Ellie shut her eyes and tried to divert her thoughts to something pleasant, because fear made it difficult to focus. Instead, she remembered the day her father taught her how to swim in the rec center pool. She bobbed in the shallow end, a pair of yellow floaties on her arms, her father beside her, watchful and encouraging. "It's only water, Ellie," he said. "We're seventy percent water. Did you know that?"

Maybe that's why the ancient sea had such a powerful hold on Ellie's soul? Was it part of her now? Had it always been? Panic diluted her memories of the pool. She could feel an ancient current flowing through her. Drowning her.

Drowning.

She remembered camping beside a lake. Tents along the shore, sandwiches and burgers on metal grills. Her older cousins were jumping from a long wooden dock, and Ellie wanted to join them. She could! She knew how to swim now.

The lake had been so cold.

She felt cold now.

How did her cousins swim so quickly? She was unable to keep up. Her leg cramped. She shouted for help. Her cousins didn't hear her.

Nobody heard her anymore.

As Ellie thrashed, gagging on dirty lake scum, she felt fingers wrap around her arm. Her father had been watching, and now he pulled her from the lake. She could remember that moment so vividly. The relief she'd felt. The warmth of his hug. The sweetness of fresh air and sunlight and . . .

Kirby slipped through Ellie's fingers; she opened her eyes, startled. The coral reef was gone, and she sat on the park bench. The world seemed normal again. But was she really home?

The sweatband-wearing jogger passed her.

"Hola!" Ellie called.

"Buenos días," he said. "¿Cómo estás?"

Ellie looked down. Although one of her sandals was gone, Kirby's shimmer sat beside her, and that was all she wanted to see. "Excelente," Ellie said. "Heel, Kirby."

As she returned to Lenore's house, Ellie searched for her missing flip-flop. She couldn't find it anywhere. It must have stayed in the realm of Devonian ghosts. Maybe she had to be touching something to move it across the barrier that separated the living from the dead.

If she had actually visited the underworld, though, Ellie needed help. She wouldn't be the first living person to make the journey. However, based on ancestral stories, Ellie was one of the lucky few to survive unscathed.

"Mom!" Ellie shouted, bursting into the living room. "Mom, where are you?"

"Over here, Ellie!" Vivian was in Gregory's playroom, supervising a game of "throw the toy frog against the wall and laugh."

"Mom!" Ellie said. "I had the weirdest experience. Oh, hi, cutie pie." She waved at Gregory. He waved back by rambunctiously swatting the air.

"What was it?" Vivian asked. "Your nose is bleeding, Ellie. Did you fall?"

Sure enough, when Ellie licked her upper lip, she tasted blood. "Ew. I'm glad a megalodon didn't smell this," she said. "You think they can sense blood like other sharks?"

"Megalodon?" Vivian looked concerned, her eyebrows scrunching closer together, as if an invisible cord between them had shrunk. "Did you wake up a megalodon ghost?"

"Not exactly. Let me start from the beginning." Ellie hesitated. "Actually, I have a question first. Is it possible for us to visit the land of the dead?"

"No!"

"It isn't?"

"Theoretically, it is. But you *didn't*."

"I don't *know*, Mom." She crossed the room and spun the airplane mobile that dangled over Gregory's crib. "I was playing with my trilobite in the park. Something I've done a hundred times."

"I know. It's always crawling around. You're going to scare somebody, Ellie. That thing resembles a humongous mutant pill bug."

"Everyone loves pill bugs. They're the insect version of hedgehogs."

"We can debate that later. What happened?"

"It started slowly. I heard a thousand other trilobites. Their feet kinda sounded like wind blowing through a field of wheat."

"Maybe you woke them all?"

"My thought exactly. At first. So I left the park. Figured all the trilo-ghosts would fall asleep quickly, as if nothing happened. Not so. Mom, none of the neighbors could see me. I shouted at them. They didn't hear me, either. The world changed, but it happened gradually. Like a slow fade. You know?"

"Changed. What did it become?"

"An ocean. Coral everywhere. Trilobites. Dozens of whales swam over my head. I could breathe, but I could also swim. You know the best part?"

"Best?"

"I hugged Kirby. Really hugged him. It wasn't like petting a force field. I even felt his wet nose."

"How did you come home?"

"It just happened. One moment, I was hugging Kirby and thinking of swimming in a pool. The next, I opened my eyes and saw the park."

"Maybe you were dreaming?" Vivian asked. The cord between her eyebrows drew as tight as it could go.

"Doubtful. I left my flip-flop in the . . . uh . . . ocean world."

"Ellie, there are stories. Old ones."

"Yeah. I remember."

"Stories about people—*living* people—who can walk between our world and the land Below, where ghosts and monsters dwell."

"Do any of these stories have happy endings?"

"Rarely," she said. "It's easy to get lost in the underworld, and ghosts will try to trick you. Stay too long, and you'll die, Ellie."

"Nobody wants that!"

"How did you open the door? What did you do? *What did you do?*"

"I don't know! Honestly, Mom." Ellie crossed her arms and tried to remember every thought and feeling she experienced on the park bench. "Hm. I guess . . ."

"Yes? What, honey?"

"It seemed innocent at the time. As I played with my trilobite, I thought about prehistoric Earth and how it's familiar. Things change, but they also stay the same, you know?"

"For safety's sake," Vivian said, "avoid philosophizing about the dead until we consult with an elder."

"I'll try . . ."

"Honey, I'm scared. Please take a break."

"A break? From what?"

"Anything that involves ghosts."

"Obviously," Ellie said, "Kirby doesn't count."

"Is that actually that obvious?" Vivian asked. "Kirby won't disappear if you spend two weeks without him."

"He keeps me safe," she said. "Plus, Kirby is right here, right now, and I haven't fallen into the underworld again."

Vivian groaned. "Let's make a deal," she said. "If you absolutely need Kirby, go ahead and wake him up. That's fine. But you can't leave the house alone. If you vanish, there needs to be a witness. Somebody who can get help. Promise me?"

"Yes, Mom." Ellie kissed her mother's cheek. A moment later, she was cocooned in a firm hug. "I'm worried, too," Ellie admitted. "Don't get me wrong, though. The ocean was incredible."

As they spoke, Ellie and her mother took turns retrieving Gregory's plush frog from the edge of the room. "I bet there's megalodons down there, too. If I ever learn how to wake up big shark ghosts without, um, putting every bite-sized thing at risk," Ellie continued, "I'll make a fortune selling tickets. People love big fish. The bigger the teeth, the better. What about you, cutie pie? Can you say me-ga-lo-don? ME-GA-LO-DON?"

Gregory giggle-shrieked, a completely respectable response.

⇜ SEVENTEEN ⇝

"A T THE LIBRARY," Ellie said, "we should use fake names. Just in case."

"Do you have any ideas?" Jay asked. He and Ellie were in McAllen, sharing a vegetarian nacho platter. Their tortilla chips were heaped with Soyrizo, cheddar cheese, and pinto beans.

"Not really," Ellie said. "I have a list of potential superhero names, but they're too fanciful for real-world undercover work."

"Can I hear them anyway?"

"Sure. Numero uno: Dog Ghost Whisperer."

"That one is probably taken."

"How about Super Natural?"

He rubbed his chin thoughtfully. "I understand the joke,"

Jay said, "but some people may interpret it literally. Like you're claiming to be very, extremely natural."

"Last one: Elatsoe."

"That's pretty!"

"Good, 'cause it's my real name."

"Ellie is short for Elatsoe? Eh-lat-so-ay? I thought you were an Eleanor."

She dropped a tortilla chip onto her plate and squinted at Jay. "How long have we known each other?"

"Forever."

"And all this time you thought I was Eleanor?"

"Either Eleanor or Elizabeth. Sorry!"

"It's my fault for not telling you sooner. I'm named after my heroic ancestor. Everyone calls her Six-Great now, but she was originally Elatsoe. It means 'hummingbird'—élatsoe— in Lipan. Well. Technically, I was named after the animal. The night before my birth, my mom had a vivid dream about a hummingbird with black feathers, which glittered like those Hubble space pictures, the ones full of galaxies. It filled her with such overwhelming joy, she thought the dream must be a sign, and the rest is history."

"I'm jealous. Mom and Dad named me Jameson because my father is James, and I'm . . . I'm his son."

"If you have a son someday," Ellie said, "he can have the name Jamesonson."

"Or Jay Junior! I love it!"

Jay's new phone played the iconic part of Beethoven's

Ninth. "It's Al!" he said. "Sorry. I need to take this." Jay pressed the green "accept call" button and treated Ellie to a fascinating one-sided conversation.

"What's up?" he asked. "Oh! I'm with her now. No. Seriously? Ronnie told you? I don't . . . Willowbee. Abraham Allerton from Willowbee . . . That's not . . . Tons of them. Just one attacked, though. I can't . . ." He lowered the phone and asked, "Ellie, how many vampires were on Dr. Allerton's lawn?"

"It was dark," she said. "But I estimate thirty? Maybe more behind the trees?"

Jay continued speaking into the phone. "Thirty. No. She doesn't trust the police . . . Okay, but be careful! Don't get killed! Have you ever heard the story of Icarus? He was a—hello? Al? You still there?" Jay looked at his phone screen. "Lost the call."

"What was that about?" Ellie asked. "Did he hear about the attack?"

"Uh-huh. Al thinks his friends—older, more connected vampires—might know about the gathering. He volunteered to ask around."

"Could be useful information," Ellie said.

During the car ride to Willowbee, Jay called his sister to confirm that she understood the risk Al might be taking. As she drove, Ellie eavesdropped; it was more interesting than the podcast about sports scandals Jay was currently playing.

"It'll help us convict the murder doctor. Hey, you stay out of it, Ronnie! He's dangerous. I never . . . well . . . Ellie can keep me safe. Ghost dog, remember? Oh! I'll tell her."

He put a hand over his phone's microphone and said, "My sister says hello! She also wants to talk to you later. After you're done driving."

"Hello, Ronnie Ross!" Ellie said.

Jay laughed and returned to his phone conversation. "We're driving to Willowbee," he said. "Research. I'll be home for supper. If she already put peas in the meatloaf, I'll eat around them. Carrots? That's perfect! Thanks! Bye!"

"So," Ellie said as Jay stowed his phone, "you don't like peas?"

"Their flavor is . . . not good."

"Fair enough. I hate tomatoes."

"Aren't tomatoes from the Americas?"

"Central and South, though trade with the North did happen. Doesn't mean I have to like them." She considered the subject. "Pizza sauce is fine."

"What did y'all eat in the old-old-olden days?"

"The Lipan?" she asked. "Tons of stuff, but you'll have trouble finding it these days. Unlike hamburgers, right? Next time you visit for supper, Mom can make our version of agave mash or nopales; they're succulent and succulents." She paused for laughter. Nothing. His loss. "Hm, what else can you eat? Tortillas, beans, wild grapes, juniper berries, and mesquite and cornmeal breads with honey. Classics."

Ellie saw the WELCOME TO WILLOWBEE sign.

She slowed and peered at the town through her window. She turned right onto Main Street and idled at a striped crosswalk. A family of three—parents and their wobbly toddler—strolled across her path, smiling. They waved. Friendly people. Ellie briefly wondered if the adults knew Dr. Allerton's secrets. If the whole town knew.

"I'm worried about Lenore," Ellie said. "The other night when Mom and I were attacked, she visited Cuz's grave. Disturbed it. She wants him to come back for vengeance."

"Are human ghosts always violent?" Jay asked. "Obviously, you're the expert, but I've heard stories about nice ones. Like . . . okay. There's this railroad crossing in South Texas. In the seventies, a school bus got stuck on the tracks. The bus driver? He'd forgotten to look both ways. A train was coming. The driver ran outside, tried to push his own bus, like one man could move ten tons of metal. The kids didn't stand a chance. Their bus was hit by a train."

"Any chance they all survived?"

"No. Half the students died. It was a tragedy. The town put a marble plaque near the railroad tracks. For a while, that was the end of the sad story."

Ellie nodded. Hopefully, it was almost the end of Jay's story, because they'd reached their destination. The Willowbee Public Library was a white, Victorian-style wooden building. Rose bushes grew along its northern wall, their flowers heavy yellow blooms that dropped thick petals on the green lawn. There were no mesquite or palm trees in sight. No desert plants or signs of drought. In fact, moisture-loving white mushrooms grew under the shade of the rose bushes. As if, like Dr. Allerton's manor, the library belonged to a different latitude.

Jay continued, "Years later, a young couple was driving home from the movies. They'd been on a date, and it was late. Unfortunately, their car broke down. After puttering ominously, it stopped on the railroad tracks. The girlfriend looked out her window and saw the marble plaque; she knew that it marked the spot where all those children died. 'We're in trouble,' she said. 'The train is coming.' They unbuckled their seatbelts and prepared to abandon the car, but suddenly it started moving! Inching forward, as if being pushed. The road was completely flat, not like they were rolling down the hill. After the car had rolled off the tracks, it stopped moving. You know the scary thing?"

Indeed, Ellie had heard the urban legend before, but Jay seemed so excited to reveal the shocking ending, she faked ignorance. "No," she said. "What is it?"

"After the car stopped moving, the couple got out and looked for the person who had helped them, but the road was empty! When they looked at the back window, though, they saw dozens of little red fingerprints on the glass. Bloody prints from six pairs of hands. Six. As if the dead kids had pushed them to safety. Now, when people stop on the tracks at night, the ghosts return to push them."

If Ellie remembered correctly, an episode of the show *Ghost Science* investigated the "children of the track." The show host, an energetic paranormal physicist with a black lab coat, could not replicate the legend's claims. Indeed, she couldn't even find records of the bus accident. "There is no reason to park your car on the local tracks at night," the host had concluded, "aside from gullibility."

"If that story actually happened," Ellie said, "I wager that the fingerprints didn't come from ghosts. They're all bad news. No exceptions."

"Even children? Babies?"

"Especially those ones." She parked near the library entrance and cut the engine. Before heat could settle in her car, Ellie popped the driver's side door open. "Actually, young ghosts are the most common ones. It's believed that they didn't have a chance to experience a full life, so they're eager to return. Makes you wonder. They're so different from animal ghosts. I wonder if they're ghosts at all or something else. Something . . . stranger."

"I'm surprised you don't already know the answer," Jay said. "As part of the secret Bride family knowledge."

"Part of that family knowledge is the certainty that so-called human ghosts are bad news. Period. Yeah, that means we shouldn't call them back to this world, but it also means we aren't supposed to dwell on them long enough to confirm any theories."

"Have you ever seen one?" Jay asked. He stepped from the car and leaned against its hood. "A human ghost?"

"Not yet." Ellie joined him outside. A breeze that smelled of magnolias cooled her face. It was a pleasant day, the kind of toasty-bright afternoon that made ice cream taste twice as refreshing. She wondered if there was a soft-serve shop in Willowbee, one that could sell her a curly-peak mountain of pistachio ice cream on a waffle cone.

"I guess it'll happen, if you do become a paranormal investigator. Right? Sooner or later."

"Yeah," she agreed. "Human ghosts are usually handled by a team. I'm not looking forward to it."

"You don't like working with other people?" Jay asked. Ellie sensed a hint of disappointment in his voice.

"That's not it," she said. "I like working with friends. People I know and respect. With these team exorcisms, you gotta cooperate with strangers. Do I really want to entrust Chloe Alamor, Hollywood Psychic, with my life?"

He smiled, and the expression lifted a weight off Ellie's back. Jay said, "Teachers say that group work prepares us for 'the real world,' like we don't already live there, but . . . well, if it does, the world needs changes."

"Yeah?" Ellie asked.

"Uh-huh. You ever notice that during most random group projects, there's one or two people who do all the work while everyone else just sits around and talks? Or there's somebody who's ignored because they don't fit in with the team dynamic?"

"I've been that person," Ellie said. "Treated like an outcast. I've also been the person to do all the work because my teammates either don't care about high grades or know that I care about them more than they do."

"Same here. Guess we're learning that life isn't fair."

"Uh-huh," Ellie said, thinking about her cousin. "Or how to recognize bad situations. I may have to work with toxic groups in school, but in the *real world*? Nope. Forget it. Chloe Alamor can find a different patsy."

"What if I wanted to work with you?" Jay asked.

"As an investigator?"

"I feel like I'm doing something important this summer. I don't know if I'm good at it . . ."

"You've been a huge help," Ellie said. "To me. To my family."

"Have I?"

"Definitely." She nodded at the library, pointing with her face. "Research is everything. Without the information you found, like those Rate-a-Doc reviews and charity ball announcements, we'd still be at square one. And your aunt? Please give her a million thank-yous."

"Can I get away with just a dozen?" he asked, smiling.

"I guess," she said. "That's plenty."

Ellie and Jay entered the Willowbee Public Library. Its interior smelled like old paper and lemon-scented cleaner; a librarian was wiping the wooden reading tables in the center of the room. Shelves of periodicals, textbooks, and new paperbacks and hardcovers surrounded the tables. A doorway with the sign CHILDREN, YOUNG ADULT, ADULT FICTION, NONFICTION was against the opposite wall and led deeper into the library. The building had a dim, musty atmosphere. Large dust motes freely spun through the dense, sunlit air. "Excuse me," Ellie said. "We're looking for your bicentennial exhibit about the history of Willowbee."

The librarian, a white woman who wore a pair of reading glasses like a crown, dropped her smudged cleaning rag on the table, as if Ellie's question required emergency attention. "Through the door," the librarian said, "and to the right. You'll find an entire room that is dedicated to local history. Is this for summer-camp credit?"

"No, just our personal curiosity," Ellie said. "I'm impressed. A whole room!"

"Of course." The librarian seemed to believe that every public library also served as a museum. Ellie had seen small displays—a few artifacts or photographs behind a glass case—within other library foyers, but a whole room? That was new to her. It certainly belonged to a prideful town, one that had a patriotic streak. The insular kind of patriotism that functioned at a county-wide, not country-wide, level.

"Thank you," Jay said. "Can you tell us . . ."

"Yes?" the librarian asked, seemingly puzzled by his hesitance.

"Never mind," he said. "Thanks for your help."

On their way to the history exhibit, Ellie asked, "What were you going to say?"

"I was going to ask her if Willowbee has lots of unexplained deaths, but she might take it the wrong way."

"Good call. We want to keep a low profile."

"Um . . . about that . . . actually, I should just shut my mouth."

Ellie stopped walking and put her hands on her hips. "Hey, now. No fair. You can't poke my curiosity like that without delivering. What were you going to say?"

They'd been speaking quietly, out of respect for the books and bibliophiles, but now Jay dropped his voice to a whisper. "As we drove through town," he said, "I noticed that people were staring."

"You mean that family on the street?"

"Not just them. There was a man walking his dog. A couple near a stop sign. A guy on his porch. Oh! When we were in the parking lot, these three women across the street. They were sitting at a table, eating lunch, and they stopped chatting and just watched us till we went inside. It was creepy."

"I didn't notice," Ellie said. "Then again, my eyes were on the road. Now, were they staring at both of us, or just me?" Although the cities around Willowbee had plenty of residents with Ellie's skin tone, she hadn't seen any in Willowbee. She stuck out, which was unfortunate, considering her desire to stay unnoticed.

"Both of us," Jay said. "I think. It's hard to tell, since we were side-by-side most of the time. They don't look angry or mean. Just curious."

"I see," Ellie said. "They're probably distracted by our beautiful faces."

Jay nodded. "That's a relief."

Ellie didn't have the heart to admit that she'd been joking. Then again, sometimes jokes were insightful, and wouldn't it be funny if she suspected the looky-loos of maliciousness when they just thought she and Jay were adorable?

The exhibit was enclosed within a square, windowless room. Ellie and Jay found the entryway between two floor-to-ceiling shelves of mystery paperbacks. "Maybe it's an omen," Jay said.

"A good one, I hope." Ellie led the way forward. The portrait of Nathaniel Grace hung on one wall, the same portrait that Brett had photographed and pasted to his report. Was he actually the town's founder? When she first read that fact in Brett's report, Ellie assumed that the kid meant "honorary founder." Willowbee was a posthumous extension of Nathaniel Grace's work. That had to be the case; otherwise, the timing made no sense. An English Pilgrim founding a town in Texas that was inexplicably celebrating its bicentennial? Then again, when it came to the history of the town, confusion seemed par the course.

Ellie had expected the original portrait to be more vibrant. Puritan colonists might not wear rainbow blouses, but they did have color in their cheeks, eyes, and clothing. However, the oil painting was downright dreary. The artist must have run out of pigments.

"It's like an old movie prop," Jay marveled. "A scary portrait hanging in a haunted mansion. The kind with eyes that follow you."

"Thanks for that mental image." Ellie paced back and forth, unnerved when she couldn't dodge Nathaniel Grace's steely glare. "So, ah, let's start looking! If we finish quickly enough, there's bound to be ice cream in town."

"That's the kind of incentive I need to speed-read!"

Books related to Willowbee were stored on low shelves beneath the portrait of Nathaniel Grace. Jay sat, cross-legged and humming contentedly, and started skimming through promising titles. Though Ellie planned to join him, she decided that a run-through of the exhibit's artifacts, antiques, and assorted displays couldn't hurt.

Ellie started her perusal at the sprawling model of Willowbee that dominated the center of the room. According to an informative plaque, a local architect had painstakingly hand-crafted miniature versions of every building in Willowbee. He glued them to a topographic model of the land. The project must have taken years, considering its rich details. Though the structures were the size of Monopoly houses, they closely resembled their real-world counterparts. Even Ellie, a stranger to Willowbee, could recognize landmarks, including the library. There were cars on the ribbon-thin streets, people lounging in the park, and thumbtack-sized trees blooming from artificial grass. The architect had even created headstones and statues for the pocket-sized cemetery. Ellie wondered if he'd marked each headstone with a name and date. She could not lean close enough to check, since the mini town was sealed within a museum-grade plastic display case. It smelled like lemon-scented cleaning fluid; the librarian must have wiped it recently, wiping away the fingerprints and smudges that inevitably multiplied on transparent surfaces.

Ellie searched the town model for something odd, a clue within the fiber of its layout, but found nothing noteworthy. Willowbee's streets didn't spell a frightful word, it didn't have a mysterious warehouse or unnamed government office, and the clinic and rehabilitation center, where Dr. Allerton presumably worked, was innocently small.

According to a paper map beside the display, the clinic fell on the intersection of Grace Lane and Sanitas Street. Each name seemed self-explanatory. *Grace* clearly referred to the town's founder, Nathaniel Grace, while *sanitas* was the Latin word for health. (To prepare for college entrance exams like the SATs, Ellie had learned dozens of common Latin roots, and she was simultaneously happy and surprised that the knowledge could be used elsewhere.) Based on street names alone, Ellie guessed that the clinic, in some form or another, was as old as Willowbee itself.

Her suspicions were vindicated by the other displays. Through a series of black-and-white photographs, antique medical equipment, and informational signs, she learned that the disciples of Nathaniel Grace founded a private clinic in Texas during the Civil War. Injured Confederate soldiers were treated for their diseases and wounds; the town blossomed around the clinic, and after the war ended, it catered to wealthy clients. The timeline seemed strange to her. If it was Willowbee's bicentennial, the town must have existed before the Civil War. Plus, the early Puritan colonists arrived during the 1600s, and Grace himself in 1702, according to little Brett Allerton's report. Her understanding of the town's history was more muddled than ever.

Confused, Ellie moved on. The next display case contained a handwritten letter to the clinic staff. Dated October 17, 1906, it was more flattering than the Rate-a-Doc reviews.

Dear Doctors of Willough-By Sanatorium:

I am mighty thankful for your healing touch. My leg works splendidly. One would never suspect that a bear nearly bit it off.

Sincerely yours,

Theodore Roosevelt

"Jay, look at this," Ellie said, momentarily forgetting to use her in-a-library voice. Jay stood and crossed the room, a stack of hardcover books cradled in his arms. He skimmed the letter, frowning at its signature.

"Roosevelt? As in our twenty-fifth president?"

Teddy was the twenty-sixth, actually, but Ellie liked Jay enough to refrain from nitpicking. "That's what the exhibit claims," she said, pointing to a picture of mustachioed Theodore Roosevelt and an old-timey doctor.

"This must be a joke," Jay said. "Roosevelt was never mauled by a bear."

"Wasn't he?"

"*Was* he?"

"I don't know," Ellie said. "Could be an exaggeration. A joke. But . . ." She turned to the portrait of Nathaniel Grace. "At my cousin's wake, Dr. Allerton claimed to be well acquainted with family secrets. And I think Grace is part of his ancestry tree."

"You think Allerton protects the Nathaniel Grace secret?"

"I think all the doctors of Willowbee have."

"Huh! Selfish, aren't they? If I knew how to make injuries disappear, I'd share the skill with everyone."

Ellie smiled ruefully. "Remember why my family guards Six-Great-Grandmother's technique to wake the dead?"

"Because it's dangerous?" Jay said.

"Yes."

His eyes widened. "Oh."

"There's a dark side to the miracles that are performed in Willowbee," she said. "I feel it."

⟫⟫ EIGHTEEN ⟪⟪

ALTHOUGH ELLIE AND JAY spent another twenty minutes in the museum, their research only confirmed what they knew already: Willowbee, founded by the disciples and progeny of Nathaniel Grace, was notable for its clinic. The small facility had an unusually high success rate. They left the library in the mid-afternoon and found a diner that sold ice cream near the public park. They each bought a cone (Jay chose rocky road, while Ellie fulfilled her pistachio craving) and sat on a bench beneath a poplar tree to regroup and plan.

"Dark secrets are usually well hidden," Jay said, squishing a mushroom under his thumb. "I guess it was silly to look for them at the library."

"Not really," Ellie said. "It wasn't a total waste. Pieces are falling into place."

"You think your cousin learned the Willowbee secret? Maybe Dr. Allerton's kid spilled during class. After that, the cult of Nathaniel Grace had to silence your cousin to preserve their healing rituals."

"I wondered about that," she said, "but here's the problem: my cousin didn't know *anything* about Willowbee's weirdness. He told me that Dr. Allerton's attack came as a surprise."

"That makes sense," Jay said. "Just based on your cousin's last words, he wasn't paranoid. He was helping somebody."

"Yeah," Ellie said, thinking of the words that were and probably always would be burned into her mind. "He was. It's like my cousin . . ."

"Like he was driving home from work?"

"Uh-huh. And then saw a car accident along the road."

"So he offered to help."

"Jay," Ellie said, so horrified that she didn't feel melting ice cream drip down her hand. "If that's what happened, I . . . I think we're close to answers. Do you have access to old newspapers? Are there any in the Herotonic electronic archive?"

"Sure. Most are digitized these days."

"That's perfect. Can you check Texas papers from mid-October 1906? Look for anything about a bear attack. The victim will have a mangled leg."

"Easy," he said. "Anything else I should look for?"

"Hm. Unexplained deaths near Willowbee. Any time

period. Maybe we can solve this mystery before the week ends."

"What about the clinic?" Jay asked. "Want to check it out?"

It was tempting. They were just a few miles away from the intersection of Grace and Sanitas. She and Jay could walk to Allerton's workplace if they wanted.

"Maybe," she said. "When me and Mom drove by Allerton's house, we got threatened, remember? The mansion was surrounded by cursed folk. One of them wanted to hurt Baby Gregory. But that was at night, and we were isolated, too."

"Yeah. If we visit the clinic, we'll be on public property in front of witnesses."

"So, it's the silver lining of that extreme attention?" Ellie wondered. Subtly, she inclined her head to the right, using her brow to indicate the diner across the street. Several pairs of eyes stared through the line of windows that faced the park; she and Jay were being watched by an elderly couple eating hamburgers, a waitress in a bright yellow apron, and a grizzled man with a shake in one hand and a fork in the other.

"Have they been staring at us this whole time?" Jay asked.

"Pretty much."

"I told you! Weirdos." He twisted, hiding his face from the observers. "I'm going to pretend that they're starved for entertainment. Considering how excited this town gets about a bicentennial, these locals must be bored." He lowered his voice to an urgent whisper. "Are they still staring?"

"Shamelessly," Ellie said. "I just held eye contact with the waitress for five seconds. She didn't look away."

"Seriously. What is wrong with them?"

"Either those diner people think windows are actually one-way mirrors, or they want us to know that they're watching us. Ugh. On second thought, I don't think it's a good idea to get any closer to Allerton without Kirby. Unfriendly witnesses can be worse than friendly witnesses."

Kirby had been sleeping all day. Ellie intended to keep her promise: no ghostly business until an elder weighed in on her brush with the prehistoric ocean. However, it was more difficult than Ellie had expected. She wanted to talk to Kirby again, tell him about life stuff. She'd always chatted with Kirby, even when he was a flesh-and-blood dog. Ellie didn't think he understood most of the stuff she said, but the springer spaniel acted like he enjoyed her chatter anyway. Dogs were perceptive. They could look at a person and glean emotions from facial expressions, body language. From the tone of their voice.

What was it about company that made a moment seem more meaningful? If she could wake Kirby, Ellie would tell him how ice cream melted too quickly in Texas. She'd ball up her hair scrunchie and throw it like a tennis ball. Their game of fetch would startle and amaze any pedestrians who noticed the wad of fabric float over the green grass. She and Kirby hadn't had time to truly play since the night of Trevor's accident. Since the surge of pain and violence sent Kirby howling through the house in the middle of a training session. It seemed like a memory from another lifetime.

"Jay," Ellie said.

"Yes?"

"It's funny."

He leaned closer, rapt, a smudge of chocolate on his upper lip. "What?"

"Texas. In the summer, it's so hot, ice cream tastes better than it ever will. But it also melts like butter on a skittle."

"The faster it melts, the sooner you can buy more," he suggested. "Can I get another for the drive back? I should have asked for two scoops. The ice cream girl just put a lump on top, didn't even fill the cone like you're supposed to. She was so mean."

"Jay, is this really about more ice cream?" Ellie asked.

"Mostly," he said, shrugging. "I guess I also want to know how they'll all react if I return. It's not like the waitress can refuse my money. We haven't done anything wrong."

Ellie shook her head, smiling. "You're so whi—I mean, right, Jay. Be sure to grab a lot of napkins, too. Mom is really strict about messes in the car; she'll notice a single crumb on the upholstery. I'm surprised that the dented roof hasn't sent her on a killing spree."

"I can't wait to buy my own car. It will have a tray just for crumbs."

"Are you sure you want a car?" she asked. "Not a motorcycle or a Segway?"

"No! I would have helmet-head every day!" Jay patted his hair. He had arrived with a springy wave of hairspray-fixed bangs, but the heat in South Texas caused the style to wilt. Now, a lock dangled between his eyes, and the rest of his bangs were tucked to one side of his forehead. Ellie had to admit that her hair was better suited for a helmet. She just had to secure it in a tight braid.

"Go get your ice cream," she said. "I'll wait outside and take care of an errand." When he got up to return to the diner, Ellie called Ronnie Ross.

"You aren't driving anymore, right?" Ronnie asked. No hellos. No how-are-yous. There might have been a time, before caller ID, when people said, "This is so-and-so. Who's calling?" But greetings like that were time wasters now, and Ronnie Ross never seemed to slow down.

"If my parents caught me using a phone behind the wheel, I'd lose both the phone and the wheels," Ellie assured her. "Plus, it's bad form. Jay said you wanted to talk?"

"Sure. *Eventually.* This can really wait, girl. You have so much on your plate."

"Not yet. Jay's waiting in line for ice cream."

"My question just seems so frivolous."

"*What* seems so frivolous?"

"In the hypothetical event of my wedding . . ."

"Hypothetical!"

". . . want to be a bridesmaid?"

"Oh." Ellie hadn't expected that. In fact, she'd never expected to be a bridesmaid, full stop. It just had never crossed her mind. What did a bridesmaid do, anyway? Besides wear a color-coordinated outfit and smile? She figured that her friends wouldn't start getting married until their twenties or later. Plenty of time to Google "wedding etiquette."

"Sorry," Ronnie continued. "I'm trying to get my ducks in a row. If, hypothetically, I get married, it'll be soon. You can say no, though. Don't even stress."

"How about yes, on the caveat that I have no idea what I'm agreeing to and may not survive the summer."

"Don't talk like that. Listen to me!"

"Hm?"

"You're part of my starting lineup now. We won't let some rich jackass hurt our own."

Too little too late, Ellie thought, but she appreciated the sentiment. "Thanks, Ronnie."

"Anytime. Also? You can bring a guest to the wedding, but nobody too weird. I get that you're asexual, so, like, it can be a friend or zucchini or . . ." She trailed off, sounding a bit uncertain. "Yeah. Just. Nobody my parents would hate. They already don't like the groom."

"Cool. Does my dog count as too weird?"

"You are *so funny*. Oh my gosh. Make a speech after my first dance or something. Okay. I'm adding you to the starting lineup messaging group. It's not just for wedding stuff. If you need help, say. All together, we can bench-press over a thousand pounds. I'm gonna hang up to add you."

"Bye."

Jay returned with more pistachio and rocky road.

"Apparently," Ellie said, "I'm on something called a starting lineup."

He raised an eyebrow. "Oh. So you're of Ronnie's bestest friends? It's a basketball thing. They're all on the same team at Herotonic."

"Huh. Does a bridesmaid have to make a free throw? Because I'm really bad at it."

"No," Jay said. "Why are you asking *that*?"

Ellie laughed awkwardly. "Oh, boy. Do I have some news to share with you!"

During the drive out of town, Ellie paid more attention to the people around them. Maybe she was just oversensitive to attention, considering the people at the diner and Jay's warning earlier, but the townsfolk did seem to stare. As if Ellie and Jay were more interesting than the average pair of teenagers.

"It's like we're a bunch of zoo animals," Jay muttered. He raised a hand, blocking the scrutiny of outsiders by pretending to hide from the sun. "Can today be any stranger?"

Ellie hesitated. Should she tell Jay about the trilobite incident? Would he worry like her mother? She hated when people fussed over her.

"Did I mention that an elder is coming to dinner later this week?" Ellie said.

"What is that?" he asked. "One of your grandparents?"

"Ah, no. Not an elderly person. An elder is an individual who is wise—that part does take time—and has plenty of traditional knowledge."

"You're entertaining a VIP."

"Uh-huh. Dan. He's on the tribal council. I need his guidance. Something weird happened yesterday."

"Uh-oh."

"I might have stumbled into the land of the dead." Ellie explained the incident in the park. How the world transformed around her. How animals born a quarter billion years ago swarmed around her feet. How whales—some larger than the largest megalodon—swam overhead, singing to one another with voices that no longer belonged to the living. How she hugged Kirby, as if he'd never died.

"You have a new superpower!" Jay said, and judging by his grin, he didn't understand that she easily could have been trapped in the Devonian reef section of the afterlife.

"I hope so," she said, "but it's probably closer to a super curse. I want Dan to teach me how to avoid the, er, underworld. See, it just happened. I didn't *intend* to visit all those pretty souls in their supernatural habitat."

"If you survived once, you could do it again, right? It's like you discovered the next best thing to a time machine, Ellie!"

"I'll ask Dan if there's a way to stay safe," she said.

"Ask him if you can bring a friend next time, too."

"Jay! *No.* You'd be safer doing backflips on the Herotonic Bridge."

"No advanced gymnastics for me," he admitted. "I'm more of a 'carry other people' cheerleader."

"You did a perfect cartwheel during the end-of-year pep rally. It was like watching the spokes on a rolling wheel."

He beamed. "You noticed! Have you watched my videos too?"

"Videos?" she asked.

"I just started an instructional series on basic tumbles and dance steps. It's called 'Improves Your Moves.'"

"If you link me the channel, I'm *definitely* watching that." As they idled behind a truck, waiting for a red light to change, they sat in contemplative silence. Beside them, a pair of men were pruning the branches of an oak tree alongside the road. One of the men stood on an elevated mechanical platform; he wore a bright yellow helmet and a bandana around his forehead that was wet with a long day's ration of sweat. Ellie wondered if Kirby could be trained to float like a balloon and trim branches from trees. Could he also rescue cats? Grab them by their scruff and gently place them on land? She imagined the city as a playground for ghosts. What would the world be like, if everybody knew how to train their departed pets?

Dangerous.

Ellie hadn't taught Kirby how to kill. But it was possible. The dead were more deadly than guns. After the Civil War ended, the souped-up United States Federal Army fell upon Texas and slaughtered the men, women, children in her tribe. With her six-great-grandmother dead, there was nobody to stop them. So the surviving Lipan people hid, and in secrecy, some escaped the genocide.

If the US had also controlled an army of dead hounds, there'd probably be no Lipan left alive. It was difficult enough to survive their deadly magic, powers that weren't the same as ghosts. Magic came from an alien place, and the use of too much corrupted the natural state of the Earth. That's what scientists were reporting, anyway. Elements from a different realm were slipping through atom-sized fissures at busy Ring Transport Centers, adding trace amounts of helium and argon and who knew what else to the atmosphere, and major spells left obvious mutations in nearby bacteria. In fact, that year, the Intergovernmental Panel on Magic Use, which was backed by over two hundred scientists, published a warning that excessive magic posed an existential threat, one nobody understood completely and very few people seemed to take seriously.

Ellie's ancestors had known—hundreds of years before any report by an intergovernmental group—the damage magic could cause.

"There! Grace Lane!" Jay said. "Look! We're about to drive past! Last chance to investigate." He pointed to a green street sign that read GRACE. It marked the first intersection beyond the stoplight.

The light turned green.

As Ellie stepped on the gas, she thought about the diorama in the library. The small-scale replica of Allerton's clinic had been so innocuous. What about the real thing? There had to be something off about it. An energy, an unwelcomeness. A conspicuously locked cellar. Barbed wire around the parking lot. "Nurses" with sharp teeth and red eyes. Something.

Then again, Ellie's parents would be lividly disappointed if she visited Allerton's den away from home. Even if she just drove by the clinic. The risk was not worth the potential reward. Right? What could Ellie accomplish by a detour down Grace Lane? How could she remain safe without summoning Kirby and potentially falling back into the underworld, Jay in tow?

She approached the intersection. Slowed. Considering. Tempted.

Jay's videos.

Would Allerton be bold enough to threaten a couple of seventeen-year-olds? Sure. He might. And if they filmed him, that would give her concrete evidence that the doctor was less kindly than he seemed.

Grace Lane, lined with breeze-rustled trees and pretty little New England–style houses, was directly to their right. *Decide now,* she thought, and she flicked on the turn signal, yanked on the steering wheel, and jerked the car to the right.

"I know this sounds like the setup for a creepy found-footage movie," Ellie said, "but we should check out the clinic and video the whole thing. Get your sister to watch us and record the stream. Just in case. What do you think?"

Hopefully, Ronnie would agree to help, because Ellie couldn't ask anybody from her family to stream the video. Vivian would revoke her car privileges for even considering the risky plan, while Lenore might get carried away and charge into the clinic with a crossbow during the investigation. If anyone was getting arrested that day, it would be Dr. Allerton.

Jay glanced at his phone, which was connected to the car's USB charging port. "Well," he said. "My battery is at ninety-nine percent. So we're safer than most found-footage characters. What's the plan?"

"Nothing too involved. I wanna see the place. Get a sense of it. If we're lucky, Allerton will incriminate himself."

Jay held up crossed fingers while Ellie drove to the joining of Grace and Sanitas.

⇶ NINETEEN ⇶

"T<small>HIS IS MY FRIEND</small> Ellie Bride," Jay said, tilting his phone camera so that both he and Ellie were in the livestream shot. "We're two-ish blocks away from Dr. Allerton's clinic. What's his first name again?"

"Abe," Ellie said. "How many people are watching us right now?"

"One. Just Ronnie."

"Okay. Nice."

"But I'm providing explanatory narration for strangers in case we need to share the video later."

Ellie leaned against her car hood and casually glanced up and down the sidewalk. Empty. Good. She'd parked alongside Grace Lane in a neighborhood near the clinic.

"We're going now," Jay said, tucking the phone in his

chest pocket. The camera's glass-covered eye peeked over the edge of his pocket, filming. "Wish us luck."

In another circumstance, Ellie would have enjoyed the walk. Well-trimmed oak and maple trees grew along the sidewalk, cooling her in their shade. The air smelled like roses and carried the voices of grackles and mockingbirds.

"So many squishable mushrooms," Jay commented, and he was right; the same small, white mushrooms grew in every lawn. As if cultivated.

"Allerton's mansion had them, too," Ellie recalled. "Strange." She noticed the green sign for Sanitas Street before she saw Allerton's clinic, which was tucked away from the sidewalk, hidden behind a screen of dense maple branches. The building, made from white-painted wooden planks and surrounded by a picket fence, was well camouflaged among the nearby residential houses.

"Is this the right place?" Jay wondered aloud. He spun once, slowly, giving the camera in his pocket a three-sixty-degree view of the location.

Ellie entered the address into a map app on her phone. A pinwheel "loading" icon spun in circles, as if unable to connect. The alert "ADDRESS NOT AVAILABLE" flashed on the screen, but it was quickly replaced by a bird's-eye view of the clinic and a little red icon labeled "YOU ARE HERE".

"Huh," Ellie said. "Weird. Even my phone had trouble believin' we're here, but we're here."

They approached the building, with Jay walking sideways

to film the property. The edge of a gravel parking lot peeked from behind the building. Ellie led the way to the entrance. There was a bronze plaque on the heavy wooden door. The symbol of a leech was engraved into the metal. "Get a close-up on this," she whispered, stepping aside.

As Jay casually leaned toward the symbol, the door swung outwards and smacked him in the chest.

"Sorry!" said a woman in the doorway. "I didn't see you." One of her arms was in a bright pink cast, and her eyes were surrounded by a mask of purple bruises. Jay politely stepped aside, holding the door open for the injured woman as she descended the two steps separating the entrance from a cobblestone path that wrapped around the clinic. As the woman passed, Ellie had a strange sense of déjà vu, but it quickly passed.

Once she was out of earshot, Jay whispered, "That looked really painful. Did she get hit by a bus?"

"I don't know," Ellie said. She hadn't expected to see actual patients in Allerton's clinic. She thought it would be private, like a Freemason building or celebrity club. Windows boarded up, entrance guarded by a stoic, muscly bouncer.

"After you," Jay said, still holding the door.

Considering Ellie's initial expectations, the normalcy of the waiting room caught her completely off guard. It was a relatively small space. Several gray PVC chairs were lined along two walls. In the center of the room was a coffee table stacked with home décor, cooking, and fashion magazines.

A box of all-age-appropriate children's toys was placed beside it. A single receptionist sat behind a counter; the sixty-something woman, who had hair as fine white as lamb's wool, eyed Ellie warily. "Can I help you two?" she asked.

"Do you have a public restroom?" Ellie asked.

"It's not exactly public, but fine. Over there." The receptionist pointed to a door beside a water cooler.

"Thanks."

Like the lobby, the restroom was disappointingly typical. It even had an emergency cord people could pull if they needed help; that was hardly sinister. She glanced in the trash can to be thorough, unsurprised to find it filled with crumpled paper towels. When Ellie emerged, Jay was sitting on a chair and reading a magazine that advertised "Fifty Recipes for the Grill!"

"Find anything interesting?" he whispered as she sat down.

"They have expensive toilet paper. Otherwise, no. What about you?"

He tilted the magazine down, showing her a picture of burgers garnished with pepper jack cheese and sliced avocado. "Pictures like this make me grateful for those new veggie patties that taste like real animals because they're made of plant-synthesized hemoglobin," he said. "We should make some."

"Plant-blood burgers? Definitely." Ellie smiled wistfully. Had it been a usual summer, they'd be grilling veg-meat and sweet potatoes in the park near Jay's house, instead of rifling through a bathroom trash can and reading month-old magazines.

Under the receptionist's watchful eyes, Ellie and Jay left the building. Instead of retracing their steps to the sidewalk, though, they followed the cobblestone path around the clinic. It led to the parking lot, which had just ten parking spaces, four of which were occupied. Ellie recognized Allerton's black Mercedes Benz immediately. It was parked in front of a sign that read: RESERVED FOR STAFF.

"He's here," she said, looking at the wide back of the clinic building. Its windows were all blocked with plain white shades. That didn't mean Allerton wasn't watching.

"Are trash bins normally locked?" Jay asked. "This one is." While Ellie had been distracted by the Mercedes, Jay had moved to the edge of the parking lot, where two large, boxy garbage bins were lined up on a strip of grass between the edge of the fence and the cement. One bin was made from bright green metal and marked by the three-arrow symbol for recycling. The other was brown, and its black lid was secured by a padlock.

"Not usually," Ellie said, approaching Jay. "The neighbors once put a raccoon-proof lid on theirs, but I don't think a raccoon could get into this dumpster. And if it was a wild animal thing, Allerton's recycling would be locked, too, right?"

Ellie's phone chimed, and a text from Ronnie popped onto the screen: "do NOT do it"

"Your sister's worried," she said. "She may think we're going to get inside the dumpster."

"Ask her to research lock-picking." He glanced at his pocket camera. "I'm joking, Ronnie. We'll stay clean."

Near the bins, the air was rank with a bitter, stale stench, one Ellie knew well. Every time she took aluminum soda cans to the community recycling center, she smelled it: stale beer.

Ellie lifted the green bin's lid a few inches, and a pungent flood of warm, ripe, beer air escaped. The bin was filled with black garbage bags and plump, buzzing flies. "Ugh," Ellie said. "I think there's a hundred old cans in here."

Jay wrinkled his nose. "And a thousand bugs. What's this much beer doing in a clinic's recycling bin? Illegal dumping? Oh! Maybe it was a work-related tailgate. Dr. Allerton and that glaring woman at reception probably know how to party."

Somehow, Ellie doubted that the fancy man hosting a whole bicentennial celebration in his mansion was the kind of boss to cut loose in a parking lot. Before she could offer another, more troubling explanation, her phone pinged with a text from Ronnie: "You're CAUGHT! Window!!!"

The camera was pointed toward the building; Ellie turned, following the phone's line of sight, and noticed one of the lower blinds swaying, as if somebody had pushed it aside to peek out. "Did you see that?" she asked Jay.

As the question left her mouth, the back door of the clinic swung open. Dr. Abe Allerton, dressed in a white lab coat, stepped outside. He paused on the stoop for a moment, his hands on his hips, the image of patriarchal disapproval. "Now is a good time to leave," he called. "Before I need to contact your parents."

"Why would you do that?" Ellie asked. "We're just standing here."

"You're loitering on private property." He crossed the parking lot with long paces. "This isn't a park. It's a place of healing and business."

"Do you usually drink at work?" Ellie asked him.

Allerton stopped a couple feet in front of Ellie and Jay, teetering on the edge of their personal space bubble. His expression went inscrutably blank for a moment, and then he smiled in a tight-lipped, reluctant way. As if he was amused, despite his better judgment. Ellie's parents used to smile like that every time living Kirby made a mess in the house.

"Of course not," he said. "That would be unprofessional. If you're referring to the contents of my recycling bin, some of the neighbors have been using it to dispose of their junk. Not a problem. Whatever encourages green practices."

He glanced at a gold watch on his wrist. It was the kind of elaborate timepiece that probably cost several thousand dollars. Ellie wondered if Dr. Allerton actually needed to confirm the time or if he just made a habit of flashing his wrist for the awe factor. "I have an appointment in five minutes," he said. "Any chance you two will make things easy and move along?"

Jay shifted, angling his chest toward Allerton. Apparently, the move wasn't subtle enough to go unnoticed.

"Are you filming right now?" the doctor asked, and to Ellie's disappointment, he sounded more amused than worried.

"Maybe," Jay said. He tucked his chin, looking down at the phone in his pocket. "Yes."

"Is this for the internet? Some kind of video challenge?" He leaned back, his arms crossed, and stared hard at both Ellie and Jay. "Wait. I recognize you now. One of you. Ellie. We met at Mr. Reyes's funeral."

"Yes," she said.

His eyes widened slightly, and he looked between her and the recycling bin. "I see." Allerton reached deep into the pocket of his slacks—

(Ellie mentally reached for Kirby, ready to call for help.)

—and withdrew his black leather wallet. He pulled a few twenties from the cash pocket. "For your family."

"Save it for your charities, Doctor," she said, recoiling slightly.

"Right." He looked down at the money, seeming lost. "Unfortunately, you cannot remove anything from our waste bins. Health concerns. So."

"How do you know my name?" Ellie asked.

He seemed taken aback. "We met," he said.

"Yeah, but I never told you my name."

He looked directly at the camera. "She did."

"Hey. My eyes are up here, man," Jay said. "Don't talk to my clavicle."

"And you are?" Allerton asked.

"Baby Oberon," Jay said.

"Right. You both need to go." He turned around, as if signaling the end of their conversation with his back. Then, Allerton hesitated. His head turned slightly, showing Ellie the edge of upturned lips and a smile-crinkled eye.

"Try visiting the library or park. They're much nicer than my parking lot."

With that, he returned to the clinic.

⇜ TWENTY ⇝

J AY PUT RONNIE on speakerphone during the drive back to the Ring Center.

"Was there a point to that?" she asked.

"Did you hear that comment about the library and park?" Jay asked. "We really were being watched!"

"By the whole town," Ronnie said. It wasn't exactly a question, but her tone seemed incredulous. "Why would they do that?"

"Could be anything," Ellie guessed. "Maybe Allerton told everyone we're troublemakers. He lies like a fish swims and a bird flies."

"Shit, I wish that I had the kind of influence to command a whole town," Ronnie said.

"No, you don't," Ellie murmured.

"Sorry, what? Bad connection."

"When will Kirby come back?" Jay asked, his tone somber. "I'm worried about you now. More worried than before."

"Soon," she promised. "Dan will visit in four days. He has an encyclopedic knowledge of stories."

"What kind of stories?" Ronnie asked.

"Stories about troublemakers, I guess," Ellie said.

"Oh, yeah," Ronnie said. "When should I pick you up from the Ring Center, Jay? Mom says—"

"The mushrooms!" Jay interrupted. "That's it! I knew they looked familiar."

"Sorry, what?" his sister asked. "You're on what now?"

"There are these white mushrooms growing all over Willowbee," Jay explained. "I mean all over. I've been crushing them all day, like they're bubble wrap, thinking: these look familiar. It's 'cause I've seen them before! They look like a fairy-ring-forming species."

"Well, damn," Ellie said. "That can't be a coincidence."

"But they weren't in rings," Jay said.

"They weren't in rings," Ellie agreed.

Late that evening, when she was alone, Ellie took her laptop outside. She sat cross-legged on a wicker chair and found a detailed satellite-imagery map of Texas on the internet. First, she entered her home address into the map's search bar and zoomed to the top of her family's narrow house. The image must have been taken before that year because Ellie could see her old red bike chained to the fence. She played with the map, scrolling down the mountain. Looking for herself or anyone she knew. But the satellite imagery was not detailed enough to re-create human faces; she just saw vaguely person-shaped blobs of color along the sidewalk.

Next, Ellie entered "Willowbee, TX" into the search bar. A minute passed; no results loaded. Ellie glanced at her Wi-Fi connection, wondering whether it had slowed. It seemed strong, but the map wasn't responding. She refreshed, tried entering the town name a second time.

Nothing.

Then, just as Ellie was about to try a different entry, the screen jumped from her zip code to the center of Willowbee, Texas. She explored the town, disappointed that the resolution was not good enough to identify areas with mushrooms (at most, she could distinguish blobs representing individual bushes and medium-sized objects, such as the sign in the library lawn). She'd wanted to search for a pattern in their growth. Maybe, they were more concentrated around the town perimeter, forming a giant ring. Maybe they were evenly distributed, which would be just as strange as a ring, considering the work required to maintain fickle little mushrooms in South Texas.

She did make note of some interesting details. For example, the color of the ground in Willowbee was uniformly dark green, with the exception of gray paved roads, and when she zoomed out, the town resembled an odd square on a yellowy-green quilt. She checked the clinic parking lot, searching for one of Allerton's old cars, but the only vehicle behind the clinic was a scuffed blue Volkswagen, definitely not his style.

During that period of time, had he been out for lunch? Driving home? When had the images been taken, anyway? Morning? Afternoon? A weekday or the weekend? Ellie wasted an hour zooming up and down Willowbee's streets. She even visited Allerton's digital mansion.

Strangely, the entire property was blurry, as if intentionally blocked.

The government sometimes blocked restricted areas from satellite-image maps, but were private citizens allowed to do the same? Probably. Allerton clearly found a way to hide.

Out of curiosity, Ellie entered one final location into the search bar: the wooded road where Trevor died.

As expected, it was empty, no sign of a staged accident. How could there be? The image had been compiled years ago. Somewhere, on that map of Texas, Trevor still lived.

And yet—

Ellie zoomed in to one of the trees along the road. There was a hint of color beside it. She zoomed in more.

The smudge of an upturned face.

She snapped the laptop closed.

When Ellie peeked at the image again, her heart beating so fast it practically vibrated, the face was gone.

⇜ TWENTY-ONE ⇝

ELLIE KNEW THAT it was possible to graft a lemon branch onto an orange tree and grow two kinds of fruit on the same plant. Perhaps that's why, in her dream that night, she woke up under a tree that had the body of a juniper and the crown of a mesquite. Black mesquite pods rattled in a dry wind and dropped, crumbling into ash as they struck the ground.

She and the tree were the only living things in sight. The earth was hard and cracked. A furrow once carved by a river split the ground in front of her. Ellie was so thirsty, but there was nothing left to drink.

"It's not just a drought," Trevor said—his voice was so close! "It's the consequence of greed."

He sat in the former riverbed. No. Not sat. He was buried to the waist.

"Are you real?" Ellie rasped, afraid to approach. In fact, she was tempted to avert her eyes and run away, but his kind smile disarmed her.

"Of course. Jeez, your voice sounds rough."

"I'm thirsty," she explained.

He shook his head. "Willowbee. They've taken all the water. They'll take everything, eventually. That's what leeches do."

"Oh," she said. "Oh, yeah."

"They don't belong here."

"But they are here," Ellie said.

"For now." Trevor drew a ring in the dirt with his finger. His nails were long, as if he hadn't cut them in weeks. "Do you know how our plants and fungi are corrupted and transformed into doorways?"

"You mean fairy rings?" Ellie asked.

"Fairy rings. That's such a cute term for wormholes that slice through reality."

"I don't know," she admitted.

"The fairies and their humans dance in circles," Trevor said. "They throw great balls and masquerades. The dances of magic users can be powerful. Their 'midnight revels, by a forest side or fountain, some belated peasant sees, or dreams he sees.' John Milton. I read his poetry in college. Not my thing anymore. I'd rather read the poetry in Gregory's book of nursery rhymes. Ring around the rosie. Pocket full of posies. Ashes, ashes . . ." He trailed off. Looked at his hands, as if confused.

"We all fall down," Ellie offered.

"Yes," he said. "Where's Little Greg?"

"He's somewhere safe."

"I was just holding him. Reading to him."

Ellie said nothing.

"Where's my son?"

Trevor's face began to darken with bruises. With a startled cry, Ellie turned around and pressed her face into the rough bark of the juniper-mesquite hybrid. A moment of silence. And then, with a voice that resembled the rattle of a mesquite pod, Trevor asked, "Can you help me? Ellie?"

She didn't want to look.

"My back," he said. "What did he do to me?"

Ellie felt a biting pain in her lower back, and the shock of it woke her up. With a startled shout, she scrambled off her cot and turned on the guest room lights. There was a pencil tangled in her sheets; its sharp tip must have stabbed her as she slept.

"Ooof," she said, sinking to her knees and leaning against the wall. "Graphite tattoo."

She tried to remember her dream, but its details were already fuzzy.

Trevor had been there. Reciting nursery rhymes. Asking for help.

Warning her about the danger of strange dances.

≫ TWENTY-TWO ≪

THE LAST TIME Ellie had an emergency one-on-one meeting with Dan, she'd just been suspended for giving her homeroom class nosebleeds.

Well, technically, it was Kirby who'd given them nosebleeds.

The howl incident began with a public-speaking exercise. Ellie, twelve years old, stood before her twenty-eight-student class; only half of the kids were paying attention.

"I can describe my summer vacation with one word," Ellie said. "*Enlightening.* Centuries ago, Six-Great-Grandmother Elatsoe, my namesake, developed a method to wake the dead." She paused for effect, peeking at her audience. All eyes faced forward. "Glad I have your attention now," Ellie continued. "Her secret has persisted through eight generations of Apache women. Nine, including me. My best friend,

Kirby, died last year. He was eighteen, which is old for an English springer spaniel. I brought him back in June. Dogs are ideal poltergeist companions, since they're easy to train. That said, anything inhuman is fair game. Grandma taught a woolly mammoth several tricks, but . . ."

Ellie stopped reading because Samuel Tanner, a kid in the first row, was waving his arm like he wanted to flag down an airplane. All his passionate hand-raising wrecked her concentration. "What?" Ellie asked.

"Actually," Samuel said, "ghosts don't work that way. They're chaotic balls of negative emotional energy."

"Actually," she corrected, "you're thinking about human ghosts, which manifest when people aren't buried right."

"Actually, Ellie, animals can't make ghosts."

"*Actually*, Samuel, they can. Did you not hear my report?"

"*Actually*, I'm calling you a liar."

"Actually, Kirby is in the classroom right now, so please shut your freaking mouth, Sam."

Mrs. Leman half-rose from her cushy teacher's chair, but before she could restore order, somebody shouted, "Make Kirby do a trick!"

"Gladly," Ellie said. She could vindicate herself and amaze the class with just one innocent command. But what? Tell him to appear? No. He still flickered sometimes, and that wasn't very impressive. Fetch? Ellie left his tennis ball at home. Ah, she had a plan! "Howl, boy!"

There are military-grade "sound cannons" that can incapacitate human targets with sonic waves. The notorious

Sargasso Sirens concert rocked so loud, eardrums burst in the mosh pit. Neither could hold a candle to the unbridled voice of a dead hound.

Kirby did not howl, not merely. His cry seized the classroom and shook it; every molecule screamed with him. The windows warped, bubbled, and cracked. Overhead, every long fluorescent bulb sparked and went dark.

"Stop!" Ellie shouted. "Stop, stop!" Buffeted by the foghorn howl, she could not hear herself scream. Could not hear a peep from her terrified classmates, though their mouths yawned with horror. The windows exploded outward, dusting the empty schoolyard with powdered glass. Students ran for the door, hands over ears, noses bleeding. The blood speckled and smeared across the tiled floor, and tennis shoes tracked it to the hallway. Ellie doubled over because her head was a nucleus of pain; blearily, she saw Mrs. Leman escape the classroom. The door closed.

Alone with his master, Kirby stopped howling.

Ellie dabbed blood off her upper lip; it stained her essay with Rorschach spatters. What the hell happened? Kirby had never howled like *that* before. Clearly, public speaking made him nervous.

Ellie looked through the window embedded in the classroom door. Somehow, its thick glass survived the howl intact. Across the hall, her homeroom class huddled against a row of lockers. Mrs. Leman had flagged down the assistant principal. Ellie ducked out of sight before either adult noticed her.

This was bad. Very bad. Suspension or expulsion bad. Ellie hadn't served detention before. She'd never survive behind bars. Would they penalize Kirby, too? The good boy was just following orders!

"Heel, Kirby," she said. "Let's go."

Ellie climbed out a broken window and ran home.

After she explained the situation to Dan, he bowed his head, as if disappointed. "Your heroic ancestor treated her dead hounds with respect," he said. "Kirby isn't your toy. He isn't your pet. Not anymore. He's a conscious grenade, Ellie. Never pull the pin unless you have a very good reason."

Years later, as Ellie told Dan about her adventure in the dead ocean, she felt uncharacteristically nervous. Would he be disappointed again? She didn't mean to visit Below. It wasn't like sixth grade. When she finished, Ellie wiped her clammy hands on her jeans and waited for Dan to speak. He was a plump man with rays of laugh lines radiating from the corners of his eyes. In fact, they were so deep, he always seemed to be smiling. Dan wore a bolo tie, yellow shirt, and blue jeans—always dressed like somebody who worked at a rodeo, even though he'd retired from that profession in his forties after one too many riding-related injuries.

"You've never been closer to death," Dan said, "than the moment you sank."

"So she *did* visit the land of the dead? God! Just like . . ." Vivian hesitated and seemed to change her mind. "What can we do?" she asked. They'd moved to the living room after supper; Lenore sat with Baby Gregory on the floor, half-listening to the conversation, and Dan, Ellie, and Vivian shared the sofa.

"These things don't happen randomly," Dan said. "Okay. Step by step, describe your thoughts, your actions, before the world changed."

Ellie crossed her arms and stared at the ceiling, sinking into her memories. "I was on a bench. It felt hot beneath me. Not painful, just warmed by the sun. Right. I woke up my trilobite."

"Trilobite," Dan said. "I've seen their fossils. Little segmented roly-poly-looking things. Is that right?"

"Yes," Ellie said. "The ghosts might as well be moving versions of their fossils. Actually, that's what I thought about as I sat on the bench. The trilobite crawled around my feet, and I thought it looked like a roach. The observation really amused me. The world changes, but it doesn't. I felt . . . this fond familiarity. Like, despite the eons that separate humans and prehistoric critters, we are all earthlings, you know?"

"I do," Dan agreed.

"Then things got weird. Other trilobite ghosts flooded the park, and the reef appeared."

"Ellie," Dan said, "besides your cousin, have you ever lost a loved one before?"

"Kirby," she said. "My dog. But he's not really lost. My paternal grandfather passed away, too. Couple years ago."

"How old was he?" Dan asked.

"Seventy-nine," she said.

"Your cousin died during the prime of his life," Dan said. Lenore looked up sharply, her jaw tense, her eyes hard.

"That's right," Ellie said. "He did."

"And have you dwelt on his death?" Dan asked.

"Every day," Ellie said. "I can't stop thinking about the . . . the *murder* . . . until Abe Allerton is in prison, where he can't hurt us anymore."

"When you coexist with ghosts," Dan said, "speak to them, and love them, you lean over the wall that separates the living from the dead. It becomes easier, then, to push you into that dangerous place, that land—or ocean, huh—that should not be experienced by anything with breath."

"What pushed her?" asked Ellie's mother. "Her cousin's death? Is that it?"

"To dwell on death, especially a premature and violent end, burdens the soul. The tragedy grew heavier every time Ellie fed it with attention. Enough weight might cause somebody to topple. Yes, it *might*." Dan shrugged. "But I think, in the park, Ellie pushed herself."

"I did?" Ellie asked.

"Yep."

"How?" Vivian cut in. "Is it now dangerous for her to wake ghosts?"

"Mom, I can't abandon Kirby."

"If I'm right," Dan said, "you won't need to stop waking ghosts, as long as you're mindful of the difference between the dead and the living." He wagged a finger at Ellie, as if lecturing a class of rowdy toddlers. "There is a difference. The dead should not seem like kin. When they do? They might devour you."

"You mean that I opened the door to the trilobite's underworld because I felt like we belonged together?"

"Uh-huh," Dan said. "That feeling of familiarity sent your soul to a dangerous place."

"Never think about dinosaurs again," Vivian said. Perhaps she realized that the statement was extremely strange, because she added, "Will that keep her safe, Dan?"

"I can't guarantee anything, Vivian. Your family line has always played with fire."

"I'm worried that it'll happen again," Ellie's mother said. "We cannot be too cautious. Ellie, I know Six-Great's secret, but I rarely use it. Maybe that's best."

"Don't worry, Mom. I can escape the underworld. I just have to think about home. Real home. It worked the first time, and it'll work again."

As if emphasizing her decision, Ellie called Kirby; he eagerly burst from the ether between the sofa and play mat. Baby Gregory uttered a shrill "Aaa?" and looked, with owlish intensity, at the ghostly shimmer. If Gregory was already sensitive to paranormal entities, he'd make a good student when he came of age. Assuming Ellie still wanted to pass Six-Great's secret down his line. She had twelve years to make up her mind.

"Is that the dog?" Dan asked, his expression so guarded, Ellie could not decide whether he was concerned or curious. After the howl incident, he refused to be near Kirby, but things had changed. Kirby wasn't dangerous anymore.

"You want to see?" she asked. "Appear, boy!"

Kirby's visibility made everyone but Ellie and Lenore jolt back with surprise. "Sorry about the jump scare," Ellie said. "I wish he could do that trick less suddenly."

"Ah," said Dan. He pointedly looked away from Kirby. "Thank you for the meal, Vivian. It's a long drive home. I should start. Once I am gone, you need to tell her the last story of your heroic ancestor. It's time."

"You're right," Ellie's mother said, standing with him. "Thank you, Dan. I'll see you out."

They left, and Ellie suspected that her mother just wanted a chance to confer with Dan alone. As if Ellie were still a child, too vulnerable and naïve to make grown-up decisions about her life.

"Are you scared?" Lenore asked, from the floor. The question caught Ellie off guard. Lenore had been sullen and quiet that evening, barely speaking at supper. Brooding, perhaps. Who could blame her?

"Scared of what?"

"Yourself, I guess," Lenore said. "What if you fall asleep in my guest room and wake up in the afterlife?"

"That won't happen."

"Is it easy to wake the dead?"

"No," Ellie said. "It's never easy. I'm just good at it."

Lenore raised an eyebrow. "How long did it take to get good?"

"A few years. I'm a natural, though." Ellie shrugged. "It's like any skill. Practice always helps, and some people excel more than others."

"What's it like? Mental math?"

"Look, I wish I could explain, but . . . the knowledge is secret. You know that."

"Worth a shot," Lenore said, smiling in a way that didn't reach her eyes. It reminded Ellie of a clown's smile, deceptive and unsettling.

"Mom may be a while," Ellie said. "Guess I'll sleep. Do you need anything? Tea? Cookies?"

"No. Thank you. I'm fine." She didn't sound fine. Didn't look fine. Wouldn't be fine until Dr. Allerton, some way or another, was punished for Trevor's death. And that made Ellie anxious. How long would Lenore wait before she did something terribly dangerous? Maybe her patience had already expired.

"We're getting close to answers," Ellie said. "Jay is looking for something right now. Something that'll confirm the freaky magic Dr. Allerton used on . . . on . . ."

"On Trevor," Lenore said. Ellie flinched at the use of his name. "Ah. So you think he killed Trevor with magic? What kind?"

"Well, I . . ."

Ellie's phone beeped in rapid succession as a flood of

instant messages rolled in. Jay was typing so quickly, his communications lacked their usual punctuation.

JAY (8:34 P.M.) – Got article bout bear attack

JAY (8:34 P.M.) – A farmer outside Willowbee found corpse in field

JAY (8:34 P.M.) – Corpse had mangled leg

JAY (8:34 P.M.) – Body never ID'd

JAY (8:34 P.M.) – Could be drifter

JAY (8:34 P.M.) – Howd u kno???

JAY (8:35 P.M.) – Forwarding article now

JAY (8:35 P.M.) – Lots of weird deaths near Willowbee

"Who was that?" Lenore asked. "Sounds like an emergency."

"Jay. Perfect timing."

"Don't leave me hanging. What did he report?"

Ellie glanced at the front door. Her mother was still outside with Dan. "Maybe I should wait until—"

"Tell me, Ellie." Lenore stood, and Baby Gregory screeched, as if sensitive to his mother's anger.

"The power," Ellie said, "to move injuries from one body to another."

❯❯❯ TWENTY-THREE ❮❮❮

As Ellie stood before her three-person audience, two women and a baby, she experienced the same broil of anxiety and excitement that a Broadway performer must feel before her first show-stopping solo piece. Ellie paced as she spoke, and Kirby, still visible, followed her heels. He thought they were playing a slow and monotonous game of chase.

"On the evening of the murder," Ellie said, "Dr. Allerton was in a serious car accident. I first suspected this at the wake. He drove a new car. Awfully convenient timing, right? He said he just liked buying cars, but I figure it's more likely that Dr. Allerton had to replace one. Especially because he drives like he's playing a real-world version of *Grand Theft Auto.* Did you see him floor it out of the gravel parking lot?"

"No," Lenore said. "I didn't see him at all at the wake." Her expression darkened. "Lucky man."

"Not lucky much longer," Ellie said, and Lenore smiled.

"There's more evidence than a new car, right?" Vivian prompted. "You found a crash site."

"Uh-huh. It's where Dr. Allerton crashed. He must have been going twice the speed limit when he swerved off the road and hit a tree. I also got reason to believe that he was drunk."

"What reason?" Vivian asked.

If Ellie told her mother about the beer-filled recycling bin, there'd be trouble. She didn't want to outright lie either, though. "Circumstantial stuff. Anyway, by the time Jay and I found the crash site with his aunt Bell, it had been cleaned up, but we found enough plastic and paint that I'm sure the car was totaled. It's also possible that Allerton wasn't wearing a seatbelt. Here's the thing: he had this accident along Cuz's route home from work. It's an isolated road near Willowbee."

"Trevor was just in the wrong place at the wrong time?" Lenore asked, and Ellie wondered if that made her feel better or worse.

"Yes. He must have noticed the wreck right after it happened. Based on Aunt Bell's psychic reading, he pulled over and tried to help. But Dr. Allerton was in a bad condition. Drunk. Injured. Maybe losing consciousness. The doctor must have realized that he could die unless . . . unless he used the terrible secret of Nathaniel Grace, a secret that has survived in the Willowbee medical community, to steal my cousin's . . ." Vivian's nephew. Lenore's husband. Gregory's father. ". . . his health. That's how Cuz got those injuries. They weren't his to begin with. Dr. Allerton must have done something. Touched him, maybe. I don't know what it takes to cast a spell like that."

"That murderous son of a—" Lenore stopped and looked at her own son, reconsidering. "You know what I mean."

"Yeah," Ellie said. "I do. It was murder. There's no doubt. After inflicting those terrible injuries on Cuz, Dr. Allerton left him to die. He didn't call an ambulance. Didn't even try first aid. No. Instead, he—alone or with cronies, I don't know—returned Cuz to his car and abandoned it on a different road. They *wanted* him to die. *Counted* on it."

"Trevor isn't the doctor's first victim, is he?" Lenore asked.

"Nah," Ellie agreed. "All these miracles Allerton has performed? The ones praised on Rate-a-Doc? Vanishing brain tumors. Repaired spinal injuries. They must come at the expense of victims. Maybe, some are willing. They can't all be. He's not a healer. He takes money from the sick to make different people sick. He isn't the first one, either. The doctors in Willowbee, probably all descended from Grace's line, have been magically swapping injuries since the town was founded."

"You said you had proof," Lenore said. "Where is it? We can contact those city police your mother knows and send them everything."

"Jay and I got proof at the library, actually. In October 1906, Theodore Roosevelt—President Roosevelt—visited Willowbee with a serious injury. A grizzly bear tore apart his leg." Ellie scrolled through the pictures on her phone.

After a few shots of melty ice cream cones and Jay's embarrassing chocolate mustache, she found the picture of Roosevelt's letter to the Willowbee Sanatorium. "Here. The president wrote Dr. Allerton's predecessors a thank-you letter after the procedure. The doctors miraculously healed everything. Not a scar! This was before penicillin, too! It would have been impossible without supernatural assistance."

"Hm," Vivian said. "Are you sure it isn't a joke? If the first naturalist president, the one who inspired the teddy bear, got mauled by a grizzly, we'd learn about it in every US history textbook."

"Unless it was kept secret," Ellie said. "Look. Jay found this article." With a swipe, Ellie opened her smartphone "downloads" folder and loaded the PDF image Jay had sent her. It was a scanned copy of a yellow-tinted newspaper dated October 16, 1906. A headline midway down the page read, "Grievous Bear Attack Claims Life."

"How's this for a coincidence?" Ellie asked. "Same week Roosevelt was a patient in Willowbee, a local farmer discovered a body in his cranberry bog. The corpse had a seriously chewed leg. Bear attack, he said. But he'd never seen a grizzly near his property, and the dead man was a stranger."

"There aren't cranberry bogs in Texas," Vivian said.

"Maybe it was a misprint?" Ellie said. "This is definitely from the Willowbee local paper."

"Do you think Roosevelt . . . knew that an innocent person would die in his place?" Lenore asked. "I always thought he was a decent man."

"Didn't he say that the only good Indian is a dead one?" Ellie asked.

"That's true," Vivian said. "And he celebrated Indian removal and the destruction of tribal land. That body in the bog wasn't a Native, though. Right?"

"Well," Ellie said, "the article doesn't mention it, so probably not. Actually, you make a good point. If Roosevelt knew that his treatment would kill a random person, he'd insist on a Native victim. Right? I bet he was ignorant. Or just ran out of time." Lost in thought, she watched shimmering Kirby scamper around the living room. He nudged Gregory's plastic blocks across the floor, playing a one-dog game of fetch.

Ellie continued, "I hope that *none* of the patients at Willowbee knew the truth about their cures."

"It's quite possible that they believe Dr. Allerton and his ilk are miraculous healers," Vivian said. "When you're hurting, dying, and out of options, few remedies seem too good to be true."

"So let's say there's an investigation," Lenore said. "The clinic *might* get shut down. Great. I still want proof that'll send Allerton to prison for murdering my husband. Where's that?"

"On your husband's body," Ellie said. "Must be. Why else would Dr. Allerton want to know its burial location? He's worried that we'll find something to link him with the death."

"DNA evidence?" Vivian asked. "Possibly, he came in contact with Allerton's blood."

They mused in silence, until Lenore offered, "What if during the spell, Allerton transferred something that could be used to identify him? A gold tooth, prosthetic hip, or . . ."

Ellie recalled her last dream of Trevor and the pain in her back that she'd blamed on a pencil.

"Or a tattoo," she said. "One Dr. Allerton got *publicly* for charity! The spell might consider inked skin to be an injury. Lenore, did the hospital document any tattoos on Cuz's body?"

"I don't know. Trevor had no tattoos, so I didn't ask."

"This one would be on his lower back," Ellie said. "It's a signature." She searched her phone and pulled up the feel-good news article about Dr. Allerton's charity tattoo. "This one," she said. "Dozens of witnesses saw him get it from the mayor."

"I'll call my friends," Vivian said, rummaging through her purse. "They can set up an exhumation. We'll also need to ask the elders for help. Thank creation that we keep grave sites secret."

Lenore grabbed Vivian's arm. "Wait," she said. "I think . . ."

"What?" she asked.

"I think I was followed."

"Followed where?" Ellie asked, though she could guess what the answer would be. Kirby stopped playing, as if he could sense Ellie's horror.

"The burial site," Lenore said. "When I visited it."

"What makes you believe that you were followed?" Vivian asked.

"I just . . . I thought I saw somebody in the woods near the grave. I noticed a shape out of the corner of my eye. It resembled a man. Or a man-shaped tree? I turned my flashlight toward the figure, but there was nobody. Still. If Dr. Allerton is friends with vampires, one might have followed me. They can be fast, right?"

"His property was crawling with vampires that night," Ellie said. "Remember, Mom?"

"Who could forget that?" Vivian said. "Here's what we're going to do: Ellie, get some rest. It's late. Lenore, I'm going to call my friends, as planned, and they will help us. The hard part—determining what happened, and why—is over. Okay?"

"I should check on his grave," Lenore said. "Tonight."

"Hon, no," Vivian said. "It won't do any good. Look, maybe you did see a tree. If so, the site is still safe. Returning tonight will only put it and you at risk."

"And if she was followed?" Ellie asked. "If his body is gone?"

"In that case," said Vivian, "it's already too late. And, I might add, a matter for the police. Be patient. Have faith." Vivian put her arms around Lenore and Ellie and pulled them into a hug.

"Faith in what?" Lenore asked, and she sounded genuinely curious and a little bit spiteful. "Justice?"

"Family," Vivian said. "It's all we've ever had." She closed her eyes, as if fighting exhaustion. "I need to speak with you in private, Ellie. Elder Dan was right. It's time for you to learn how your six-great-grandmother died."

⫸ TWENTY-FOUR ⫷

ELLIE AND VIVIAN moved to the backyard patio. They lit a mosquito-repellent candle, and Vivian waited for its scent to wash over them before she spoke, as if concerned that insects might eavesdrop.

"This story cannot be repeated." Vivian held up her index finger. "You will hear it once and must only share it once."

"Huh! Seems dangerous," Ellie said. "Maybe we should wait until the Dr. Allerton situation is resolved."

"It's riskier to wait. Come on. Don't you wonder how your six-great-grandmother died? She wasn't immortal."

Truthfully, Ellie never dwelt on that question. To her, Six-Great *was* immortal; the stories made her that way. They carried her personality through generations. Ellie was worried that the final story would be like a second death. A final one.

"I've had my fill of bad news lately," Ellie said. "Don't cram my head with more sad stuff. Let's watch a comedy movie instead."

"Every year, when I teach my students about the law of buoyancy, I begin the lecture with a story. Once upon a time, in ancient Greece—"

"If this is about Icarus, I've already heard it, Mom."

"—a king commissioned a goldsmith to make him a special crown. It was a finely sculpted piece: golden leaves and vines twisted into a metal wreath. However, the king was a cautious, suspicious man. He feared that the goldsmith had diluted the gold with silver, a less expensive metal. But how could anybody tell? Pure gold and impure gold looked very similar, and in those days, people didn't have complex technologies, like spectroscopy, to analyze metals.

"The king summoned a genius named Archimedes. 'You're a brainy man,' he said. 'Devise a way to test this crown. If you succeed, I'll give it to you. If you fail . . .'" Vivian ran a finger across her throat, miming a knife. "Archimedes asked, 'Do I have a choice?' And the king just laughed. He wasn't very nice. In fact, deep down, he hoped that Archimedes would fail almost as much as he hoped that the crown was a fake. Both of those outcomes would lead to bloodshed. Something the king relished more than precious metals.

"Poor Archimedes pondered the question all day long. He was so nervous, his robes became soggy with sweat, and he started to smell . . . ah . . . like an athlete's sock. It happens to everyone, even geniuses! So he decided to take a bath. In ancient Greece, there were public baths, places where people shared big tubs. Archimedes was so eager to wash off, he hopped into the water, causing it to slosh over the edge of the tub. That's when he had a revelation! He knew how to solve the king's problem! 'Eureka! Eureka!' he shouted, much to the dismay of the other bathers. 'I have it now!' The man was so excited, he leapt from the tub and ran through the city streets, naked and dripping wet! How did Archimedes solve the king's riddle?"

"Oh, yeah, I've heard that story before," Ellie said. "Gold is denser than silver. That means a gold coin weighs more than a silver coin, if they have the same volume. Archimedes just needed two things: a bucket of water and a bar of pure gold that had the same weight as the crown. He'd put the crown in the bucket. Measure how high the water level rose. Take out the crown. Put the bar in the bucket. If both were pure, they'd have the same volume and displace equal amounts of water. You know that probably didn't happen, though? The story was first spread by some guy centuries after Archimedes died."

"But you *knew* the story," Vivian said. "Somebody told it to you?"

"Yeah. A teacher. I can't remember which one. Could have been during English class a few years ago."

"Did it help you learn about volume, density, and displacement?"

"Uh-huh. It's hard to forget a story about Archimedes

streaking through a city. The mental image alone is burned into my mind."

"It helps my students, too," she said. "That's why some stories are particularly important. They're more than entertainment. They're knowledge."

"So we've circled back to Six-Great-Grandmother." She sighed, gagging when the deep inhale filled her nose with the sickly, sweet-bitter scent of bug repellent. "Maybe I don't want that knowledge."

"You aren't the only Elatsoe to visit the underworld, Ellie," she said. "You're just the only one to return alive."

"Wait. Mom. That's how she died?"

"Yes. I warned you, didn't I? There are many stories about people who visited that place, but few have happy endings." Vivian clasped her hands in her lap. "This is hers. It started during foaling season. A mild, sunny spring. Your six-great-grandfather loved all his animals, but one—a quick mare with a dappled coat of gray and black—was special. They had a bond; he delivered her, raised her, trained her to run through mesquite fields and over mountainous terrain. She was pregnant with her first, overdue by several days. Six-Great-Grandfather was worried about poor Dapple, so he spent his free time near her, just in case she had trouble.

"Sometimes, foals were born at night, so your six-great-grandfather camped outside, near the horses. He slept on a bedroll in the grass. Alone.

"That night, a gunshot woke Six-Great-Grandmother. Either the gunshot or her dogs. They were howling and whining. The dead ones, anyway. As if they knew what had happened."

"They did," Ellie said, softly. "Like Kirby the night Trevor died."

"I believe it. Dogs are extremely sensitive when they're alive, and without a body to restrain them, great feats are possible. However, the whining and howling could not save his life. By the time your six-great-grandmother reached the campsite, the men who shot her husband were gone, along with several horses. Thankfully, they did not take the dappled mare. The poor creature wouldn't leave her master's body."

"That's . . ." Ellie hesitated, searching her vocabulary for a parent-appropriate substitution for her preferred curse. "That's terrible. Why would somebody murder Six-Great-Grandpa? Was it a revenge thing? Did the monsters target him to hurt Six-Great-Grandmother?"

"Only one kind of monster uses guns," Vivian said. "They were . . . uncommon in the eighteenth century, but the Spanish, British, and other invaders used them, especially for military purposes. I believe that muskets were the gun of choice for soldiers. The long, unwieldy kind that used musket balls and had to be loaded with each shot. Unreliable things. Hard to aim, unless they were fired at close range or enchanted. Your six-great-grandfather was on his bedroll when he died. They must have surprised him."

"That still doesn't explain why. I mean. I know that lots of settlers hated us, but he wasn't doing anything."

"True. That happened before there were bounties on Apache scalps, but it could have been a message. A warning for the rest of our people. He was an easy target. And yes, your six-great-grandmother had a reputation as a formidable warrior. She was very successful at defending her family. So you may be right. It could have been a retaliation assassination. There was no good reason for anyone to hate your six-great-grandfather personally; it's not like shy horse whisperers make many enemies."

"I get it. I don't *like* it, but I get it." Ellie crossed her arms and bit the inside of her cheek. It would have been easier for her to accept Six-Great-Grandfather's murder if some two-faced fish or blood-sucking ancient creature had been responsible.

"The dappled mare threw a fit when men removed your six-great-grandfather's body," Vivian continued. "The poor thing had to be restrained with ropes and tied to a tree. She almost uprooted it."

"Aw!"

"It had to be done. Everybody was afraid that the mare, if freed, would follow them to the burial ground, remember its location, and return to her favorite human's grave again, again, and again, until the rhythm of her hooves reanimated his ghost like a heartbeat.

"For two days, your six-great-grandmother mourned with her children, sisters, brothers, cousins, and friends. On the third day, after the dappled mare gave birth to a healthy foal, your six-great-grandmother conferred with her eldest daughter. 'I will find the people who stole our happiness,' she said. 'Take care of things until I return.'

"'Bring somebody with you, mother,' said her daughter, a practical woman to the core. 'For company.' In truth, she was worried about your six-great-grandmother's health. Not only was she burdened with grief, she carried the aches of a punishing life; her knees locked after too much activity, her hands curled with arthritis, and she could no longer see the horizon clearly.

"'I have the dogs,' your six-great-grandmother said. 'Be good, child.'

"That night, Six-Great left, and she did not return home until the summer. Nobody knows what happened during that period of her life because she refused to speak of her journey. However, she brought all the stolen horses home. I suspect that the murderers faced justice.

"And that was that. For a time. A good man had died, been buried, and avenged. If this came from a standard book in a typical library, the story would have ended with her homecoming. That's what your English instructors teach you, right? Stories have a beginning, middle, and end. A tidy little plot. A main character who changes, usually for the better."

"That's what I've learned," Ellie said. "Yes."

"Reality doesn't always work that way. So neither does this story. Your six-great-grandmother could not find peace. His name was always whispering through her mind, if not her lips. She stopped traveling. She rarely slept a full night.

She spent more time with her dogs and horses than with human company.

"One day, her eldest daughter said, 'Mother, you worry me.'

"'I've heard that before,' your six-great-grandmother said, because, as I said earlier, her daughter was a sensible woman. Naturally, she fretted whenever her mother left the safety of home to fight encroaching threats.

"'Auu. You've never worried me like this before,' her daughter said. 'Will I lose both of my parents this year? Stop sending your thoughts in the earth with him!'

"'When you have an itchy bug bite,' your six-great asked, 'can you will the sensation away?'

"'No. Thinking about it makes the itch worse.'

"'The grave is an itch,' your six-great said. 'I hear him in my dreams. Every night, his voice is louder. Soon, it will rage like thunder. He tells me to avenge him. That I haven't done enough.'

"'That isn't his voice, Mother! It must be a ghost, and you know that they are terrible things.'

"'Of course I know.'

"'You need to visit a healer.'

"'Nobody can help me,' your six-great said. 'For sixty years, I've been a path between the underworld and ours. My dogs have crossed the gulf through me. Now . . . something dangerous has found the path too.'

"'What will you do?' her daughter asked.

"'Instead of waiting for him to come to us, I will go to him.'

"'You must be joking!' her daughter said. 'Why?'

"'Deep in the underworld, where our ancestors dwell, your father's goodness waits for us.'

"'Of course. So? What are your plans? That place is not for the living. You'll become lost and trapped. As good as dead!'

"'Not necessarily. Some people have visited the underworld and survived. Let me try. Maybe, if I tell the good part of him that his horses are safe and his murderers are no longer a threat, the news will dampen his ghost's fury. Maybe there is a way to bring him back. His body is no use, but there are other vessels . . .'

"'Maybe? *Maybe!*' her daughter cried. 'And maybe the sun will rise from the west. Please, reconsider!'

"Your six-great-grandmother hugged her daughter tightly. It would be their last hug. She said, 'It is a careless and dangerous plan—'

"'It is!' her daughter agreed.

"'For him, I will be careless.' Your six-great-grandmother stepped back and bowed her head, as if ashamed. 'If I'd been there . . . if I'd camped with him that night . . . if he hadn't been alone . . .' She had to pause to collect herself. There's nothing shameful about crying, but sometimes, parents are afraid to do it in front of their children. It's a matter of protectiveness. Anyway, when your six-great-grandmother could speak again, her firm tone made it clear that she would not change her mind. 'I go tonight. Whatever happens, be certain of one thing: you are stronger and wiser than I'll ever be. Mind the family. Protect our knowledge. As for the dappled mare and its foal? Let your brother care for them. I leave my newest puppy to you. He'll be a good companion once you teach him a few tricks. Forever, I hope.'

"'Yes,' her daughter said. 'It is good.'

"As the story goes, she went to the underworld at sunset. Your six-great-grandmother walked to the west, surrounded by her hounds, and as the horizon extinguished the red sun, she vanished. And that was that."

Vivian blew on the candlewick, snuffing its flame with her breath. A thin stream of smoke coiled from the smoldering wick.

"The end?" Ellie asked.

"C'est la fin."

"So . . . maybe she didn't die!"

"Ellie, no. You completely missed the point. Your six-great-grandmother, slayer of invaders and monsters, was defeated by the underworld." Vivian put her hands on Ellie's shoulders and held them firmly, as if afraid that her daughter would vanish like a magician's assistant. "She was an elder. You are seventeen. Understand why I'm terrified? It's miraculous that you escaped once."

"To be fair," Ellie said, "Six-Great intentionally journeyed deep into the underworld. I just saw a pod of whales and bailed."

"Elatsoe . . ."

"I won't do it again."

Vivian scowled. "This is my fault. I never should have named you after her."

"Technically, you didn't," Ellie said. "I'm named after the bird."

"That's true."

"Do you think it was really a special dream?" Ellie asked.

"Perhaps. Sometimes, guilt haunts us more intrusively than ghosts. Maybe your six-great-grandmother just thought she heard his voice."

"No, not *that* dream. I meant the one you had before I was born. With the hummingbird."

Vivian hesitated. In the silence, cicadas hummed. "Yes," she finally said. "I do."

⭈⭊⭆ TWENTY-FIVE ⭆⭊⭈

E LLIE DREAMED ABOUT FAMILY that night. Her parents, grandparents, aunties, and uncles stood in a straight line. Holding hands, they faced away from a gnarled mesquite tree. Its branches grasped for them, crackling with every swipe, but the human chain was out of reach. Wind rustled through waxy leaves and rattled heavy seed pods; the tree seemed to groan and whisper.

"Mom," Ellie said, approaching the chain. "What are you doing? Is this a game?"

"Hush," her mother said. "Turn away. You must not look at him. You must not listen to him. You must not take his hand."

"Him?"

"Me," Trevor said. "It isn't fair. Why do the living disown the dead?"

Ellie could not stop herself; she looked at him, listened to him. Trevor stood under the mesquite canopy, his legs still half-buried in the earth, as if he'd sprouted from his grave. He wore slacks and a cheesy checkered sweater, the kind that was uniquely well-suited for teachers.

"We never disowned you," she said. "We'll be reunited someday. All of us. Every generation."

"How many generations will there be, after us?" he asked. "Selfish men have salted the earth." The mesquite tree blackened, its leaves crumbling like ash. "Our children," Trevor continued, "cannot be sustained by cruelty and poison. Each generation will wither until there is nobody left."

"You think so?" Ellie asked.

"Think?" He crossed his arms, exasperated, as if Ellie had forgotten to do her homework.

"You know," Ellie said.

"I know. You do, too. Don't wait until it's too late. Do something. Act. You promised to protect my wife and son."

"I have!" She took a step closer, still separated from Trevor's grave by the chain of people. "We know what happened now. Dr. Allerton won't get away with murder."

"He's just one man." Trevor leaned forward, rooted to the grave. "There are millions more who will continue to treat our family and land like garbage. Think of them like pests."

"Pests . . ."

"Termites in your house. Locusts in your field. It doesn't make any difference if you crush just one insect. The swarm will devour your home." Trevor held out his hand, reaching for her. "Please," he said. "Help me."

Ellie's living family, the human wall that protected her from the ghost, faded away. As they vanished, the sky burned bright as embers, as if four suns lay behind every cardinal direction. East, west, north, south. Ash motes danced between the desert and sky. They resembled gnats.

"Come on," Ellie said. "Trevor, people aren't insects."

"Yeah," he said. "They're much worse." He lunged at her, reaching for Ellie's face with talon-sharp nails, but the ground held his legs securely. Its grip prevented him from ripping off her nose. With a startled cry, she ran back.

"Ellie, I need you to pull me out!" he said. "Please! I can't escape without help!"

"You're a ghost," she said, turning away from him. Refusing to look. "You don't get my help."

"I'm still your cousin! Don't abandon me, Ellie. Freedom is so close. Just help me. Help me, and nobody will ever hurt our family again. I won't let them! *Look* at me!"

She did not turn around.

"I want to see my wife," he said. "I want to see my son! One last time. It's cruel. I died alone!"

She promised herself that he'd see them again someday. It was the only way Ellie could stay strong.

"Gregory?" There was a hint of triumph in his voice. Was he trying to deceive her? Trick her into peeking? "Gregory," Trevor shouted. "Gregory! Greggie-bug, come here. Come to Dadda. Hello, my smart boy!"

A baby squealed with delight. Ellie whirled around. Gregory was crawling across the cracked earth, a mostly toothless smile on his cherubic face. He reached for his father's hand. Trevor knelt, allowing Gregory to grasp his index finger in a plump little fist.

"Damn it," Ellie swore. "No!"

Of course, it was too late; when he touched the soul of a living being, Trevor's final connection to the underworld severed. He rose from the ground, cradling Gregory in his arms, and approached Ellie with slow, inevitable steps.

"I knew my boy was talented," Trevor said. "He found me. Just like you, Cuz. Promise you'll teach him the family secret? It'd be a terrible waste if you didn't."

"Give him to me," she said, holding out her arms. "I promise to teach him everything."

When Trevor handed over Gregory without hesitation, Ellie knew that he was not the man she used to know. She protectively cradled Gregory against her chest and stepped back.

"Is this a dream?" Ellie asked.

"Sort of," Trevor said. "You and Little Greg are both sleeping." He closed his eyes, tilting his face up, basking in magma-hued light. "But I'm wide awake."

The sky darkened, as if the setting suns had burnt out, extinguished by the cold breath of terrible gods.

"See you at the party, Elatsoe. This will be the last time their dance corrupts our earth."

⇶ TWENTY-SIX ⇷

WHEN ELLIE AWOKE, she felt something wriggle against her arm. With a startled gasp, she rolled over. Baby Gregory was lying stomach-down on the cot beside her. He wore the same yellow onesie from the dream, and his face was scrunched with profound confusion, the same kind that he experienced during peekaboo.

"Hey, little guy," Ellie said. "What are you doing here?"

Gregory's crib had high bars, his nursery was across the hall, and the guest room door had been closed all night. He couldn't crawl into her arms without help. Did one of the adults move him? Or . . .

"Kirby," she said, sitting up and cradling Gregory against her chest. "Kirby! Appear! Heel!"

Kirby stood at attention beside her cot, his feathered tail held high. His ancestors had been hunters; their white-tipped tail was easy to spot as they pursued prey through long grass. Kirby whined, a powerful sound that made Ellie's teeth ache. Was Trevor's ghost nearby? Could Kirby stop it from attacking?

"Mom!" Ellie called. "Mom, where are you?" According to the tabletop alarm clock, it was only half past seven. The adults normally slept until eight. After a steadying breath, Ellie stood and padded across the room, followed by her anxious dog. She balanced Gregory on one arm and pushed the door open. The hallway was dim and quiet. No sign of a haunting. No blood, no broken vase, no eerie writing on the walls. She tiptoed to the living room, drawn by the sound of snoring. There, her mother dozed on the plush sofa. According to Vivian, it was more comfortable than an air mattress.

"Mom, wake up," Ellie said. "We're in big trouble."

Her mother sat up stiffly. "Trouble? What? Where?"

"Trevor's ghost." There was no use avoiding his name anymore. "He's awake. He said humans were worse than termites, and—"

"Ellie," Vivian interrupted. "Did you wake him up?"

"No!" Ellie shook her head so quickly, her sleep-mussed hair flipped across Gregory's head. He laughed and shoved a lock into his mouth. "In the dream, I turned away from Trevor," Ellie said. "Wouldn't take his hand. He begged me for help, but . . . no! I couldn't. I'd never! Gregory was the one who woke him."

"The baby?" Vivian sounded more than a little incredulous.

"Yes! He must have . . . I don't know . . . sensed his father? Gregory is really receptive, Mom. Ghost stuff comes easy to him. Same as me. Obviously, he doesn't know the difference between life and death yet. Or . . . or understand how dangerous ghosts can be."

"Are you sure, Ellie? Sometimes, a nightmare is just a nightmare. You've had a lot on your mind."

"Am I sure?" She sat beside her mother. "I don't know. I've dreamed about him several times. Maybe some of those instances were one hundred percent imaginary. But. This dream was definitely wrong. When will somebody check his grave? Look for the tattoo? I'm worried that it's too late. That Allerton or his people have already . . ." She trailed off before voicing her fear: already dug him up. It was too horrific to contemplate.

"Soon," Vivian said, patting Ellie's shoulder. "A team is going to the burial ground this morning. In the meantime, Kirby will protect us. Right, good boy?"

Kirby sat near the sofa, alert but relaxed. He tilted his head, as if acknowledging the praise.

That's when Ellie's phone, charging on the coffee table, rang. She was surprised to see Jay's name on the caller ID; he normally texted first. She passed Gregory to her mother and answered the call.

"Hey, Jay," Ellie said. "What's up?"

"Um . . ." Jay said. "Ronnie really wants to talk to—"

His sister's voice cut in. "Hey! Have you seen Al?"

"Not recently," Ellie said. "What's wrong?"

"He never returned from the mission."

"Um. Whoa. *What* mission?"

"The one you sent him on." Ronnie sounded terse, a concerning departure from her typical boisterous, confident cheeriness. "The intel mission."

"He wasn't supposed to go anywhere!" Ellie said. "Al said his friends might know about gatherings in Willowbee. That's all."

"A friend knew a friend sent Al to the Cursed Man Club. Vampire-only bar in Austin. Apparently, the manager knows all about Willowbee."

"So Al never returned from the club? Have you called the police?"

"What can they do? He's only been gone thirtyish hours. My own parents believe that he ditched me. As if! We're soul mates."

"I wish I could help somehow."

"You can." Ronnie lowered her voice, conspiratorial. "My friends and I . . . *spoke* to the manager last night."

"Yeah?"

"He says that Al might be in the Allerton mansion. Young vampires go there and never return." She made a sound that was half sob, half furious shriek. "If anything happened to my baby, I'll . . ."

"I'm so sorry, Ronnie," Ellie said.

"Abe Allerton is the one who needs to apologize. I'm going to wring his freaking neck."

"You can't just stroll into the mansion. We need a plan."

"Sure I can. Isn't there a party today?"

"Yes. A bicentennial ball, but . . ." Ellie remembered, in blood-chilling detail, the conclusion of her dream. Trevor's promise.

"But what?" Ronnie asked.

"No. No, no, no."

"What?"

"Put Jay on the phone."

"I'm not done ye—"

"My cousin's ghost," Ellie said, "is going to turn the Willowbee bicentennial party into a bloodbath, and nobody is safe! Not me. Not Al. Not even the sixth-grade-spelling-bee champions. They're guests of honor! He's going to slaughter a bunch of innocent spelling nerds, Ronnie! Put Jay on the phone!"

"Me again," Jay said. "Ellie, do . . . do you think Al is okay?"

"I wouldn't put anything past Dr. Allerton and the butchers of Willowbee."

Jay paused a beat before saying, "He just wanted to help."

"He wanted to help *you*," Ellie said. "You: his new little brother. Keep that in mind during the wedding. Especially when the minister says, 'If anyone has objections to this union, speak now or forever hold your peace.'"

"I will," Jay said. "We need to find him!"

Ellie looked at her mother, borrowing strength from Vivian's supportive nod. "My cousin is awake," she said, "and he's haunting the Allerton mansion."

"Wh—haunt? You mean . . ."

"Yeah. This will be much worse than rattling chains and mysterious bumps in the night." If Kirby could burst light-bulbs with a howl, throw objects across the room, and jump through walls, what could a human do? Trevor had the self-awareness, intelligence, and motivation to fully exploit his powers.

"Let's call exorcists," Jay said. "The best in Texas!"

"If Al is trapped in the mansion, an exorcism might hurt him. They tend to get chaotic. Violent. Lots of collateral damage."

"What can we do?"

"First, find Al and free him," Ellie said. "There's several hours till the masquerade ball, and my dog can track people using—"

"Ellie," Vivian interrupted. "What are you planning?"

"Hey, I'm on the phone! Wait a second." She theatrically ducked her head, as if protecting the conversation from prying ears. "Kirby needs a scent to follow. Do you have unwashed clothes that belong to Al?"

Ellie heard muffled voices on Jay's end. A moment later, he said, "Yes! His sweater. Will that work?"

"Perfect."

"Can you meet us at the Ring Transport Center in an hour?" he asked.

"Count on it," Ellie said. "Kirby and I will be there." She glanced at her mother. Vivian wore a steely expression, the kind that teachers used to wordlessly check rowdy students. "Mom is probably coming too," Ellie amended.

Once the call ended, Ellie clasped her hands, imitating penitence. "How much did you hear?" she asked her mother.

"Enough to understand."

"Hundreds of people might die. I have to do something."

Vivian smiled. "I know," she said. "Me too. Before we leave, be sure to eat breakfast. I need to speak with your father. Hopefully, he won't be busy with surgery all day."

They hugged, and part of Ellie—the part that she usually repressed—wondered if it would be their last.

In the bathroom, after splashing her cheeks with cold water, Ellie contemplated her reflection. Her black T-shirt was emblazoned with green 0s and 1s, binary code. Ellie had not understood the message when she first bought the shirt, but it intrigued her. Rather than checking the clothes tag for a translation, she had decoded it in the store using her phone and a "binary to English" converter. The message was inoffensive. It declared: *Hello, world!*

Perhaps the shirt was a good sign, a tribute to solved mysteries with pleasant endings. Smiling, Ellie fastened her hair in a braid and rubbed sunscreen on her face, neck, and arms. Thus readied for action, she ran to the kitchen, toasted two strawberry tarts, and shouted, "Mom, let's go!"

Her mother stepped from the guest room; Vivian wore sunglasses and a white suit with magnificently wide shoulder pads. "Here's the rules," she said. "We're going into the lion's den, but that doesn't mean we should poke the cat. You. Your friend. Your friend's friend. Y'all will be livestreaming. Film everything. If Kirby senses danger, we leave. If Allerton or his cronies get violent, we also leave. No fighting. We have a single goal: evacuate the party."

"And look for Al."

Her mother crossed her arms. "Yes. If Kirby picks up his scent. I'm not entirely convinced that Al is being held prisoner in the mansion. However, we won't know unless we look."

Ellie returned Gregory to his crib while her mother checked on Lenore. When they regrouped outside, Vivian seemed perturbed.

"What's wrong, Mom?" Ellie asked.

"Probably nothing. Lenore was awake. And . . ."

"What?"

"She smiled at me. Big one. I haven't seen her smile like that since before the funeral. She didn't even try to come with us."

The two women jumped into Vivian's minivan, buckled up, and pulled out of the driveway. "She knows that Trevor is back," Ellie said. "His ghost visited her, too."

"Seems likely."

A call came in during the drive. That morning, a team of close friends and family reached the mesquite tree that grew beside Trevor's grave. They found a hole in the ground. His body was missing.

Stolen, no doubt, by the man who first stole his life.

⊰⊱ TWENTY-SEVEN ⊰⊱

A T THE RING Transport Center, Jay led a procession of women through the exit turnstile. Despite the sweltering weather, they all wore chic matching trench coats and cargo pants. The coats were olive green and hand-decorated with rhinestones and silver-colored studs.

"Hey!" Ellie called. "How many sisters do you have?"

"Just one," Jay said. "Introduce your peanut gallery, Ronnie."

The tallest woman, Ronnie Ross, stepped to the front of her group. Ronnie and Jay had some sibling similarities, like their wide-set eyes and small noses. Ronnie wore her bottle-black hair in a chemically solidified bouffant. It arched from her forehead like an inky wave. "Thanks for meeting us," she said. "These are my friends Jess, Martia, and Alice. Actually, you know them already. Just not in three dimensions."

Jess was a white woman with shoulder-length hair and an upturned nose. Martia and Alice each had black hair and brown skin, but Martia's face was oval-shaped, while Alice had a rounder face with plump, bright cheeks.

"You're the basketball bridesmaids?" Ellie asked. "Which one of you can bench-press ten thousand pounds?" While Jay was a cheer squad star, his sister played a mean basketball center. Nearly six feet tall, she towered over Ellie and Vivian. Ronnie's friends ranged between five four (Alice) and five eleven (Jess), and they moved with the unconscious unity of a well-trained team.

"Herotonic University varsity," Ronnie said, her eyes crinkling fondly.

"I hope you didn't bring more," Vivian said, "because my van only has room for eight."

"Just us, ma'am," Alice said. "We don't mind close quarters."

"Last season, we sat three to a seat on the bus to Dallas," Jess added. "By the end of the trip, I was in Martia's lap."

"Good times," Martia said. "Until my legs fell asleep. How do mall Santas do it?"

"Let's be serious for a moment," Ronnie said. "If anyone wants to back out now, that's fine. I won't hold it against you."

Her friends made an assortment of sympathetic sounds.

"I'm serious," Ronnie continued. "This will be a hundred times more dangerous than last night."

"Last night?" Jay asked. "Heeeey. Did you guys beat up that bar manager?"

"We didn't have to," Ronnie said. The "but we could have" was obvious.

"Let's find Al," Alice said. "Nobody wants to back out."

That settled, the rescue party crammed into the van. Martia and Jess took the far-back seats. Ronnie, Jay, and Ellie took the middle (Jay, ever polite, volunteered for the dreaded *middle* middle seat). Alice snagged shotgun. Kirby spent the trip on Ellie's lap; to his credit, he didn't weigh a thing, so her legs survived.

"We stay together," Vivian said, repeating herself, as if she could guarantee something by saying it enough times. "We stay together, we be quick, and we avoid confrontation whenever possible. When we reach the mansion, I'll park on the street outside the driveway. Ellie, wait in the car with Jay. Be our getaway drivers, okay? The women and I will enter the mansion."

"Wait," Ellie said. "I have to go, too. You need Kirby!"

"You seem to forget," Vivian said, "that I can also communicate with ghosts." She locked eyes with Ellie's reflection in the rearview mirror.

"We understand," Jay said. "I won't let you down, Ms. Bride."

Ellie said nothing.

The Willowbee welcome sign had been decorated for its bicentennial. A pod of yellow balloons with pink ribbons was fastened to its post, swaying in a gentle breeze. White, fleecy clouds drifted overhead. No chance of rain. The town's 200th birthday would be well attended, and that made Ellie nervous. Judging by the news articles online, Dr. Allerton's public events drew crowds from across South Texas. They had bouncy houses, live entertainment, and carnival snacks. How *good* of him. How *charitable*. However, Ellie suspected that charity was the least of Dr. Allerton's motivations. The parties diverted attention from his sins.

"Phones charged?" Ellie's mother asked, and everybody checked their respective devices.

"Yes, Ms. Bride," Jay said.

"Ninety percent," Ellie said.

"I'm at forty," Martia admitted, "but that'll last a couple hours."

"What if the ghost cuts the cell phone signal?" Jay asked, biting his lower lip in a profoundly anxious manner. "Can . . . they do that?"

"Ghosts are like superheroes, in a way," Ellie explained. "They have an inexplicably wide range of powers. The real question is: can *he* do that? Which . . . well, I don't know. Maybe."

"If he cuts the phones," Vivian said, "we'll retreat."

Ellie looked out the window and watched the small town pass. There were picnics—wicker baskets on checkered blankets—in the lush town square. The librarians hosted a book sale outside the library. An ice cream truck idled on the street corner. Families, couples, and groups of townsfolk milled around, chatting, enjoying the day. Children played with the unbridled enthusiasm that summer vacation, devoid of early mornings and deadlines, permitted.

"I suspect that most people will stay in town until later," Jay said. "The big dance begins at sundown. There's just lawn-party stuff at the mansion till then."

"Fingers crossed," Ellie said.

Their hopes were dashed a few minutes later; the gates to the Allerton mansion were open, and dozens of parked cars lined the driveway to his house. Two men in green shirts waved Vivian toward a spot near the gate. From that position, Ellie could see part of the lawn, but the trees blocked the house, except for a couple chimneys and the occasional sliver of brick wall.

Everyone poured out of the minivan. Ronnie and her team were dewy with sweat, but none removed her fancy coat. Ellie wondered if they had a secret arsenal hidden under the sparkling fabric.

"This belonged to Al," Ronnie said. She handed Ellie a vanilla-colored cable-knit sweater. It reeked of cologne and pomade.

"Kirby," Ellie said, dangling the sweater low, "scent it!"

Kirby's shimmer flowed toward the item. After a moment, Ellie said, "Track!" and he blinked out of view. "If Kirby picks up on the scent within, oh, a square mile of this place, he'll return and yap once."

"How long will it take?" Ronnie asked.

As if responding, a sharp, excited bark rang out. The

269

starting lineup all reacted with varying degrees of surprise. Alice gasped. Martia and Jess leapt back-to-back, steeled for an attack. Ronnie took a defensive pose, her legs and arms spread wide.

"Ghost dogs," Jay said, shrugging. "They sneak up on you sometimes."

"He found the trail!" Ellie said. "Can you see him, Mom?"

Vivian nodded. She tucked her phone into her blazer pocket; its camera peeked out, filming on the sly. Streaming straight to Ellie's screen.

"Kirby," Ellie said, "lead." The shimmer slowly circled the van before flowing up the driveway. Everyone but Jay and Ellie followed him toward the lawn party. In the distance, a group of revelers cheered. Somebody tooted on a horn. "Let's sit in the shade," Ellie suggested, nodding toward a nearby maple tree. "If anyone asks, we needed a break from the excitement and came here to hang out."

Jay flopped beside her and leaned close enough to watch the video on her phone. They shared a pair of earbuds; he had the left, and she had the right. "Is that a mime?" Jay asked. "And a juggler?"

"Clearly an extra special day for the doctor."

There were performers outside the mansion, painted acrobats with jester hats that jingled when they danced. A jester in green guided Vivian to a crowded courtyard behind the mansion. The scene resembled a country fair. To one side, food carts served guests popcorn in paper cones, lemonade in plastic cups, and fried dough on disposable plates. A fortune teller, a balloon animal artist, and a magician entertained throngs of people under separate tents. The main event, however, was a country music show on a portable stage. The performers must have been famous, because several people in their audience wore T-shirts emblazoned with their band name: Shiny Cowbirds.

"Kirby went into the house," Vivian whispered; she must have tucked her chin, putting her mouth over her phone, because the sound transmitted well. "I'll try to finagle a way inside too. Damn. Dr. Allerton thought of everything. He has outdoor toilets." Vivian turned, pointing her phone camera at a blue portable bathroom. It was over twice the size of a typical porta-potty model. Handicap accessible. If Ellie didn't know better, she might have mistaken Allerton for a good man.

"I'm putting you on mute," Vivian said. "If you need anything, text me or call Ronnie."

"I feel faint," somebody off-camera—Alice? It sounded like Alice—said. "It's too hot for leather sleeves."

"What are you kids doing?" boomed a voice. "Party's up there!" One of the gate guards stepped around the van and approached Ellie and Jay. He twirled an orange traffic wand like a glee-squad leader with a baton.

"We're taking a break," Ellie said. She lowered her phone, angling it screen-down over her lap. When the guard seemed unmoved by her excuse (he *did* just see them arrive), she added, "And waiting for friends. They're supposed to meet us here."

"They're late," Jay added. "They got lost."

"Out-of-towners?" the guard asked. "I can help with directions. Been living here all my life."

"Uh. No need," Ellie said. "It's sorted. Thanks."

"Don't go wandering," the guard said, tipping his cap. "Guests aren't allowed in the wooded lawn. It's a liability, see. If some kid climbs a tree and falls, his parents can sue. So I'm telling you right now: stay near your car."

Ellie nodded. "Got it," she said. "No wandering."

He pointed to his eyes, as if miming *I'm watching you*, and strolled back to the open gate. Along the way, he whistled a tuneless song.

"How'd I do?" Jay asked, and Ellie didn't have the heart to point out that he looked pale and shaken.

"Convincing bluff," she whispered. "Need a drink of water? There's bottles in the trunk. I can . . . oh! Hold on. Mom's got in the mansion! Look."

Her phone displayed a view of a long hall. It had wall-to-wall white carpeting, a testament to Allerton's wealth. It was difficult to expunge stains from anything absorbent and pale-colored, yet the carpet was bright as fresh snow. The walls also celebrated Allerton's disposable income. A variety of elaborately framed oil paintings hung from gold hooks. They depicted country scenes, pretty young women, and Impressionist gardens. It was difficult to appreciate the art's finer details, since Vivian moved quickly, but Ellie suspected that the paintings belonged to a range of time periods and painters.

"Great!" Jay said. "How'd they do that?"

He had his answer shortly. A woman in black ushered Vivian to a pale green sitting room. It had teardrop-shaped mirrors on every wall.

"She can lie down," the woman said. "Somebody will bring the doctor. You, ah, might consider removing that coat, miss."

"Air conditioning," Alice sighed. Her friends carried her to a pine-green sofa. "I feel better already."

Vivian's voice piped up, "Thank you. How long will Dr. Allerton be?"

"A few minutes," the woman said. "Do you need anything else?"

Although Vivian responded, Ellie was distracted by a dark blotch in the western teardrop mirror. It swayed beside Vivian's reflection.

"Do you see that?" Ellie asked, pointing.

"It's a . . . face," Jay said. "Really dim and blurry, though. You think they're wearing a stocking, like some bank robber? For the masquerade?"

"Maybe, but who does it belong to? I don't see anyone else in the room except your sister, her friends, Mom, and that woman."

"You think . . ." Jay's voice broke mid-question. Ellie chalked it up to fear, and she completely empathized.

"Call Ronnie," Ellie said. "Tell her to evacuate *now*."

"On it!" Jay pressed an icon on his screen and held it against his pointy ear. Normally, his curls hid its sharp tip.

A recessive trait, very few descendants of fairy folk had "elfin ears," and he disliked drawing attention to them.

"It's ringing," he said. Simultaneously, through her earbuds, Ellie heard a faint *tweet-tweet* in the sitting room. Vivian turned away from the mirror and faced Ronnie Ross.

"It's my brother," Ronnie said, answering. "Yes?"

"Retreat!" Jay said. "Trevor's ghost is in the room."

"Hah. Why are you asking that?" Ronnie said. "Even if they opened a pool, it's not the right time."

"Did you hear me?" Jay said, shaking his phone, as if trying to jiggle a loose chip into place. "I'm not talking about swimming. Ronnie, get out of the mansion. Now!"

"I love you too."

"What? Ronnie? Ronnie, don't hang up!"

"Shh," Ellie said, patting Jay's arm. "The guard might hear."

"She hung up!" he said. "It's like we were having two different conversations!"

"I noticed." Ellie stood, shifting from foot to foot, indecisive. Because they were still connected by earbuds, Jay stood with her and mirrored the side-to-side motion.

"We should . . ." Ellie trailed off. What should they do? Vivian wasn't facing the mirror anymore; had Trevor's visage disappeared, or was he still grinning at the women? Why did Ellie and Jay see him so clearly, while nobody else seemed to notice? Had Trevor interfered with the phone call to Ronnie?

"It has to be Trevor. He wants us to enter the mansion," Ellie said. "It's a trap, obviously, but I'm not unprepared."

"Whatever happens, we stick together," Jay said.

"Trevor probably just wants me," she said. "You don't have to step in the trap too. It's not necessary."

"Neither are socks, but I choose to wear them! Happily! It's my choice."

"Huh," Ellie said. "That's a weird example. Still. It works."

"Dang right! Let's hurry!" He sprinted up the driveway. Jay must have forgotten about the earbuds, because his momentum almost plucked the phone from Ellie's hand. She made a spirited effort to catch it, lunging forward like an outfielder grasping for a baseball, but the phone brushed her fingertip and struck the ground with a soft *thunk*. Thankfully, the grass softened the impact, and the video remained connected.

"Cool your jets!" she said, scrambling after him. "We almost lost the phone. It's our evidence! Remember that your partner has short legs!"

"Partner?" he called over his shoulder. "I'm not your sidekick?"

"You never were!"

Jay slowed, allowing Ellie to catch up. "We're both Kirby's sidekicks," he said.

"That's too true."

Ellie glanced at her phone screen; the video was choppy, freezing and buffering every few seconds. She held it a bit higher, hoping that the connection issue would resolve itself. Dreading that it would not.

"C'mon," she encouraged her phone. "You survived the fall."

As they neared the mansion, four jesters danced in front of their path.

"Poor guys must be melting," Jay said, already winded by the heat. The performers were covered head-to-toe. Each wore a long-sleeved jumper, gloves, and knee-high boots with spurs on their heels. A hood-and-hat combo covered everything but their faces, which were slathered with stage paint: white foundation, black lips, and red diamonds around their eyes.

"No need to run, children," the red-garbed jester called. "There's plenty of fun to go around."

"My mother just called!" Ellie said. "Our friend got sick. She was taken inside the house."

"We need to see them," Jay said. "We're minors!"

"Poor thing," the green jester cooed. "That's a risk of the season, regrettably. Come. I'll take you through the catering entrance."

"What's that?" Jay asked. "A back door?"

"Yes," the green jester said, hiding his grin behind a politely lifted hand. "It's a discreet way for servants to enter and exit the house. Rich people are so easy to offend."

"I wouldn't know from experience," Ellie said.

"Are you sure about that?" The jester led them around the

house, his steps emphasized by tinny *cling, clang, clings* from the spurs.

"Am I sure that I don't know lots of rich people?" Ellie asked. "Yeah."

The jester cackled. "I said 'offend,' not 'know.' Good job, by the way. Abraham hasn't slept well in weeks." He stopped outside a white door that was half hidden by a rose bush.

"You know who we are?" Ellie asked, taking a step back.

"Half this party knows who you are. I'm surprised there aren't 'Wanted' signs pinned to every tree in town. 'Wanted: offensive teenagers. Only dead. Not alive.'"

As the jester unlocked the door with a skeleton key, Jay whispered, "Ellie, did you see his teeth?" The two of them started to back away.

"What's wrong with my teeth?" the jester asked, kicking open the door and whipping around. "They work magnificently." He grinned, flashing a pair of vampiric canines. Sharp as half-inch knives, they could easily puncture skin, rip apart veins.

Before either Ellie or Jay could react, the jester grabbed them and shoved them through the doorway. They stumbled into a long, featureless corridor, clinging to each other for support. The fluorescent lights embedded in the ceiling turned on, as if motion-activated, and the door boomed shut.

"Why are you doing this?" Ellie shot out. She and Jay put their backs against one wall and faced the jester. He removed his silly hat, lowered his hood, and kicked off his boots.

"Don't feign ignorance," the jester said, rolling his dark brown eyes. "Your fainting spells tricked . . . oh . . ." He held up his gloved hands, wiggled his fingers, and then curled them into fists. "Nobody. Where's the ghost dog, kids? Waiting to pounce? Ellie, you should have kept him secret. Tried to surprise me. As it is, you have no surprises left."

"We're just here to help Al," Jay said. "He's a vampire too! One of your own kind!"

"I prefer the term 'cursed man,' if you don't mind," the jester said. "I was born human, you know. Still am human, where it counts. It's been a couple hundred years since I ate a solid meal, though." He shrugged. "Oh, well. I'm no gourmand."

"Wait. If you're two hundred years old, how did you survive the sunlight out there?" Ellie asked. "Your face should be a fireball."

"Ah. Blood lust. Explosive sunburns. Heightened sensitivity to *Allium*. All symptoms of a progressive disease." The jester winked. "All you need is the right doctor."

"Of course," Ellie said. "Dr. Allerton is your buddy. Why doesn't he give his minions better uniforms?"

"I don't understand," Jay said, linking arms with Ellie.

"Yes you do, kiddo," the jester scoffed. "You're just stalling."

"I'm not!" Jay insisted. "Is Al alive, or not?"

"Oh, Al again," said the jester. "He's alive for now. A couple lawyers from New York are embroiled in a bidding war for him. But you? You can—"

"How much does it cost?" Jay blurted out. "How much do people pay for Allerton's magic? How much is Al's life worth?"

"More than yours," the jester chuckled. He bared his teeth theatrically and shouted, "As I was saying . . . you can run, if you want! Boo!"

Ellie stepped in front of Jay, intending to protect him, but he did a clever step-and-spin move that reversed their positions.

"Really?" Ellie asked, amused despite the peril.

"You can be the brave one next time," he said.

"There won't be a next time," the jester said, and he sounded vaguely exasperated.

"Oh yeah?" Ellie asked. "My name is Elatsoe, daughter of Vivian. We are Lipan Apache, and you are not welcome in our home!"

For a moment, the corridor was silent, except for the shrill hum of fluorescent lights. Then, the jester spoke.

"My name," he said, softly, almost reticently, "is Glorian, and I was born along the bank of our fertile Kunétai over two hundred years ago. In those days, I had a different name, a Lipan name, bestowed by parents whose names I do not remember anymore. Curses are strange things, Elatsoe. Illogical magic. I have cut all ties to my family and culture, but because this land was once mine, it always will be home. And your trick? *Useless*."

"Oh." Ellie said. "Um."

"Indeed," Glorian agreed. "Oh. Um. Ruuuun."

Jay and Ellie ran.

⇒⇒ TWENTY-EIGHT ⇐⇐

"TEN," GLORIAN BOOMED. "Nine. Eight . . ."

Normally, Ellie would call Kirby and rely on his protection. However, Kirby was with her mother. What if Trevor's ghost started haunting the mansion in earnest? Vivian needed protection too.

Was Kirby the only option? Ellie could summon wild animals, but without training, they'd cause indiscriminate damage. A grizzly bear, for example, didn't know the difference between evil minions and good-hearted teenagers. It might tear everyone apart before, satisfied by its bravery, it fell back to sleep.

Ellie and Jay reached a heavy metal door at the end of the corridor. It was cracked open, an enticing escape route, but they wouldn't have enough time to blink once Glorian finished his countdown. At two hundred, he must be quicker than a striking rattlesnake. Jay tugged on the door, straining against its weight.

"Four!"

"Get in!" Jay said. The door was open wide enough for one person to squeeze through. "Hurry!"

As the number "one" slipped from Glorian's black-painted lips, Ellie had an idea. From her training with Grandmother's beloved mammoth, she knew that the animal responded to one powerful command.

Ellie did not, however, know how the mammoth would fare without her beloved Grandma, especially in a claustrophobic hallway. In fact, Allerton's mansion was crowded, confined, and noisy. Hopefully, the mammoth recognized Ellie as a friend. She concentrated and called her spirit from a corner of the underworld where the Ice Age never ended.

Three things happened in rapid succession:

The hallway shimmered.

"Time's up," Glorian said.

"Charge!" Ellie shouted.

The invisible mammoth shot forward, a giant bullet through a chamber, and collided with Glorian. The cursed man flew through the air and slammed into the far wall. He slumped to the ground, his nose bleeding, his limbs twisted, as the shimmer faded away.

"Is . . . is he . . . dead?" Jay stammered.

"I don't know." Ellie took a tentative step forward. "Hey, you! Hey!"

Glorian's hands curled into fists, and he groaned.

"Okay," Ellie said. "Definitely not dead. Go, go, go!"

The door behind them led to an aluminum staircase that descended at least two stories. Much like the staircase in their high school, it was wide enough to walk four abreast, so Jay and Ellie shared steps, each holding their own rail. Ellie to the right, Jay to the left. Near the bottom, they leapt to the landing and pushed through industrial, windowless double doors. The swinging doors snapped closed behind them, cutting off all but a sliver of light.

"Where's the switch?" Ellie asked, patting the wall. It felt cool and smooth. "Use the light on your phone."

"Or I could do this! Aha!" A white will-o'-the-wisp blossomed over Jay's palm. It shone as brightly as a sixty-watt bulb. They were in a large, clinically sterile room with cement flooring, white walls, and rows of long, silver boxes on the ground. Several cabinets lined the far wall, and a medical-grade freezer was against the left. To their right, Ellie saw another pair of double doors.

"Are those coffins?" Jay asked. "Oh my gosh!" His light flickered erratically, as if tethered to his emotions. Indeed, the heavy metal boxes resembled futuristic coffins. They could easily contain a six-foot-tall adult.

"Found it," Ellie said, shoving her palm against three push-button switches. They activated recessed, rectangular ceiling lights.

"If I lock the door behind us," Jay said, "am I protecting us, or trapping us? Glorian wanted us to run this way. I'm sure of it." He slid a deadbolt into place.

"Nobody has popped out of the freezer," Ellie said. "For now, we're safe. But . . . Kirby? Hey, it's Kirby!"

A dog-shaped shimmer guarded a corner coffin. He yapped once in acknowledgement.

"Why isn't he with your mom?" Jay asked.

"She doesn't need him. That's great news." Ellie pointed between Kirby and the box. "You know what else? I think he found Al!"

Al's techno coffin was fastened by four heavy screws in its lid. Fortunately, each had a butterfly-shaped knob that allowed easy removal. Jay tentatively knocked on the lid and pressed his ear against the surface, listening. After a few seconds, he gave Ellie a thumbs-up. "Somebody tapped back," Jay said. "Al's alive."

"I hope you're good at opening pickle jars," Ellie said, as she started twisting one of the fasteners.

"I don't like pickles." He started working on another.

"Do you eat anything in a jar?"

"Oh, sure! Marmalade."

"I hope you're good at opening marmalade jars."

As it happened, they both were. Ellie and Jay unsealed in two minutes flat. Jay shoved one of the gigantic screws into his pocket. The butterfly handle poked out conspicuously. "It's for self-defense," he said, when Ellie gave him a look. "If Glorian charges, I'll stab him in the heart."

She disregarded a litany of jokes because, to be honest, Ellie didn't want her last words to involve screw-related puns.

"Help me with this lid," she said. "It weighs a ton."

They braced themselves, knees bent, and shoved the lid forward. It budged a couple millimeters, if that. Ellie had used the value "ton" figuratively, but now she wondered how close her guess had been. Was the lid filled with lead? There were handles at the head and foot of the coffin, but it would take considerable strength to lift it, even with two people. If Ellie had more time, she could scrape together a system of ropes and pulleys. More time and more ropes.

"Can Kirby help?" Jay asked.

"I haven't trained him for this."

"What about the mammoth? She can knock the lid off!"

"In this little room? She might crush us instead!"

A knock rang out, but it didn't come from the coffin. Glorian started pummeling the locked double doors. He laughed as his fists drummed a catchy rhythm. "Good one!" Glorian shouted. "Send another ghost! I relish the excitement!"

"Time for one hundred and twenty percent, Ellie!" Jay said, spinning his hands in a twirly maneuver that would look much nicer with pompoms. They threw their weight against the lid again, and it rumbled forward at a snail's pace.

"Can you do a . . . cheer . . . to block out that loser's voice?" Ellie asked.

"I can't remember any!" Jay confessed.

"It's cool."

"One reason I struggle with exams," he said. "Anxiety wipes my brain clean."

"I'll try," Ellie said. "Go, team, go."

"Go, team, go. We're dynamo?"

"Yes! It's cheesy, but it rhymes!"

An inch. Two inches. The knocking stopped. Ellie glanced worriedly at the second pair of doors. They had no deadbolt lock. She wondered how Kirby would fare against a man like Glorian. So far, the English springer spaniel was, at his meanest, all bark and no bite. In contrast, Six-Great had trained ghost hounds for war. Her heroic pack could rip apart an enemy in seconds. Howl so terribly, entire fields withered. Ellie always reasoned that Six-Great lived in a more violent era, one that transformed pacifists into warriors. Six-Great didn't fight because she enjoyed it; she had to protect her family and friends from genocide.

There were still people to protect. That, Ellie now realized, would never change.

Ellie concentrated, mentally reaching for the dogs of her ancestors. She could sense their jubilance, their loyalty. They were so close . . .

But Ellie was afraid to call for them. Afraid to fly too close to the sun.

"Almost there!" Jay said, his face red with strain. "Keep pushing!" They weren't *almost there*, though. The coffin was barely cracked open. Four white fingers shot out, wiggling. "Hungry," Al croaked. "Too weak. Help . . ."

"I'm hungry, too!" Glorian shouted.

The unlocked doors at their right burst open.

⇶ TWENTY-NINE ⇜

ONE MOMENT, GLORIAN was charging, and the next,
Ellie felt like she'd been hit by a tidal wave. She flew
back, struck the cement ground, and rolled once before a
metal coffin broke her inertia. Her elbows and knees ached.
They'd been bruised by the impact, but at least nothing
broke. Ellie crawled behind the coffin and peeked over its
top. Glorian was thrashing, as if fighting an invisible swarm
of hornets. His leg bled where Kirby held it. A canine growl
hummed through the room. "Atta boy!" she shouted. "Jay,
wherever you are, stay down!"

Swallowing her winces, Ellie sprinted to the medical
freezer and opened its swinging door. Crisp, chilly air flowed
out, heavy, pooling against her face. As expected, the fridge
was crammed with blood bags. Each bag was labeled with
barcodes and eleven-digit numbers.

"I need backup!" Glorian shouted into a walkie-talkie as he strained against Kirby's hold. "Don't send cursed men. She's Native!"

"Location?" the walkie-talkie crackled.

"Dungeon B," he said. "It's infested by meddling kids and their ghost. We need an exorcist, too."

Ellie grabbed a couple bags and ran back to Al's coffin jail. She shoved one bag through the crack, relieved when it fit without bursting. "Cheers," she said. "Drink up."

Glorian swung his arms, slashing the air with yellow, talon-sharp nails, straining against Kirby's hold. "You shouldn't have touched me, creep," Ellie said. "You're my ghost's chew toy now. By the way, if you turn into a bat, he'll swallow you whole!"

Across the room, Jay pushed a cabinet in front of the unlocked doors. It screeched like nails on a chalkboard as metal scraped across cement.

"We have exorcists on staff," Glorian taunted. "Like I said: your ghost isn't a surprise."

"If they send Kirby to the underworld," she said, "I'll just call him back."

"How clever! What if they send you to the underworld first? All the security guards carry guns. Actually . . . so do I!" Glorian drew a handgun so quickly, Ellie was surprised that she didn't hear a sonic boom. As he whipped the gun at them, Al kicked the metal coffin lid; it flew off and knocked Glorian aside. The gun discharged with a tremendous *crack*, firing a bullet into the wall. As Ellie dove for cover, Al tackled Glorian. The two men wrestled for the weapon, evenly matched. The older vampire had been crushed by a mammoth, and Al was recharged by a fresh meal. Plus, Glorian's leg bled profusely, unable to heal around Kirby's spectral teeth, which stubbornly held fast.

"Get food to the other prisoners!" Al shouted. "They can—hey! Stop it! No biting, asshole!" Al wrenched Glorian's teeth from his shoulder. "Hurry, Jay! He's like a bloody snapping turtle!"

Ellie and Jay hastened to unfasten the neighboring coffin. They didn't even need to push its lid; the prisoner was stronger than Al had been, and once the screws had been removed, she freed herself, gorged on a bag of blood, and stalked over to the wrestling match between Glorian, Al, and Kirby. The freed vampire was Black, with short hair, bat-shaped gold earrings dangling from each earlobe, and a sprinkling of freckles over her nose and cheeks. She grabbed the gun, yanked it away from Glorian, and emptied its chamber, clearly no stranger to firearms. "There are kids present," she said, "so we should lock him in the coffin. Keep things PG. Make no mistake, Glorian: I am tempted to cut off your head and write angry poetry with your blood."

"We're at least PG-13," Ellie said. "*At least*. But I appreciate your consideration. If we can survive the night without more death, that'd be lovely. Kirby, come!"

Kirby gave Glorian's leg a final shake before relinquishing his bite. Kirby excitedly ran circles around Ellie and Jay, his shimmer tail whipping side-to-side. Al and his new ally wrestled Glorian into a coffin and sealed it shut. "You should have killed me," Glorian taunted, his voice muffled by three inches of metal. "I finish what I start."

"What did you start?" Al snarled, smacking the coffin. "Well? 'Cause this is pathetic. Who brags about attacking a couple of harmless nerds."

"Nerd?" Jay asked. "Hey!"

"I'll accept nerd," Ellie said, "but we aren't harmless. Are you okay?" Al's clothes—black pants and a white undershirt—were wrinkled, and his hair direly needed a fresh wash and spray. It drooped over his brow.

"Yeah," Al said. "Thanks to you. I almost died! You know what Dr. Allerton does?"

"Heals ancient vampires by exchanging their developed curses for the health of young vampires?" Ellie asked. "We gathered."

The bat-earring woman whistled, impressed.

"Well, uh, yes. That's exactly right," Al said.

"I'm glad you're okay," Jay said. "Sorry about all this. And I'm sorry that my parents had a fit about the wedding. Ronnie loves you. That's the important thing. And I, well, I . . ." Jay flashed a pair of thumbs-ups. "I think you're swell."

"Does this mean that you'll be my best man for the wedding, brother?"

"Uh."

"I'll let you take everyone to an arcade for the bachelor party."

"Then yes," Jay said. "Yes, I will." The two sealed the deal with a firm side-hug.

"Get out of here," the bat-earring woman said. "Before other security arrives. I can free the remaining prisoners."

"Okay, Lily." Al jogged to the door without a barricade and unlocked the bolt. "Let's go."

"We can't leave without my mother," Ellie said.

"And Ronnie," Jay added.

"Ronnie?" Al looked over his shoulder, whiplash-fast. "Where?"

"They're upstairs," Ellie said. "A green room with fancy mirrors on its wall."

"Okay," Al said. "Change of plans, kiddos. We go upstairs, retrieve family, and then run!"

"Careful," Ellie said. "The mansion is . . ."

Al opened the door.

A body was lying on the staircase landing. A dead body. Definitely dead. Ellie didn't need to check for a heartbeat, because the body's head was twisted one hundred and eighty degrees.

"Haunted," she finished.

⇶ THIRTY ⇜

JUST IN CASE, Ellie checked the body for signs of life. Pre-
dictably, she found none. No pulse, no breath. Although
the skin still felt warm, it had a waxy pallor.

"Did he fall?" Jay asked. "An accident?"

"Not likely," she said. "A fall can't make a head . . . look
like . . . are the prisoners okay? We should hurry."

"Everyone fed and free," Lily said. She and four others
clustered in the doorway. "What the hell happened?"

"Glorian called for backup," Ellie said. "I don't think they
made it to Dungeon B alive." She stepped away from the
body, trying to forget the way his skin felt. It had been so
still. Like touching a warm, soft mannequin. "Stay behind
me. Kirby will sound the alarm before an ambush."

"Should we bring his gun?" Al asked, gesturing at the
dead man's weapon in its holster.

"No!" Jay said. "No. It's . . . just no."

"Bullets won't help us," Ellie said, starting the ascent. "They didn't help him."

The lights flickered once, as if winking in agreement. She took the staircase two steps at a time. There were drops of blood on the railing and a red handprint on the wall. How many people had responded to the walkie-talkie summons? Hopefully, just one: an exorcist. However, exorcists usually wore a specialized trade uniform. Their features varied, based on methodology. Some exorcists wove bones and hair into voluminous cloaks. Others draped themselves in mineral crystals precipitated from dead seas. The man on the landing—the *body*—just wore a black suit, like run-of-the-mill security. What were the chances that a security guard worked alone?

When Ellie reached the top of the stairs, with Jay, Al, Lily, and the freed prisoners on her heels, she heard Kirby whine timidly.

"Is there a problem?" Lily asked, her voice a secretive whisper.

"I don't know," Ellie admitted. "Get ready for anything." Cautiously, she opened the door. As if preparing for a jump scare in a horror movie, Ellie covered her eyes with one hand and peeked through her fingers.

Violence marked the corridor.

Broken bodies slumped against the walls and sprawled, in pieces, across the floor. She counted six men: one wore a red robe, the others dressed in suits. Nobody had fired a gun. Maybe they realized that bullets could not deter the dead. Maybe they never had a chance.

"You didn't have to kill them," she said, hesitating in the doorway. "There are other ways."

A walkie-talkie on the nearest body crackled, and Trevor's voice hissed, "Can't let an exorcist ruin our fun tonight, Cuz."

"You're strong. He wasn't a threat."

"Are you a threat?" asked the walkie-talkie voice. "Or ally?"

"We just want to go home," she said. "Will you let us pass?" Ellie took a hesitant step forward, into the corridor. "I won't appeal to your compassion, Trevor, since it's far away, but consider the cost. Are we worth the trouble?"

All six walkie-talkies responded at once: "Go." Ahead, the exit door exploded open, thudding against the outer wall with enough force to chip brick. It was dim outside, as if the sun decided to call it quits. Had storm clouds flooded the clear blue sky? Texas weather could change on a lightning-strike whim. None of the meteorological forecasts predicted this and the weather icon on Ellie's phone still displayed a cartoon sun.

"Go," Ellie said. "Double time! I'm right behind you. If anything attacks, I'll send the mammoth." She waved the escapees forward. Al, Lily, and the four other prisoners hustled toward the exit. Ellie kept a wary eye on the dead bodies, half-expecting their guns to float in the air and riddle the hall with bullets. She and Trevor watched the Indiana Jones trilogy together; he had ample inspiration for deadly traps.

Thankfully, the bodies did not pounce, and the guns remained silent. All but Jay and Ellie reached the exit safely. "Kiddos, c'mon!" Al called. He rested a hand on the doorway. Ellie had an alarming vision: Trevor slamming the door and severing Al's fingers. Could vampires regrow digits? Old ones, maybe. Not new vampires like him. "Give us room!" she whispered. "Al, step back! We're going to run. Okay, Jay, your turn. Sprint like you're at the end of a marathon."

Jay tried to take her hand, but she delicately brushed him away. Trevor had lured Ellie into the house for a reason. He might not want her to leave so soon—or at all—but maybe Jay could escape.

"Together," he said, smiling, because Jay was the kind of optimistic fellow who believed every cheer he endorsed in-uniform. Even surrounded by corpses, he had the audacity to see the glass half full, and maybe his optimism was as con-tagious as his smile, because . . .

Jay's shirt bunched up in the back, as if an invisible hand grabbed it. He toppled with a yelp and slid down the hall, pulled by his shirt. "Let go!" he cried. He thrashed, kicking, but the force that dragged him was stronger than any living human. Trevor flung Jay out the door, and Ellie didn't see whether Al managed to catch him, because the exit shut with a *thunk*.

"Kirby," she said. "Heel."

A tremor ran through the corpses. One by one, they trem-bled and flopped, like fish out of water. Ellie closed her eyes.

They might have been bad men, but she didn't want to see their bodies treated like puppets.

The sounds of movement ceased, except for a whisper of fabric. She felt the air around her shift, as if somebody was leaning close, and a sour odor tainted the air.

Ellie opened her eyes. She was face-to-face with the exorcist's corpse. His mouth hung open, locked in an unending yawn, and his skin was waxy-looking, his blood pooling in his feet. The body did not frighten her, however. It was just an empty shell.

Trevor frightened her.

The walkie-talkie in the exorcist's cloak hissed and sputtered. Through it, Trevor said, "He was wrong."

"Who?" she asked.

"Samuel Tanner, that insufferable know-it-all in your sixth-grade class. He was wrong. We aren't just balls of negative energy."

"What are you, then?" Ellie asked. "Honestly. You aren't my cousin. He'd never . . ." She thought the implication was obvious, but just in case, Ellie pointed at one of the bodies. "*Never* do that."

"You're right. I'm not your cousin."

She waited for Not-Trevor to continue.

"I am," he said, "an impression Trevor made. I am his spiritual footprints in the earth. I am, Ellie, an emissary of a murdered man, unleashed to right a terrible wrong. His suffering filled me like a breath of air, and now I have purpose.

Everything I do tonight will be for him. For justice." The exorcist corpse's head flopped to one side, as if trying to study Ellie with its cloudy eyes. "He loved you," the emissary said. "He loved all his family."

"I love Trevor," she said. "Always will."

"Someday, you'll be reunited," the emissary promised. "If you want that day to come sooner rather than later, interfere with my vengeance."

"Vengeance?" she wondered. "Didn't you say 'justice' a moment ago?"

"In this case, they're the same."

"No," she said. "You've already gone too far."

"Not far enough," it said. "Not far enough until Willowbee is salted by the blood of its people. They're despicable leeches. Young and old. They've suckled upon centuries of suffering." The corpse puppet touched a red splatter on the wall. The hissing walkie-talkie voice continued, with a trace of sorrow, "They are worse than vampires, Ellie. Cursed men drink blood indiscriminately, but Willowbee puts a bounty on the Indigenous, the poor, and the *vulnerable*. Its familial line of doctors steal health to glut the rich. The influence of its founder, Nathaniel Grace, still desecrates our bodies and our legacy with hideous magic. You think the townsfolk here are ignorant? Hah. No. They just don't care. I'll make them care. I'll teach them what it feels like to be powerless. To mourn."

"Teach? Listen to me. Trevor taught some of the children at this party! He cares for them too! They're like his second family. He'd never—"

"Ellie!" screamed every speaker in the hall. "I thought we already established that I'm NOT! YOUR! COUSIN!"

The emissary's voice transformed into a shrill hum that shattered the light fixtures. In the darkness, silence fell. Judging by the meaty *thunk* beside her, the exorcist's corpse had collapsed, its puppet strings cut. Ellie winced as a piece of glass pricked her palm. She felt more shards in her hair and on her shoulders.

The emissary continued, "We must exist for a reason."

"Who?" Ellie asked, shaking her arms. *Clink, clink* went the glass that rained from her sleeves.

"Me," it said. "Others like me. There are so many. So, so many emissaries of vengeance trapped between this world and Below. If you tried, could you free us? We're not *too* different from animal ghosts."

She heard the air ring; the glass shards were floating, colliding, and although she could not see them, their tinkling voices were too close for comfort. "Does anything exist for a reason?" she asked, biting back nervous laughter. "Ask that question to a room full of philosophers, and they might start a brawl."

"Another time, perhaps," it said. "Right now, I'm asking you."

"You're strong enough without an army."

"Not nearly. I'll mince this party, but there's more work to accomplish. Willowbee is just one town."

"I can't help you."

Ellie felt a razor-sharp edge slice through her upper arm.

It happened so quickly, at first, there was no pain. Then, a sharp sting pulsed through the wound.

"Kirby," Ellie said, sticking her fingers in her ears. "Big howl."

If his voice could disperse a river of trilobites, it might also prevent her from dying in a glass tornado. Kirby's howl reverberated in the hall, drowning out the sound of falling glass. Ellie ran to the exit. Twice, she stumbled over the dead. Were they screaming, too? Or had Kirby's howl split into a dozen separate voices, each resonating in a different key of anguish? Before her, the door opened, bathing Ellie in a pale rectangle of light. She dove outside, dripping blood from her right nostril, and wrenched the door shut. Beside her, Jay and Al were doubled over, clutching their ears, aching from the bombardment of sound that flew from the hall when they opened the door.

"What the nine hells was that?" Al asked.

"My dog," Ellie said, wiping her nose. Kirby, blessedly silent, appeared at her side. She petted his shimmer affectionately.

"Is that what he did during the howl incident?" Jay asked. "Back in sixth grade?"

"Yep. My whole class got nosebleeds. Glass rained everywhere. Why is it so dark out here?" Ellie looked up. There were stars overhead, the bright ones that appeared at dusk. "It's night?" she asked. "How? We just . . . we only . . ."

"Look at this," Jay said, holding up his wrist. He wore a watch with a woven blue strap. "My wristwatch says it's noon. But my phone jumped ahead to 8:00 P.M. when I landed outside. We got stuck in some kind of freaky ghostly time pocket!"

"That means the masquerade has started," Ellie said, "and everyone has gathered in Dr. Allerton's mansion. They're worse off than fish in a barrel!"

"Lily and the other vamps went for help," Al said, grimacing. "What's our next move?"

"We save the day," Ellie said. "I mean. Night. Hurry. The vengeful thing won't stay gone long." She shook a few persistent glass fragments from her hair and pointed to the mansion. "Ready?"

"Onward!" Jay said.

They ran to the grandiose, columned front entrance. The jesters were gone. In fact, Ellie couldn't see anyone outside. A crowd of elegant masked people mingled beyond the windows. At least the partiers were in good spirits, unscathed by the emissary of vengeance. Ellie tried the front door. It did not yield.

"Locked," she said, "though I don't know if it's physically locked or just jammed by the emissary's poltergeist powers. Who wants to break a window? Anyone see a brick?"

"Oh! Oh! Another way in!" Jay pointed to a second-floor balcony. The party had spilled outside; two children in papier-mâché masks were using bubble guns to shoot soap bullets over the balcony railing.

"Easier to climb than a bridge," Al said. He spider-crawled up the brick wall and jumped onto the balcony, popping a bubble underfoot. The children shrieked and ran inside. "Sorry!" Al called after them.

"How are we supposed to get up there?" Ellie asked. "Can you lower a . . . Jay. No." Jay had knelt near the balcony and extended his hands, as if he wanted Ellie to step on them. She'd seen him do a similar move during pep rallies. The stunt usually ended with a cheerleader balanced on his hands above his head.

"Trust me," he said. "I've been one-person base with tons of fliers."

"What are those? Birds?"

"I've thrown and lifted lots of people," he amended. "Al will catch you! Right, Al?"

Maybe Kirby would catch her if Al missed his chance. The pup was good at fetch. With a muttered apology for her dirty tennis shoes, Ellie stepped on Jay's palm. "I hope you know what you're doing," she said. "Because I don't."

"Tuck your chin," he said. "It reduces the chance of neck injuries. Okay. Three! Two!"

"Neck injuries?" Ellie asked.

"One!" Jay stood and threw her in one quick motion, and if Al hadn't grabbed her by the arm, Ellie would have wobbled and plunged to the grass.

"We actually did it!" she cheered, her legs bicycling in midair as she dangled from Al's grasp.

"Maybe you can join the squad next year!" Jay said. "You're a natural flier."

"Hey, kiddos," Al said, "we aren't done yet. Ellie, you need to climb, because I can't pull you through these bars." To reach her, he'd shoved his arms through gaps in the railing. "Lift me just a bit," Ellie said, and Al obliged. When she felt a metal bar against her hand, Ellie grabbed it, flipped to face the building, and pulled with all her strength. Al, now free to move, helped guide her over the rail.

"Now me!" Jay called. "Lower a rope!"

"We don't have a rope," Al said.

"Can you carry him on your back?" Ellie suggested. "You're extra strong, right, Al?"

"Huh." Al crossed his arms. "Come to think of it, I could have carried you, too. Or . . . both of you. At the same time."

"Yeah," she said, lowering her voice, "but he's so proud of that throw. Look at his smile. Don't mention it, okay?"

Al winked and pretended to zip his lips.

It took a minute for the group to reconvene on the balcony. They followed the sound of laughter and chatter through an empty guest room and down a hall. A woman in a devil mask pointed them toward the ballroom. She giggled when Ellie asked, "Is everyone alive?"

"I haven't seen any zombie costumes, if that's what you're asking," the woman said, sipping bubbly liquid from a glass flute. "Hurry, hurry! You don't want to miss the giveaway. Somebody is going to win a trip to Hawaii!"

"Where are you going?" Ellie asked. "It's a great night. You should step outside." If nothing else, she wanted to spare one person from the emissary's violence.

"I have business in the lavatory!" the devil woman said,

raising her glass. "Second time tonight. There's so much to drink."

"During your trips, have you seen a green sitting room?" Jay asked. "Or a bunch of women in matching outfits?"

The woman closed her eyes and tapped her chin, as if trying to remember a complex mathematical formula. "Ye-eees," she said. "During the spring luncheon, I ate cucumber sandwiches in a green room." She pointed down the hall. "That way. Somewhere. Now, if you'll excuse me, I need to make room for more of these." She finished off the bubbly drink and sashayed around a corner.

"The ballroom is a tinderbox," Ellie said. "I can't waste any more time."

"You two go ahead," Al said. "I'll find the green room."

"Good luck, bro," Jay said.

Al nodded once, and the group divided and went separate ways. At the ballroom entrance, Jay and Ellie hesitated. They turned around, looking back. Al was gone.

"He'll find them," Jay said.

The two friends linked arms and stepped into the ballroom. Designed for hundreds—if not thousands—of guests, it was a vision of opulence. Its auburn hardwood floor shone, somebody had painted a Renaissance-inspired fresco on the ceiling, and palatial marble arches with gold accents leapt around the ballroom's perimeter. A cello, a drum set, a baby grand piano, and an electric guitar were arranged on the low stage. The musicians were on a break. Without music, the throng of guests mingled under the golden lights of electric chandeliers. The hum of their combined voices was loud enough to drown out a high school cafeteria during lunchtime.

Ellie skimmed the crowd, searching for anyone she recognized. Masks seemed to be optional because most of the attendees had exposed faces. One person was eerily familiar, a woman with bright red hair. Had she been the waitress in the Willowbee diner?

"I'm going to call my mother," Ellie said. She dialed Vivian, and this time, the emissary did not interfere. Ellie was right where he wanted her, after all: in the haunted house.

"Mom?" Ellie asked. "You there?"

"Yes, honey. What's wrong?"

"Listen. We freed Al, but a spirit of vengeance that formed during Trevor's death wants to reenact the bloody prom scene from *Carrie*."

"Slow down. You found Al already? How?"

"It's night! You've been in that room for *hours*. We need to evacuate now!"

Ellie heard muffled conversation from her mother's end of the call. "On our way," Vivian said. "Ellie, I want you to—"

The phone call was dropped as a hush fell over the ballroom. From her vantage point at the edge of the crowd, Ellie could see Dr. Abe Allerton step onto the stage with a wicker basket in his arms. He was dressed like Uncle Sam, with red-white-and-blue-striped pants and a star-spangled suit jacket. Allerton tipped his blue top hat at the crowd. Smiling, he sidled up to the microphone and tapped it twice.

"Happy birthday, Willowbee!" Allerton said, his voice buffeted by applause. "Ladies, gentlemen, and spelling bee champs, this is the moment you've all been waiting for—"

A delicate scale in D minor danced across the piano keys. The doctor turned, one eyebrow cocked, and the room burst into a fit of good-natured laughter. "We have a prankster in our midst," Allerton said. "Who did th—"

With a discordant clang, every key on the piano slammed down.

"Run!" Ellie shouted. "Get out of here!"

Her warning didn't have the intended effect. Nearly every head in the ballroom turned to look at her. Some people seemed confused. Others smiled, as if they mistook Ellie for a performer, just another one of Allerton's jesters. And some of the people—including the red-haired waitress—stared in a hard, guarded way. Like they wouldn't do what she said for a million bucks. And in that moment, when the guests were distracted, it happened.

The piano flew up as if seized by a tornado, sailed over Dr. Allerton, and plummeted toward the now-screaming crowd.

⇒ THIRTY-ONE ≪

V IVIAN WONDERED IF SHE'D made the right decision by bringing Ellie to the party. She admired her daughter's courage. Of course she did! But the world presented too many opportunities for brave people to risk their lives. Wisdom helped reduce those risks; the inexperience of youth increased them.

If only Ellie could see things from Vivian's perspective.

"How long has it been?" Ronnie groaned. She'd been pacing the green room since the butler left, hands thrust into the deep pockets of her trench coat.

"Ten minutes," Vivian said, glancing at her phone. "Let's wait another five before we start breaking things."

"Sit down," Alice said, patting the sofa cushion beside her. "We need to save our energy."

Vivian wondered what they expected would happen. A

ballroom blitz? "What's with the matching outfits?" she asked. "I hope you realize that it's my nature to get nervous when I see kids in trench coats. I'm a teacher. You could be hiding anything."

No matter how many times she confiscated smartphones from her students, they pulled new ones out of the ether the moment she turned her attention back to the dry-erase board. To be fair, Vivian understood the utility of a device that could communicate at a global scale and pull knowledge from every corner of the internet, but did they have to be so small? So easily hidden in purses and pockets?

The basketball team exchanged sly glances, and then Ronnie opened her coat. Vivian had the sudden mental image of a street vendor flashing his counterfeit Rolexes in a dim alley. But Ronnie wasn't carrying ten pounds of fake gold. Thin, metallic stakes, the kind used to secure camping tents, hung from loops in the lining of her trench coat. There had to be ten on each side.

"What are those supposed to be?" Vivian asked. "Do you all have them?"

"Silver-coated stakes," Ronnie said.

"They're important," Martia said. "You know what this place is?"

Jess interjected, "Before he went missing, Al learned that King—the cursed guy who owns King's Ranch down by San Antonio, you know?—he visits Willowbee every few years, and he isn't the only big guy who does."

Vivian was vaguely aware that Mr. King, an oil baron

and cattle dealer of some ilk, was one of the oldest vampires in the country. However, it was said he didn't associate with people outside the wrought-iron gates around his ranch. She always assumed that he was too wracked with bloodlust and sensitive to light. But if he visited Willowbee on the regular, that couldn't be the case.

"Okay," she said. "And the weapons? They're for him?"

"Anyone, really," Ronnie said. "Powerful vampires travel with entourages. Big ones. I heard about the gathering you interrupted. It's lucky you escaped. We might have to fight our way out of these walls."

"Silver stakes," Vivian mused. She drummed her fingers across the arm of her sofa, gazing thoughtfully at her reflection in one of the many mirrors. "Have you ever killed somebody before?"

Alice laughed in a strained, forced way, like she was responding politely to a terrible joke.

"It's a serious question," Vivian said. "If the silver is pure, those stakes can kill. They'll *need* to kill, in the situation you just described."

"No," Ronnie said. "Have you?"

"Yes."

Now, everyone was looking at Vivian, but she continued watching her reflection. Her hair was the kind of shimmery, ethereal gray that an even mixture of white and black hair produced. Not unlike the silver that the girls had carried against their chests. "Do you know about the power of my lineage?" she asked. "We can wake the dead."

"That's the opposite of killing," Alice said, smiling, and Vivian suspected that she was the kind of person who couldn't abide a serious situation without jokes to break the tension.

"We know," Martia said.

"My mother," Vivian continued, "is allergic to dogs. Cats, too. So we never had them growing up. I didn't mind. We lived in New Mexico. I love Texas, but the land of my father will somehow always feel more like home. It's difficult to describe the beauty of those plateaus. Or how vast and clear the sky can be when you're standing on a mountain filled with millions of old bones. Fossils, mostly. I think that's how my mother got the idea to make an extinct thing her companion."

"A dinosaur?" Ronnie asked. No longer pacing, she sat cross-legged in front of Vivian. "Oh! You can raise an army of dinosaurs to help us!"

"A mammoth," Vivian said, nipping that idea in the bud. "Really not much different than your typical elephant, except for the tusks. They're also much larger. Fluffier, too."

"Wow," Alice said. "You could see it?"

"Sometimes. Usually, it was just this massive, shimmery bulldozer that rumbled through the desert behind our home. Ma would spend hours training it after school. She started in the wilderness, miles from our house, in case the beast was unruly. After a few years, the trust between them was such that Ma did her training sessions near my playhouse. It was actually an old car. Broken down, no tires. Dad let me play in it because I begged, and it wasn't like anyone needed the thing, even for scraps. After school, I'd sit on top of my car, shaded by an umbrella, and watch her shout commands to the shimmer. When I came of age, she taught me how to shout commands too. By that time, the mammoth was well-behaved, and I think it loved us both. They're very much like elephants in that way too. Capable of affection. Intelligent." She exhaled through her nose, making a discontented *hff* sound. "People don't give animals enough credit sometimes. Or maybe they give humans too much credit."

She checked her phone again. Only three minutes had passed since she last looked at its thumbprint-streaked screen. Three minutes? Was that all? She thought it had been longer.

"What happened?" Ronnie asked. "Who did you kill?"

"Don't rush stories," Vivian chided. "That's sacrilegious."

"Sorry. I'm just . . ." Ronnie rubbed her face and groaned. "Angry."

"I know. So am I. But this is important. That's why I'm sharing now, of all times." She looked again at her reflection. "I loved the land so much. Sometimes, I'd go for long walks through the desert, looking for lizards and bugs. My favorite time for these was late afternoon, when the sun was low enough that these long, cold shadows stretched from the plateaus. It felt like walking among giants. I'd follow this red, sandy road between them. It was mostly for locals. Outsiders often had the wrong kind of car for our roads; you needed something light with good tires. Sometimes, a tourist would get lost and become stuck in the fine red sand. My father liked to tow them free and provide directions to the nearest paved street. They'd try to pay him for the kindness, but he refused. My mother would tell him to get over his pride. That we needed the money. Didn't have much back then, except for each other.

"Anyway, when I saw the pickup truck, I figured a tourist took a wrong turn and was driving in circles, trying to get to the road home. I was thirteen years old at the time. Small for thirteen, though. Didn't have my big growth spurt till later that year. So a stranger might have taken me for ten or eleven.

"As the truck approached, I went closer to the roadside. Naïve, yes, I know. But I hadn't been afraid of strangers since Ma taught me how to wake the dead. The power went straight to my head.

"It happened quickly. The truck stopped right there in the middle of the road—nobody around for miles, so it's not like the driver had to worry about causing an accident. A man exited. He was tall, maybe forty-something. To children, adults look old, and it's hard to tell thirty from forty or fifty. I remember that his body language frightened me. It was aggressive and confident. He strode around the car, carrying a knife in one hand and reaching for me with the other. The blade seemed this big—" Vivian spread her hands two feet apart, like somebody describing a fish she'd just caught. "—but that's because I was afraid. It was probably a little hunting knife or Swiss Army knife. Something people carry in case of emergencies."

Momentarily, Vivian lost her train of thought as she remembered the pocket knife Trevor used to own. He'd been so confident that it, with all those foldable gadgets, would protect him from life's unexpected crises.

Ellie had the knife. Was that wise? Maybe it should have gone into the earth with Trevor's body. Or maybe, with an object valued for its utility, a burial was the worst possible fate.

"Did you know him?" Martia asked, and she sounded furious, as if the attack had happened that day instead of thirty years ago. "Who does that?"

"No. I'd never seen him before. That might have been the first time he drove through our neck of the desert. Like I mentioned, it was an isolated place." She crossed her arms. "Back then, I didn't know many white people. Mostly saw them when my family visited cities like Flagstaff. I'm sure I would have remembered him if we met before."

Vivian noticed that everyone but Ronnie seemed amused by that.

"Do you . . . miss that?" Ronnie asked.

"I just miss being around my family," Vivian said, "and people who understand my rare in-jokes. It's been a long time since I lived in New Mexico. My parents divorced when I was fifteen, and Ma took me to Texas."

"What happened to the man?" Jess asked. "How did you kill him?"

"Hey, now. How do you know that he's the one who died?" Vivian asked.

"Just wishful thinking, I guess."

She chuckled at that. Her smile dropped quickly. "I think he was the kind of monster who drives around and looks for . . . opportunities. Lucky for him, there I was. He said one thing: 'Get in the car.' I remember wanting to scream but realizing that any sound I made would be swallowed by the vastness around us. I also wanted to run but was afraid that he'd stab me in the back. So I called for the mammoth.

"She appeared as a shimmer beside me. The man didn't seem to notice. Still. It's not like he had any chance to react. The mammoth must have realized that I was in trouble. They're smart. Protective. Before I could say a command, she reacted. It happened quick as a snakebite. One moment, the man was reaching for my arm, and the next?" Vivian clapped. "Flying through the air like a rag doll. Head over heels. Clutching that knife the whole time. He landed in the middle of the road about twenty feet behind the truck. Alive.

"When I was in college, I went to a rodeo with my friends, and we saw this spirited bull immediately knock off his rider. But that wasn't enough. The one-ton animal rounded on the fallen cowboy and tried to stomp and gore him to death. Thankfully, a circus clown saved the day.

"That's what the mammoth did to my would-be kidnapper. Stomped and stabbed. But she was six times heavier than a bull. Angrier, too. I watched her invisible feet flatten him limb by limb. She stomped until I couldn't tell he was a person anymore. Until his bones became mash and his blood dyed the earth a deeper shade of red. Believe me when I say this: the mammoth saved my life. I don't know what that man planned to do—or what he'd done to others—but I'm confident that the truck was my coffin.

"Despite that, his death is the most horrible thing I've witnessed. I don't feel guilt, but I wish that I could have kept my innocence just a little longer. The lucky will go their whole lives without witnessing such violence. It changes you in unpleasant ways. Do you understand?" Vivian looked at each of the young women—they were still children, in her eyes, barely older than the students she taught—and was pleased to see them all nod in agreement.

"Ma'am," Martia said, "do you still go on walks with the mammoth?"

"No. It's been a long time since I saw her. I can't wake the dead like I used to." She glanced at her phone to check the time. "Well! I know my stories tend to drag on, but this can't be right."

According to the analog clock projected on the screen, it was well past nine in the evening. Maybe, her phone had switched to the wrong time zone. Glitches like that happened in the presence of ghosts. Vivian stood, moving to open the door.

Before she had the chance, it flew open, narrowly missing her outstretched hand. A disheveled Al stood in the doorway. Wide-eyed, he looked around, his gaze finally settling on Ronnie.

"Babe!" she cried.

"Babe!" he agreed.

Each leapt forward, colliding in a hug.

"You escaped!" Ronnie said.

"Jay and Ellie helped. Quick. We need to get out of here. Trevor's ghost is on the warpath."

Vivian cleared her throat. "You mean he's awake?" she corrected. "Where's my daughter?"

"We split up. She and Jay are evacuating the ballroom. It's on the way out."

How was that possible? The ball wasn't supposed to start until evening. As Vivian jogged into the hallway with the rest of the group, she found her answer through the window: it was dark outside. She heard rain pattering against the roof, as if a storm had swept in while she and the starting lineup were trapped in some kind of time pocket.

Her phone beeped four times.

Missed call from Pat: 4:48 P.M.

Missed call from Pat: 7:00 P.M.

Missed call from Pat: 7:15 P.M.

Missed call from Pat: 8:50 P.M.

The double doors connecting the eastern wing to the central ballroom were closed, but Vivian could hear a tremendous commotion behind them. It wasn't the kind of noise she expected at a party. The voices were panicked. A few clear cries for help raised above the overall discordant hum:

"Help us! Oh God!"

"You're crushing me!"

"It doesn't work. Do something!"

The sound she'd mistaken for raindrops was actually dozens of fists rapping against the wooden doors. The walls also trembled with muffled knocks, like the whole ballroom was trying to get free.

Vivian grabbed a bronze door handle and pulled. When that didn't work, she pushed with all her weight. The door wouldn't budge. "Ellie!" she shouted. "Can you hear me? Are you there?"

The others tried to help. They kicked the wood, and Ronnie even whaled against it with a pair of silver stakes. Unfortunately, their combined efforts did little more than dislodge old chips of paint, baring the raw underlying material. It was a dense, grayish wood that peeled away in fine splinters.

Behind the door, a swell of terror-raised voices suggested that the situation in the ballroom was not improving.

"Stand back!" Vivian shouted, retreating to the far wall. "The doors are blocked with a supernatural barrier!" She didn't know what could wield such tremendous power. Trevor's ghost? Allerton's magic? Whatever the case, Vivian knew the best battering ram in Texas.

She just had to call her.

What did innocence feel like? Vivian used to sit on the roof of her playhouse car and watch plumes of dust rise between distant juniper and sage as the mammoth played.

A creature of the Ice Age, it must have found the sweltering desert to be strange and endlessly surprising.

Like young Vivian, a child who marveled at every pretty stone and bug she encountered during her ambling walks. Back then, she'd pretend to go on adventures, inspired by the stories of Five-Great-Grandmother. Saving lives, slaying monsters, meeting new people. She and her best friend, Miss Mammoth, would become new heroes.

Wake up, Vivian thought, extending her heart to the cavernous Below. *We need you, Miss Mammoth.*

A whispering responded. She was coming. She'd save them.

No. She was enormous. It was too dangerous! She'd *kill* them.

In her mind's eye, Vivian witnessed the doors bursting inward, an explosion of splinters, wooden shards impaling frightened people. The charging mammoth would crush bodies underfoot. She was summoning a bloodbath!

Or maybe the mammoth would crack the supernatural barrier that trapped Ellie in a room with certain death.

Vivian had to take the risk. But she couldn't hear the whispering from Below anymore. All she heard were muffled screams. Voices pleading for an escape. She squeezed her eyes shut, balled her hands into fists, and searched for the sense of calm that amplified her inner voice. Normally, meditation helped, but there wasn't enough time for that.

Wake up, she thought. *Wake up!*

Nothing happened.

Please! Wake up! Ellie needs you! Please, wake up!

"Ms. Bride," Ronnie said. "What are you doing?" She and her friends stood with their backs against the wall, waiting.

"I'm trying to open those doors," Vivian said. "I'm *trying*!"

"Maybe there's another way in," Ronnie said. "An underground route! We have to try."

With a shriek of frustration, Vivian threw herself against the door and wrenched its bar. "Ellie!" she shouted. "Can you hear me? Wake the mammoth! Knock the doors down! Get out of there, Ellie! *Elatsoe!* I'm coming!"

As Vivian backed away from the door, following Ronnie's group down the hall, she wondered if anyone could hear her in the ballroom above the cries of terror.

❧❧❧ THIRTY-TWO ❦❦❦

T HE PIANO LANDED on its side. It splintered upon impact, shards of hardwood rim and lid popping outward. Keys clattered across the floor, and wires twanged as they snapped free. Ellie and Jay tried to reach the accident site, running against a flood of screaming, retreating people. Somebody elbowed Ellie in the ribs. Another guest almost knocked Jay to the floor. Kirby barked, but nobody seemed to notice.

"Did it hit anybody?" Ellie asked, finally reaching the piano. A ring of Good Samaritans rushed around it.

"Yes!" one man said. "Careful, miss. Stand back." He and several other men lifted the piano's main body, including its inner iron plate. They heaved it to one side. A shattered, bleeding body lay among the remaining pieces of piano scrap. Ellie gasped and clasped her mouth with a trembling hand.

"Doctor Allerton!" somebody shouted over the roar of the room. "Help him!"

Dr. Allerton remained on the stage, his expression inscrutable. Ellie preferred the blank face to his arrogant grin, but she expected at least a sign of horror or anger from the murderer.

His victim had returned.

The body in the piano rubble was Trevor's. Bruised, bleeding, dying Trevor. The same Trevor who first visited Ellie in a dream. He'd returned. Had the emissary been in the ballroom the whole time, invisible and waiting for the perfect chance to demonstrate his wrath?

"Tonight," Trevor's body whispered, and it *was* a whisper, but Ellie heard it so clearly she wondered if the emissary could transmit its voice directly into her skull, "you'll wish that you had died in your Mercedes-Benz. Murderer."

Ellie was vaguely aware of a frenzy behind her, of people throwing themselves against doors that wouldn't open, of fists pummeling windows that cracked but didn't shatter. Her gaze, however, remained fixed on Dr. Allerton's face. On his eyes. Dr. Allerton looked down at the people on the ballroom floor. At Trevor. At Ellie. At the frightened guests who could not escape.

"What are you?" Dr. Allerton asked. "Death at my red masque? Come to teach old Prospero the error of his ways?"

"You murdered my cousin!" Ellie shouted, striding toward the stage. "Trevor was just being a decent man! Just trying to help! And you *murdered* him!"

"Frank!" Dr. Allerton shouted, ignoring Ellie; he wouldn't even look at her anymore. "Frank! Frank, I need you up here now!"

"If Frank's your exorcist, he's gone," Ellie said. "Vengeance killed him. Tell everyone about the night my cousin died! Tell them how you kill the poor to heal the rich. Confess!"

Dr. Allerton leaned toward the microphone. "Please stay calm, everybody!" he announced. "My team of exorcists will make quick work of the devil that has attacked my home!"

A pair of hands, ghostly manifestations, popped from the stage floor and grabbed Dr. Allerton by the ankles. The fingers seemed to be rotting, and Ellie couldn't help but think about B-grade zombie movies, about the dead emerging from their graves, hands first, to feast on brains. Trevor used to love those movies. He'd watch them with a bowl of popcorn and shout instructions at the characters on TV. "Don't go in that graveyard! Don't split up! Don't forget your cell phone!"

What would the real Trevor shout at Ellie? What would he tell her to do now? She wished that she knew.

"He won't confess!" the emissary boomed. Its voice was amplified by the microphone speakers, which had been turned up to the maximum volume. Ellie covered her ears, cringing at the thunderous sound. It was almost as loud as Kirby's howl.

"He won't confess, ladies and gentlemen and spelling bee champions," the emissary continued, "so how about a demonstration? The last time Abe Allerton was gravely wounded—by the way, how fast were you driving, Doctor?

Twice the speed limit? Faster? FASTER!—he transferred his injuries to a local schoolteacher, Trevor Reyes, a devoted father and husband. An unwilling sacrifice. But I suppose that's old news to most of you. So tell me: who will be Abe's victim tonight?"

Invisible hands dragged a child across the polished dance floor and toward the stage. "Mom!" the boy cried. "Mom, help!" A woman tried to grab the child's hand, but the emissary flung her back into the crowd of dancers.

"Our volunteer," the speakers boomed, "is a brave kid named Brett. Place your bets. Who thinks Abe Allerton will kill his own son?"

"Stop him!" Dr. Allerton shouted. "For the love of God! Hurry! You don't need to demonstrate. They *already know*!"

The crowd was evenly split between those who were trying to escape at the perimeter of the ballroom and those who watched the confrontation between Dr. Allerton and the emissary with rapt horror. None of the bystanders moved to help Brett. They seemed rooted in place, although no ghostly hands held their feet. Then, a dozen red-robed people emerged from the crowd.

Ellie recognized their outfits; the dead exorcist had worn something similar. Of course a man like Allerton would be amply prepared for a haunting, especially after robbing a grave. She almost called out, "Cuz, watch your back!" but the impulse was extinguished by one look at Brett's terrified little face.

That *thing* wasn't Trevor, anyway. Her cuz wouldn't want

anybody to suffer, least of all his former student. That was, perhaps, the worst part of his death. So much cruelty and suffering had filled the gulf that Trevor had left behind.

"They already know what I can do," Allerton said. "They *know.*"

"Ah," the emissary said. "Is the wager unfair? Have you killed another son befo—"

"Stop," Allerton interrupted; his voice, loud as thunder, almost drowned out the speakers. "This is my confession. I am descended from Nathaniel Grace. No better wizard has ever existed, and I inherited his wisdom, his magic, his responsibilities, and his town. If I die, Willowbee rots with me." He spreads his arms. "The people in this room understand why your death was *necessary.* I do not keep secrets from my own."

Ellie looked at the people around her. Most had removed their masks during the chaos, baring ordinary faces. "How could you?" she whispered.

The piano fragments floated and started revolving around the emissary's battered body. Glass flutes, loose jewelry, utensils, cell phones, and every miscellaneous sharp or hard ammunition in the ballroom flowed into the spinning mess. The galaxy of odds and ends moved sluggishly, as if caught in molasses.

"Jay," Ellie said. "We need to find cover."

She could not see any available hiding spot.

The ballroom lights buzzed and flickered, promising greater mischief. Except for the exorcists, people crouched in defensive postures, waiting for a tornado to strike. They shielded their heads with purses and arms; many adults used their bodies to protect children and partners.

"House's choice, you Jedi-looking freaks," the emissary said, nodding at the nearest exorcist. "Do you want to move first, or should I?"

"What now?" Jay whispered, kneeling with Ellie. Kirby paced around them.

"I can help send the emissary to the underworld," Ellie said. "But the exorcists have to act."

Every cell phone in the ballroom rang. Electronic *bring-bring-brings*, techno beats, classical melodies, and cheesy jingles trilled in a mismatched chorus. Soon, the sound shifted from music to voices. Ellie heard her mother weeping and screaming; the sound came from the phone in her pocket. Others must have heard personal horrors, too, because smartphones (and a few flip phones) skittered en masse across the polished floor, cast away like venomous scorpions. Some were stomped underfoot; the broken electronics joined the tornado of junk that spun around the emissary.

The floating phones continued to speak. Ellie heard one ask, in a child's voice, "When will my head stop hurting?"

Another phone begged, "Stop it! Please! Oh, please! Why won't you stop?"

In a synchronized motion, the exorcists whipped knives from their cloaks and sliced their own palms from pinky to thumb. They charged the emissary, their bleeding hands extended.

"Damn!" Ellie said. No time to retreat. She threw herself over Jay. "Kirby, don't let us die!" It wasn't a command he knew. Ellie hoped that, on some level, he understood that flying objects could injure his mistress.

Wood, glass, metal, and stone exploded outward, riding a psionic blast. With the ease of a fetch-master, Kirby blocked the junk that sailed at Ellie and Jay. An invisible wall knocked the two on their backs, but it did not hurt. The crowd, which cowered at the edge of the ballroom, toppled over like bowling pins.

The lights went out. Every phone squealed and crunched—the sound of a car accident. Ellie could feel the wooden floor warp beneath her.

A tremor shook the mansion.

"Big howl, Kirby!" she shouted, hoping that the sound would distract the emissary more than the exorcists. Ellie didn't want the ballroom to become a mass tomb.

As Kirby keened, the floor stopped writhing, and the emergency lights turned on. Three exorcists, the only ones left standing, descended on the emissary with their red-slicked, outstretched palms. "Traitor," screamed the phones and speakers. "Elatsoe, you are a *traitor*!"

The floor beneath Ellie dropped. No. She wasn't falling. She was floating. Every person in the ballroom rose. The emissary wanted to lift them toward the dome ceiling. Let them touch the cherubs and clouds on the fresco before they plummeted three stories. A fall like that could kill. Even survivors, the lucky people who landed just right or were cushioned by other bodies, would have serious injuries. Broken bones, punctured innards, permanent aches and hardship.

Thankfully, one exorcist reached the emissary. He slapped its back, leaving a bloody handprint. The print glowed exit-sign red and expanded, transforming into a giant, three-dimensional hand. Its fingers wrapped around Not-Trevor's chest and squeezed. The emissary cursed, and his concentration must have faltered because Ellie suddenly stopped rising. For a disorienting moment, she simply hovered.

Then, Ellie fell. She dropped three feet and landed on her side, slightly winded. In front of her, the emissary thrashed like a fly ensnared in a spider web. The glowing hand was sinking, pulling him below the floorboards. Not-Trevor seemed unable to break free.

"Just go," Ellie said. "Please."

With a pained grimace, the emissary of vengeance looked at her. The anger leached from his eyes, leaving nothing. His last word, before vanishing from the world, was a quiet, "Why?"

"Ow!" Jay said. "Ah, ow, ow!"

"Are you okay?" Ellie asked, turning away from the emptiness in Not-Trevor's wake. Although the main lights had not turned on again, the emergency lights were bright enough to cast everything in dim relief. She couldn't make out details across the ballroom, but she could see Jay's pain-pinched face. Blood dried on his upper lip.

"My tailbone," he said. "I've felt this before. It's just bruised." He crawled closer to Ellie before collapsing face-down on the warped floor. The hardwood planks resembled solid waves. Nobody would dance on them again, but the ballroom could be converted into a challenging skate park. "Is it over?" Jay groaned.

Ellie rewrapped her bun as the town of Willowbee, led by Dr. Allerton, staggered and limped toward her. A long sliver of wood protruded from Allerton's chest. He wheezed, as if one or both of his lungs were injured. "Not yet, Jay," Ellie said. "Don't let him touch you."

Dr. Allerton ripped the stake from his body, flung it aside, and shook hands with the man beside him. The hole in Dr. Allerton's body closed as a red spot blossomed on his ally's shirt. "Thank you, sir," the doctor said. "I appreciate your sacrifice."

"Anyone is fair game, huh?" Ellie said. "You don't care who dies. Including your own."

"He's fine," Abe said. "That puncture wound is surviv-able, even without my treatment."

"Why didn't you keep it, then?" she asked.

"I'll need my strength to clean up this mess." He rubbed his face and sighed, as if deeply exhausted. "Not my best dance."

"Why bother?" Ellie asked. "After tonight, your minions

won't be the only people who know Willowbee's secrets. *Your* secrets. Some of the guests here are from other cities."

Now that the emissary was gone, the few innocent guests could leave the mansion, and they were evacuating quickly. Ellie didn't see anyone phoning for help—the phones must have been fried by paranormal energy—but it was only a matter of time before dozens of witnesses shared their experiences with uncorrupted police, reporters, lawyers, and social media.

"You can't possibly believe," Abe said, "that I'm a one-trick pony? That we, the children of Nathaniel Grace, have escaped persecution for centuries because of luck?"

"Persecution?" Jay demanded, standing. To his credit, he barely flinched when the movement jostled his bruised tailbone. "People don't want you to kill them. That's self-defense!"

Behind Dr. Allerton, the Willowbee minions closed their eyes and bowed their heads, as if praying. Static electricity crackled between them and lifted filaments of hair, as if they'd rubbed their scalps with balloons. There were many powerful magic users in the town; that was unusual. Willowbee must have close ties with the fae realm.

"I am a neutral force," Dr. Allerton said. "My healing balances my harm. Ellie, I tried to help you and your family. Did you know that I collected scholarship money for Trevor's child? Well? Enough to pay for college! For grad school! You just wouldn't let it go. Everything is a mess now."

"Shut it," Ellie said. "All the scholarships in the world can't be a father to Gregory."

"So I should have died that night instead? Taken Nathaniel Grace's strongest spells with me? Left *my son* without a father?"

"Yes?" she said. "Obviously? Why is that a question?"

He had the gall to appear insulted.

"Just stop," Ellie said. "Let us go. All the magic in the world can't sweep this mess under the rug."

"You're wrong," Abe said. "We've recovered from worse. History is intrinsically malleable. Even without magic. It's carried in our minds, our records. Enchanted tongues spin convincing lies. With a spell, we'll persuade the world to forget this night. To forget you, Ellie, and your family. The town . . . we'll have to move again. Where now? West coast?"

"Near the sea," a Willowbee minion suggested. He was a forty-something man with bushy black eyebrows and a slightly oversized suit.

"Not enough room," argued a sixty-ish woman. She wore a long-sleeved black sequined dress. "The coast is packed."

"I can't stand another desert," a third person huffed. He was a gray-haired guy with a well-trimmed, pointed beard.

"Wait, did you say *move* Willowbee?" Jay asked. "Like a mobile town? How?"

"Nathaniel Grace secret, I'm afraid," Abe said. "Willowbee was founded in Massachusetts. We've only been in Texas, oh, about thirty years. All land is ours, and no land is ours."

That certainly explained the abundance of strange vegetation in Willowbee and its New England architecture. The whole damn town was a sinister ball of magic, slithering through space to escape its sins. She wouldn't be surprised if Willowbee had existed, in some form, before the 1700s. If it had drifted across the Atlantic Ocean with Nathaniel Grace when he thoroughly infuriated his home country. Its migration, she guessed, powered by a strange breed of fairy-ring mushrooms that fed on extravagant dances.

"You backed me into a corner," Abe said, as if that absolved him of all sins. "Ready, my siblings?"

His so-called siblings raised their hands, grotesquely imitating a rapturous choir. Buzzing arcs of electrical light zipped between their fingers. Their digits resembled rods in a Jacob's ladder.

As the air sparked with magic, Ellie realized that Dr. Allerton was going to get away with everything. *Again.* He'd erase all evidence of his crimes, reinvent history, move somewhere else, and continue profiting off others' misery. There would be no justice for Trevor. No justice for any victim of Willowbee.

No.

Dr. Abraham Allerton would not get away with *anything.* If Ellie had to fly into the sun to stop him, so be it. She'd fly into the sun. She wasn't Icarus. She was Elatsoe, daughter of Vivian, Pat, and the Kunétai. Six-great-granddaughter of a hummingbird woman who protected her people.

"Jay," Ellie said, "tell my family that I love them. I love you too. Be good."

She closed her eyes, exhaled slowly, and summoned the dogs of her ancestors. *All* of them.

✦ THIRTY-THREE ✦

IF ELLIE FOLLOWED her family tree to its ancient roots, she'd find few people who did not depend on one or more animals for companionship, protection, or labor. The dogs of her ancestors were numerous enough to rule their own underworld country. Ellie had sensed them, these marvelous dogs who recognized her as part of their extended family. With all her strength, she summoned the pack. Ellie called to them in every language they might understand: English, Spanish, Lipan.

Dog! ¡Perro! Né łe!

They sprung from the warped hardwood, leapt through the walls, and rained from the ceiling: hundreds of dogs, yapping and whining and barking, anxious but not yet aggressive. Their invisible bodies resembled a mirage tsunami that surged over the people of Willowbee. The magic-users lost their balance and sank under a wriggling layer of ghosts. Ellie nearly laughed at the way they floundered. They were trying to swim in ghosts! Each dog that the exorcists sent back to the underworld was immediately replaced with another. Only Ellie and Jay escaped embarrassment. The good dogs were thoughtful enough to respect their human's personal space.

"They're beautiful!" Jay said. He tentatively reached for the nearest shimmer and petted its intangible head. The ghost made a contented sound, something between a sigh and a bark.

"My pack," Ellie said. "Wish I knew how to make 'em all visible."

She walked toward Dr. Allerton. He knelt beneath the ghosts' paradoxically heavy bodies. The pose was rather pathetic, but she didn't have time to gloat.

"Hey, Doctor," Ellie said, putting a hand on his shoulder. "You're coming with me." He pulled back, trying to escape her grip, but could not throw off the dog pile.

"Going where, exactly?" he asked, strained.

"You'll see." Ellie returned to the feeling that had drawn her into a dead ocean: familiarity. Her heart brimming with grief, she sought for similarities in sorrow. Wasn't the underworld a vast and frightening place? Wasn't the Earth vast and frightening, too? The Above and the Below were two sides of the same coin, and Ellie could feel hurt and lost in each.

The dogs appeared gradually, in pieces. They swarmed

as a mix of floating black noses, wagging tails, and attentive brown eyes. A pup brushed against Ellie's hand, and though she could not see its back, she felt its wiry fur.

"Jay," she said, turning, wondering whether he'd fallen through the door she opened.

He was gone, though a Jay-shaped shadow darkened the wooden planks. Jay's shadow ran back and forth, at one point passing through her. He called her name, his voice far-away and fading. "Ellie! Ellie! Please, Ellie!"

Gradually, his shadow faded, too. Ellie and Dr. Allerton were the only humans in sight, Allerton now partially concealed by furry bodies. "It's like we crashed a doggy ball, Kirby," she said. "Can I have this dance?"

His floppy ears perked up. With a pleased cheer, Ellie wrapped her arms around Kirby and lifted him bridal-style. "So heavy!" she said, giving his forehead a big smooch. Kirby wiggled until she let him go free. With a sharp yap, the kind that meant "Let's play!" he scampered around Ellie's legs and wagged his tail so enthusiastically, his whole butt wagged too.

"We'll visit the park tomorrow," she said. "With a Frisbee. No googly-eyed skulls. Never again. I *promise*, you sweet little guy."

By the time Dr. Allerton escaped the dog pile, the ghosts were indistinguishable from the living.

"You can go now, Doctor," Ellie told him.

"Go where?" He stood very still, as if afraid that sudden movements would attract violence. However, the dogs paid him little attention. Satisfied that Ellie was safe, they dispersed. Some jumped through the broken ballroom windows. Others, unconcerned with finesse, trotted straight through the wall.

"Dunno," she said, shrugging. "Pick a direction and start walking."

Dr. Allerton sidestepped to the nearest window, never turning his back toward Ellie. He stood against the wall and peeked outside. "You moved my house!" Dr. Allerton cried. "How?" He actually sounded betrayed, as if Ellie had broken a promise to respect Willowbee's spatial autonomy.

"It's a secret," she said. "Much stronger than your trick. What do you see?" Ellie dared not approach the walls.

"Mesquite trees," he said. "That's all. It's the middle of nowhere."

"Great. Goodbye." Ellie meditated on home, ready to return, but Dr. Allerton's blabbing broke her concentration.

"Who's that? You there! Hello?" He leaned outside, his brow furrowed, and then leapt away from the window. "God! Oh, God, no! Ellie, don't leave me here! Please!"

She put her fingers in her ears and tried to ignore him. Home. Think of *home*. Think of her mother, her father, and her cheerleader. The toxic river behind her house. The high school she almost missed. The movie theater and summer blockbusters with . . .

"I'll cover your college tuition," Allerton said. "That's a blood oath."

. . . popcorn that cost more than the movie tickets, and . . .

"They're between the trees! They're everywhere! Listen to me!" Allerton leapt toward Ellie and tried to grab her by the elbow, but Kirby lunged between them, his teeth bared.

"They're coming into my home," Allerton said, his hands up and then clasped penitently. So it *was* possible for the man to look regretful. "Don't let them. Please."

Faces peered through the window. They looked like they belonged to people. Ellie suspected otherwise, however. Their jaws were tense with fury. Their eyes were wide with delight. The emissary of vengeance had asked Ellie if he and other emissaries had a purpose. She still could not answer his question.

"Do you know them?" she asked, stepping back, moving to the far end of the ballroom because the other side was filling with angry people. "Are they your victims, Doctor?"

"Am I yours?" he spat back.

"You tried to kill me."

"What do you want?"

"You tried to kill my friends and family."

"*What do you want?*"

"You killed . . ."

"Be merciful. Help me."

The emissaries had stopped crawling through the windows and walking through the walls. Slowly but deliberately, they approached. Their steps resembled a terrible march.

"Trevor tried to help you once," she said. Dr. Allerton's victims were so plentiful, they couldn't even fit in the ballroom.

"This," Ellie said, her heart breaking, "is me showing mercy to the people who will live now that you're gone."

In Dr. Allerton's stunned silence, Ellie put her hand on Kirby's head and thought of home.

The emissaries charged.

Dr. Allerton charged too.

He collided with Ellie. She fell on her back, and when Dr. Allerton tried to wrap his hands around her neck, she kicked him in the stomach so hard he wheezed. As Ellie scrambled away, she felt a sharp tug on the back of her head; he'd grabbed her by the braid.

If she tried to return home now, Dr. Allerton would tag along like a tick. Or a *leech*.

If she didn't return soon, the emissaries might kill them both.

Ellie grabbed Kirby by the scruff and drew Trevor's Swiss Army knife. With a violent swipe of the two-inch blade, she chopped off her braid.

Home, she thought. *Finally. Home.*

Dr. Allerton grasped for her again, but before he could touch Ellie, Kirby broke free and attacked. Dog bit man, and then dog shook man, flinging Dr. Allerton side-to-side like a rag doll. As the underworld slipped away, Ellie called for Kirby. "Here, boy! Come!"

His ears perked up attentively.

"Leave the bad man!" she urged. "Come!"

Kirby turned and looked at her with his bright, dark eyes. Then, panting happily, he began to run.

"Good boy!" she praised. Just one more leap, and they'd be together. The world seemed to shimmer, as if little more than a reflection in a pool of water. Ellie reached for her dog, expecting to feel his soft head beneath her fingers.

Instead, she grasped her mother's hand.

"Elatsoe!" Vivian said. "My baby."

Ellie felt herself squeezed in a vise-tight hug as she looked around her. They and other party survivors sat outside the Allerton mansion. Above; no sign of Allerton or the emissaries. Ellie did not see anyone she recognized from Willowbee either. Perhaps, adrift without their leader, they all fled. "The doctor?" Ellie asked. "Is he . . . did I . . ."

"That jackass disappeared. There's no telling where he went."

"I know *exactly* where he went, Mom," Ellie said. "Where's Jay?"

"I'm right here!" Jay peeked around Vivian. "But you *left* us!" He knelt, taking Ellie's hand and patting it twice, as if confirming that she was real. At least Jay didn't poke her in the forehead this time.

"It's okay now." She gave Jay a gentle hug, careful not to upset his bruises. "Is Ronnie safe?"

"She is," he said. "Al, too. And the bridesmaids."

"Can you stand?" Vivian asked. "We should drive to the hospital. Your father is a couple minutes away."

"Dad's here?"

"He took the first available flight when I told him about the bicentennial."

"Everyone's safe, then. Except . . ." Ellie called for Kirby. Waited.

Nothing.

It was normally so easy to wake him. Second nature, like typing on a keyboard or riding a bike. Why didn't he respond? Those vengeful emissaries wouldn't hurt a dog, right?

She mentally shouted his name, and when that didn't work, she called it out loud, too. "Kirby, come! Here, boy! *Kirby!*"

He did not respond.

At last, Ellie wept.

⤜⤛ THIRTY-FOUR ⤚⤙

Hours later, Ellie and her parents left Willowbee for Lenore's house in a rental car while Jay, Ronnie, Al, and the bridesmaid trio used Vivian's van. Ellie was grateful to be in the less crowded vehicle. Grief felt like a stone in the pit of her stomach, and she wanted to let its weight drag her into the deep-sea depths of quiet suffering.

"He'll come home," Vivian said. "Dogs always find a way."

Alone in the back seat, Ellie nodded unenthusiastically. Her mother might be right, but she couldn't stop thinking about the death of heroic Six-Great. One of the world's best adventurers stepped into the underworld and never escaped. What if the same thing happened to Kirby?

Listlessly, Ellie watched the sun rise through a streaky window. She, her parents, and her friends had spent all night dealing with the Allerton fiasco fallout. The manor had been swarming with federal agents. She didn't know how they'd reached Willowbee so fast, but at least they weren't evil wizards like the local cops.

"In one mile," the built-in GPS intoned, "turn right."

Ellie jolted in her seat, startled by the deep robotic voice. It had been especially unsettling because the backseat speakers were directly behind her head. For a moment, she thought some ghost had followed them from the manor.

Ellie's father turned off the highway, taking a road that cut through the semi-wilderness outside Willowbee. It looked so familiar. The bridge, the ditch, the juniper and mesquite.

A cold realization: it was the road where Trevor died.

"Dad, what are you doing?" she asked.

"Huh? What? Are you okay?"

"Why are we here?"

"It's the fastest way home, I guess. If you trust robots."

Of course he didn't understand. Ellie's father had been hundreds of miles away when she and Jay discovered the real crash site. Plus, the wilderness had started concealing most of the damage. Pale leaves sprouted from the half-crushed bushes, and fresh weeds carpeted earth that had been stripped of vegetation by rubber wheels.

How long would it take for the earth to heal? When would the sap on the metal-scarred tree harden into amber? It seemed odd that an act so violent and cruel could leave gemstones in its wake.

A minute after they passed the crash site, a woman dressed in jeans and a worn gray T-shirt stepped from the nearby tree line and stuck out her thumb. Her brown hair was restrained in a fluffy ponytail, and she carried a paper bag emblazoned with a waffle logo.

"Should I stop?" Pat asked.

"No stopping," Vivian said. "She may be a cultist."

As the car passed, the hitchhiker shouted something that sounded like "Hey, wait! Please?" Reflexively, Ellie turned to look out the back window. "Dad!" she shouted. "Stop!"

He slammed on the brakes. "What?" he asked. "Is there a squirrel in the road?"

"No. *Look*."

The hitchhiking woman was gone. Or, more specifically, her human form was gone. In the woman's place stood a coyote. The takeout bag from the waffle place dangled from her toothy mouth.

"Is that a coyote person?" Ellie asked. "I've never seen one before. Reverse, or something. We have to give her a ride!" The animal people had been in hiding for so long, it was beyond lucky to meet one. A blessing, really.

"Well," Pat said, "I'm obliged to help all critters in need. It's the Hippocratic oath of veterinarians."

"She can sit in the back with Ellie," Vivian said. She sounded less than enthusiastic, but it had been a long twenty-four hours.

Ellie rolled down her window and waved. In response, the coyote trotted up to the car, and with a mirage-like shimmer, she was in human form again: a weathered-looking woman of indiscriminate age with a mane of pale brown hair barely restrained by her hair tie, fine laugh lines around her eyes, and a hopeful smile. "Give me a ride?" she asked.

"Where to?" Pat asked.

"Anywhere," the coyote said. "It doesn't matter."

"Huh! Then why do you want a ride, Auntie?" Vivian asked.

"Because I feel like it." She looked up, and her human-shaped nostrils flared and wrinkled as she scented the air. "Something changed last night. It's safer."

"Get in," Ellie said. "We're going anywhere."

She opened the door and scooted over. With a thankful nod, the coyote woman climbed inside and placed her take-out bag on the narrow middle seat between them. The bag reeked of breakfast sausages. The savory aroma—grease and spices—quickly overpowered the bottled new car smell, a definite improvement.

For a moment.

Cheap sausages reminded Ellie of Kirby. When he was alive, he'd sit beside the dining room table every morning and beg for scraps of bacon and eggs. As the world became blurry through a haze of tears, Ellie thought she saw the coyote transform into a wiry canine. She wiped away her tears and realized that it hadn't been an illusion; the coyote had dropped the human facade. She was about the size of a medium dog, but lankier and scruffier than most. Perhaps mistaking Ellie's astonished stare for hunger, the coyote nudged the bag with her paw and said, *You can have one.*

In the way of animal people, she did not speak with her

mouth, instead using a language that all living things could understand. It blossomed in Ellie's head like a dream, a series of thoughts she did not consciously control.

"No, thank you," Ellie said. "I filled up on doughnut earlier."

Why are you sad, then?

"My friend is gone."

Gone where?

"Below," Ellie said.

Oh. Sure, sure. Many of my friends have gone there, too. The coyote lowered her yellow eyes and sighed. It was a distinctly canine sigh, a too-quick whuff of air through her black nose. *More there than here. Have we met before? I meet so many people. It's hard to remember every face. Sometimes, I see a stranger that makes me feel something. So I think: maybe this is not really a stranger.*

"What do you feel when you look at my face?" Ellie asked.

Friendship. Also worry.

"How old are you?" Ellie asked. She frowned. "Is that rude? If it is, I'm sorry."

Not rude. The coyote tilted her head. *Why would it be? Older than you. By a lot. I don't count the years.*

"Maybe you knew my six-great-grandmother. There's also my five-great-grandmother, my four-great-grandmother, my three-great-grandmother, my great-great-grandmother, my great-grandmother, and my grandmother. They've all lived the kind of life that makes people worry. Especially friends."

Huuuuhm, the coyote said. *Maybe. Let me mull it over.* She closed her eyes, and her ears swiveled on her head, as if searching for radio signals. A minute passed.

It was Vivian who broke the silence. "I once said that your six-great-grandmother was too stubborn when it came to danger," she said, twisting in her seat to make eye contact with Ellie. "Personally," she continued, "I used to consider that part of her to be a character flaw."

"I know," Ellie said, smiling faintly.

"I might have been wrong."

"What?!" Pat blurted out. "Are you unwell? We pass a hospital on the way—"

"Stop it," Vivian said. "I'm trying to make a point."

"But if you need medical attention—"

"I don't."

"—the offer stands."

"That's very generous of you," she said.

"You're welcome."

"What were you going to say?" Ellie asked, leaning forward until the seat belt resisted. Briefly, she wondered if the coyote should be buckled up. Kirby used to have a harness for the car. When he was alive. When he was with her.

She focused on the memory of Kirby, reaching for him, calling his name with the part of her soul that sang the language of all living things.

There was no response.

"She knew herself," Vivian said. "And never doubted what she knew. No matter how many times people said, 'It's too dangerous. Don't do it.' Your six-great-grandmother *knew* that she was capable of wonderful, dangerous things. That isn't a flaw. It's . . . enviable."

"But she made a mistake, Mom. In the end."

"No. She took a risk for love. That isn't a mistake. It isn't even a bad decision."

"I'd go one step farther," Pat said, "and say it's a *good* decision."

Me too, the coyote agreed. She yawned wide and curled up in a ball, tucking her nose under her tail. Her mournful yellow eyes peered up at Ellie. *What happened last night? The air felt . . . taut. Like its threads were ready to unravel.*

The car turned, and sunlight spilled through Ellie's east-facing window, warming her face. "I guess I should start from the beginning," she said. "When I was a kid, my parents took me to the pound. That's where I met a dog . . ."

She'd say his name and tell his story. Maybe, someday, he'd follow the words home.

⇜ THIRTY-FIVE ⇝

A FEW DAYS LATER, as Ellie shoved her folded clothes into a backpack, packing for the return trip home, her phone buzzed. A message from Lenore popped onto the rectangular screen:

Meet me in the park.

Instinctually, Ellie felt to Kirby, calling, "Walk, boy!"

Five minutes later, she left the house alone.

It was strange to feel the sun against the back of her neck. As Ellie walked through the calm neighborhood, she wondered how long it would take for her hair to grow below her back. She was tempted to keep it short until she stopped mourning.

How long would that take?

Lenore sat on a bench in the park, Gregory dozing beside her in a hooded baby carriage. She wore round sunglasses and a short white dress. There was a small cardboard box on the ground.

"Hey," Ellie said, sitting beside Lenore. "Funny story: this is where I got swarmed by trilobites."

"Eek." Lenore lifted her feet gingerly, as if protecting them from a roach. "Do you want to move?"

"No worries. That was a one-time mistake."

"I'll miss you," Lenore said. "Please visit. Okay?" She had decided to sell her house in the Rio Grande and move in with her good friends, a married couple. The women lived alongside the Mojave Desert and had a large guest house.

"I promise," Ellie said.

"You're always welcome. Always. Oh! I have a gift for you." Lenore nudged the cardboard box with one of her feet; she wore a pair of shiny red pumps with silver heels. "Did you know that I used to work at a comic-book store?"

"No way!" Ellie said. She used Trevor's Swiss Army knife to cut through the masking tape around the cardboard box, revealing stacks of graphic novels. They included indie titles she'd never seen before. Rare and unique oddities about jilted sirens, unhappy psychics, and unlucky starlets. All very elegant and melancholy, just like Lenore Moore.

"When I was in college," Lenore said. "The job paid for my degree, but I also enjoyed its perks. Like a twenty-percent employee discount."

"Are these all yours, then?" Ellie asked.

"Mm-hm. They used to be." She looked away, almost self-consciously. "Trevor mentioned you like comics too."

"I do!"

"They're yours now." Lenore put a hand on Ellie's shoulder. "Something to read during the long trip home. When are you leaving?"

"Tomorrow morning."

"One more supper together."

In silence, they watched a father push his daughter on a swing in the park. The girl was laughing, "Higher, higher!"

"He was a good dad," Lenore said. "And a good man."

Ellie knew exactly who she was talking about. No names required.

⇜⟫⛏ THIRTY-SIX ⛏⟪⇝

"S NICKERS," ELLIE SAID, "play dead!"

The brown labradoodle rolled onto his back.

"*Dead*," Ellie repeated.

His pink tongue lolled out.

Jay whistled, impressed. "How'd Snickers learn that in a *week*?"

Had it really been just seven days since her father brought the dog home? Ellie felt like she'd known Snickers for years. Granted, he was no Kirby. That was fine, though. She didn't want a replacement.

"He's the most food-motivated dog I've met," Ellie said. She passed Snickers a pea-sized treat. He revived in a heartbeat and swallowed it whole. "I could train him to vacuum my bedroom for a slice of bacon."

"I'm surprised that nobody wanted him," Jay said.

"Sadly, I'm not." Ellie gave Snickers a firm squeeze. He leaned into the hug and tickled her cheek with his floppy ear. "People don't go to the shelter for eight-year-old dogs. They want young 'uns and puppies. If Dad hadn't agreed to foster him . . ."

The underworld must teem with unwanted pets. She hoped that, in death, they finally found love. Maybe, Kirby integrated with a pack in the labyrinthine Below. Ellie wondered if she'd have to wait until her own death before they'd be reunited. If they'd be reunited at all. Could she risk another visit to the underworld? Return just long enough to call Kirby's name?

"Just foster?" Jay asked. "Great! I'll adopt him! Awyeah. Doggy maid."

"Sorry to crush your dreams," she said, "but Snickers is joining my family. You can visit any time, though."

Ellie winked and returned to the center of her bedroom. There, balsa wood, paint, and superglue were scattered across an unfolded newspaper. A half-finished bridge dried atop the comics pages. The semester had just started, and she was already working on a group project. Fortunately, she and Jay were in the same structural physics class. With a partner like him, Ellie finally enjoyed group work.

"Another one!" Jay plucked a page from the newspaper mat. "Hah. 'Senator resigns after Willowbee connection revealed.' It's the guy from Texarkana! Can I keep this for my summer scrapbook?"

"Feel free." She prodded the bridge delicately. "Needs a few more minutes."

"This Willowbee thing got so big," he continued, folding the newspaper into a tidy rectangle, "I've had to start a *second* book for news articles. Mom thinks we can use the publicity to get scholarships. You . . . still want that, right? College?"

Considering her role in the Willowbee scandal, Ellie could easily start her own business after high school. Although her parents guarded her privacy with every trick they knew, the occasional interview request, fan message, or angry screed broke through their barrier. If one third of the people who contacted her were serious, she had enough potential clients to fill years of work.

Dear Ellie Bride,

My son has been acting weird lately. He hears rats in the walls, but there are none! Is our house haunted? Other strange events include . . .

Dear Ellie,

I live in an apartment near El Cementerio del Barrio de los Lipanes. My girlfriend thinks that the original burial ground was larger, but developers built on it. Please tell your dead tribe that I'm sorry for living over their graves. I can't afford a better location right now. My girlfriend won't stay the night until I do something. We've been together three years . . .

Hello Miss Bride,

What are your opinions on alien abductions? Namely: can an alien ghost abduct a human ghost? Please respond . . .

Dear Ellie Bride,

Abraham Allerton is not alone. There are other wizards on our land, self-worshipping people who corrupt reality itself. Be careful.

"There's a lot I want to learn," Ellie said. "My mother, her mother, and my grandmother's mother taught me about the way of our land, our dead, and our monsters, but the times have changed. I need college to prepare for the next Willowbee."

Ellie threw Bear Buddy across the room; Snickers caught it midair and crawled under the bed, wringing squeaks from the toy with his teeth. Unlike Kirby, he did treat fetch like a game of keep-away. The habit would take more than a week to break.

"Will there be another Willowbee?" Jay asked.

"You can bet on it." Ellie knelt and tried to grab Bear Buddy, but Snickers just wiggled farther back. Groaning with mild annoyance, she dropped to her stomach and used her elbows to scoot halfway under the bed.

"At least we're prepa—AAAAH! What the hell! Run!"

Ellie felt Jay grab her by the foot and pull. If she hadn't been wearing overalls and long sleeves, the maneuver would have caused serious carpet burn.

"What?" she cried.

"That!" Jay pointed. A googly-eyed skull bobbed across the room, carried in the mouth of an invisible dog.

It took a moment for Ellie to regain speech. "Appear, Kirby!" she said. "Appear!"

In an instant, he turned visible. There stood Kirby in all his floppy-eared, feather-tailed glory. Ellie made a joyous sound that verged between a shriek and a wail. She threw herself at him, squeezing his intangible body, and he wagged his poltergeist tail so enthusiastically, it scattered balsa wood slivers in a preternatural wind. "You aren't afraid of it anymore," she said.

Snickers poked his nose into the open, intrigued.

"This is your big brother," Ellie declared. "He's a ghost."

The dogs circled each other twice. Neither seemed to care about life or death, living or dead. After the silent introduction, they bounded around the room, and Jay narrowly rescued the bridge from destruction. Eventually, when Snickers grew tired of play, he and Kirby curled side-by-side on the doggy bed. Ellie was torn between watching them sleep and gathering both dogs in her arms in a tight, joyful hug.

"I knew that Kirby would find a way home," Jay said. "Dogs always do. Huh. What's that?"

He stooped and picked up a dirty, torn doll from the ground. It was made of leather and rattled when Jay tossed it across the room to Ellie's outstretched hand. Kirby and Snickers perked up, their eyes trained on the toy.

"I've never seen this before," Ellie said. The doll was no marvel of craftsmanship. Just a sock-shaped tube of leather with a smiling face painted on one side. A long braid of fibrous material dangled from the top of its head, and the rattle, which reminded Ellie of dry mesquite seeds shaking in their husks, came from its belly. "It looks like a dog toy, though. Maybe Kirby brought it with him."

"From Below?" Jay asked. "You . . . do you think it's cursed?"

"It took him forever to warm up to Skull Buddy over there," Ellie said. "I *really* doubt Kirby would be in the same room as a cursed dollie. Hm. I wonder . . ."

Ellie thought that her happiness would sprout a pair of wings and fly through the window, over the house, higher than Owl, and above the sun. Fly so high, that the ground would disappear and there'd be nowhere to fall.

That night, she and Jay finished the bridge together, and once the glue dried, they decorated its beams with acrylic paint. There were no broken hearts.

ACKNOWLEDGMENTS

I wrote a "novel" when I was in first grade. It was a forty-page mystery about a girl who found a box of opals and a riddle in her attic. I only remember fragments of the plot. Somebody was poisoning a butterfly garden in the neighborhood park, and the protagonist cracked the case (don't ask me how; it was related to the opals . . . maybe).

So there I was, a seven-year-old author with a finished manuscript. I gave it to the only beta readers I knew: my parents. Luckily, my dad, an English/writing professor with a strong background in Shakespearean lit, not only read the book (and praised my writing!), he edited all forty pages.

Keep in mind that we were still learning the alphabet in my homeroom class. To put it lightly, I didn't have the strongest grasp of English grammar.

Dad explained his edits, and I corrected my manuscript on a nineties-era computer that was good for two things: typing and Tetris. Then, Dad taught me how to write a query letter (gotta be succinct and polite!), and I sent my manuscript to a real book publisher.

You can probably guess their response. I still have the rejection letter. Dad framed it, proud of my persistence and big dreams. Proud of me. He figured I could hang it alongside my first acceptance letter as a reminder of my journey.

When it comes to my writing, Dad has always been my

biggest teacher, supporter, and advocate. This book wouldn't exist without a lifetime of his guidance.

I am also thankful for the friendship of my writing community at the "cafe"; for the linguistic guidance of David Gohre; for the breathtaking art of Rovina Cai; and for my agent, Michael Curry, who not only found a home for *Elatsoe* but also provided suggestions that helped it become a richer, more cohesive work.

Finally, I'd like to acknowledge the wonderful team at Levine Querido (Arthur A. Levine, Alexandra Hernandez, Antonio Gonzalez Cerna, Meghan Maria McCullough, and Nick Thomas), who have been incredible champions for *Elatsoe*. In particular, I am exceedingly grateful for my editor, Nick Thomas, whose keen editorial insights helped *Elatsoe* shine. Nick, it's been a privilege working with you.

And to my readers:

xastéyó.

ABOUT THE AUTHOR

Darcie Little Badger is an Earth scientist, writer, and fan of the weird, beautiful, and haunting. She is an enrolled member of the Lipan Apache Tribe of Texas. *Elatsoe* is her debut novel.

SOME NOTES ON THIS BOOK'S PRODUCTION

The art for the jacket and interiors was drawn by Rovina Cai on an iPad, and then edited, shaded, and textured in Photoshop. The text was set by Westchester Publishing Services in Danbury, CT, in Cochin Lt Std, from the Cochin font family, a serif Italian old-style typeface designed in 1912 by Georges Peignot. The display was set in Dear Sarah, designed in 2007 by Christian Robertson and meant to evoke the feel of hand-writing. The book was printed on 98gsm Yunshidai Ivory FSC™-certified paper and bound in China.

Production was supervised by Leslie Cohen and Freesia Blizard
Book jacket and interiors designed by Sheila Smallwood
Edited by Nick Thomas

LQ
LEVINE QUERIDO